PRAISE FOR

Delia Suits Up

"In *Delia Suits Up*, her *Wall Street* meets *Freaky Friday* experience forces Delia to rethink everything that she values in life and puts a whole new spin on girl power."

—kc dyer, author of *Eighty Days to Elsewhere*

"A delightfully fun yet thought-provoking page-turner. Ms. Aksel delivers a smart, sexy tale of a woman determined to smash the glass ceiling who discovers that sometimes the most courageous thing you can be is yourself."

—Melanie Summers, bestselling author of *The Royal Treatment*

"[A] clever and funny first-person 'I woke up like this!' novel. . . . Delia's experiences as a man in the workplace are thought-provoking."

—*Library Journal*

"*Delia Suits Up* is a hilarious, laugh-out-loud, thoroughly entertaining story from the first page to the last."

—*New York Times* bestselling author Helena Hunting

"See life through a different lens in this thought-provoking, creatively told skewering of societal norms—perfect for fans of *Freaky Friday* and *She's the Man*."

—Julie Valerie, bestselling author of *Holly Banks Full of Angst*

"*Delia Suits Up* is warm, witty, and absolutely wonderful. A winner."

—Meredith Schorr, author of *As Seen on TV*

"A funny take on gender roles and how society sees them, this is a humorous look at the world of finance and women in business, especially in male-dominated fields."

—*Parkersburg News and Sentinel*

"A quick, easy summer escape."

—*Booklist*

No Funny Business

AMANDA AKSEL

JOVE
NEW YORK

A JOVE BOOK
Published by Berkley
An imprint of Penguin Random House LLC
penguinrandomhouse.com

Library of Congress Cataloging-in-Publication Data

Names: Aksel, Amanda, author.
Title: No funny business / Amanda Aksel.
Description: First edition. | New York: Jove, 2022.
Identifiers: LCCN 2021059712 (print) | LCCN 2021059713 (ebook) |
ISBN 9780593201633 (trade paperback) | ISBN 9780593201640 (ebook)
Subjects: LCGFT: Romance fiction. | Novels.
Classification: LCC PS3601.K74 N6 2022 (print) | LCC PS3601.K74 (ebook) |
DDC 813/.6—dc23/eng/20220121
LC record available at https://lccn.loc.gov/2021059712
LC ebook record available at https://lccn.loc.gov/2021059713

First Edition: July 2022

Printed in the United States of America
1   3   5   7   9   10   8   6   4   2

For my dad,
who loved comedy,
especially on vinyl . . .
And for his beloved Jeep

No Funny Business

One

sn't life funny? Both ha-ha and strange. Lately I've been wondering exactly how I ended up with my tush glued to an ergonomic chair beneath migraine-instigating fluorescent lights, reviewing commercial real estate contracts and pretending I give a hoot. My glazed-over gaze falls on the tray of business cards behind my keyboard. If only they read my stage name, *Olivia Vincent*, with the title *Stand-Up Comedian* replacing my current one—*Staff Attorney*.

Because the thing is, there's nothing funny about drafting legally binding contracts. Sometimes I'm tempted to slip a joke in between the lines *indebtedness secured hereby* and *successors thereto* just to liven the damn thing up. It's all so serious. Stuffy. The enemies of humor.

Bzzz. Bzzz.

My phone vibrates on my desk against my heavily used coffee mug. It's Bernie, my booking agent, and at the moment, a very welcome disruption. "Hi, Bernie," I say, rebalancing my eyeglasses and distancing myself from my dreaded duties.

"Olivia, I got somethin' for ya," she spits out in her raspy Queens accent. Just the thing I need to escape my corporate punishment.

"Oh my god, Bernie. Your timing could not be better."

"How would you like a feature spot at Funnies?" Twenty minutes of stage time at my favorite downtown comedy club? Yes, please!

"That's a no-brainer. When is it?" I snatch my trusty yellow legal pad and jot down the words *Funnies* and *feature* in the margins next to the newly scribbled jokes I'm planning to workshop at an open mic tomorrow.

"In an hour but you'd need to be there at least fifteen minutes early. I know it's short notice but the guy bailed last minute. Can you make it happen?"

I glance at my watch, remembering that I'm supposed to be at a client dinner in an hour. Hmm, maybe Bernie's timing *could* be better. In the business of comedy, timing is truly essential. It's one of the first things I learned in comedy class. (And in case you're wondering, there are no squeaky red noses or banana peels involved—just a group of misfit jokesters.) It doesn't take long to grasp that when the timing is off, the punchline won't land, and the whole thing's a disaster. Because no matter what anyone says, there's only one reason a stand-up takes the stage. It's the reason we, the misfit jokesters, were put on this earth to begin with.

To make people laugh.

Oh, those glorious ha-ha-has, he-he-hes, and ho-ho-hos.

Okay, maybe you only get the ho-ho-hos if Santa's taking up two chairs in the audience with sugar cookie crumbs scattered over his beard. The point is that no matter the shape, sound, cadence, or volume, we stand-ups love getting the laugh. In fact, I love it so much that I'm going to ditch that client dinner and claim my birthright.

"Of course I can. You know I'll take any stage time I can get."

"Thanks, Olivia," Bernie says. "I'll email you the details."

I end the call and silently thank the idiot who backed out at the eleventh hour.

Since I work as a full-time attorney at the law firm of Whitley, Bauer, Carey, and Klein, it hasn't been easy for a Texas transplant like me to catch my big comedy break. That's why I'm using the Jim Gaffigan plan. That's right—America's favorite pale comedian with the Hot Pockets bit. Don't we just love a famous funny guy with their wife jokes, sex quips, and wacky impressions? And every now and then, America will love a famous funny gal too. As long as she doesn't joke about menses. But she should because the word *menses* is hilarious.

Anyway, legend has it he worked his corporate job to support his family while pursuing stand-up until he hit the showbiz jackpot. I may not have a family to support, but judging by the size of my monthly student loan bill, you'd never know the difference. Funny (not ha-ha), since we all know laughter is in fact the best medicine. But do we, the comedians of the world, get the credit and compensation psychiatrists and physicians do for the endorphin-inducing, cortisol-reducing, calorie-burning service that we provide?

Uh, no.

As it stands, if I pursued comedy full-time, I'd be subjected to a steady diet of generic foam-cup ramen until I booked enough gigs to afford the name brand. Though, sometimes it seems like a fair trade-off when I've been sitting in a three-hour legal meeting and my ass cheeks are numb.

"Knock, knock," a friendly voice calls in sync with a couple taps on my doorframe. It's my best friend and roommate, Imani, dressed in a perfectly pressed ginger-colored jumpsuit complete with a popped collar and gold layered necklace. She tilts her head with a funny expression. "What's that goofy grin for?"

"I just hung up with Bernie. She snagged me a feature spot tonight."

"Oh, yeah? Don't you have a dinner meeting?" Sure, Imani and I work at the same firm but we're in different departments, so I wouldn't expect her to know my calendar so well.

"How'd you know that?"

She shrugs with a sweet innocence that rivals mine. "You mentioned it this morning. And since you have other plans, I wanted to come by and see if it's cool that I borrow your black stilettos. The ones with the gold ankle strap."

"My horny heels?" I can't help but smirk at the special shoe request. "Who you doin' tonight?" She's been working round the clock, pulling for a promotion at the firm, which doesn't leave a lot of time for sex and dating. An issue that plagues us both.

"No one. Just meeting a guy for a drink thing." Her gaze trails off as she swipes her glossed lip with the tip of her ring finger, showing off her new ombre manicure.

"What guy?" I could ask myself the same question but it would mean something completely different.

"Just a guy. I swear I'll tell you all the dirty details later if I can borrow your shoes."

"So there will be dirty details?" I press the issue.

"Liv! The shoes?"

"Sheez. Someone needs a little hoo-hoo in her hmm-hmm," I say under my breath.

"I heard that," she says. "And you're one to talk."

"Can't argue with that, but tonight, the shoes are yours. Just don't forget to leave on your finder app."

"I always do."

Real-time GPS locators are one of the best things to happen to single women in the city. And stalking ex-girlfriends. Imani and I use it regularly to look out for each other when the other is out late alone. And seeing as I'm moonlighting as a stand-up, that's pretty often.

"So who are you opening for tonight?" she asks.

"Um . . . I forgot to ask." I pull up my email on my phone, scrolling for details from Bernie. When I see that it's ten after and add up the twenty-plus minutes it'll take to get downtown, I set the finer points aside for the commute. I can't be late.

"So how exactly are you going to get out of your meeting tonight?"

I grab my bag and shut my laptop. "Don't you worry about that. Just enjoy the shoes."

She waves me off and I hurry down the hallway, stepping as lightly, but swiftly, as I can in my pumps. What I wouldn't give to wear my stage Converse in the office. Sneakers are even frowned upon on casual Friday, which occurs only monthly instead of weekly at our firm. I turn the corner and run smack into Mr. Whitley, one of the partners and my boss, nearly headbutting his silk tie.

"Oh, shiii— Sorry," I say, managing to curb my words.

"Whoa, where's the fire?" Mr. Whitley brushes himself off with his usual stony expression.

"No fire," I say, catching my breath and flashing a toothy smile. "Just need to unload all this coffee in my system."

"I'm not following." If I spoke in heretos and therefores, perhaps he'd get my drift. "But since I've run into you, please make sure you show Mr. Fenwick a good evening. As you know, he's a very important client."

This may seem like the opportunity to ask to skip the client dinner but I find that managing partners don't take too kindly to associates prioritizing activities that don't include billable hours, which include but are not limited to family taco night, martinis with friends, tickets to *Hamilton*, and of course performing stand-up comedy. In my experience, it's better to ask for forgiveness rather than permission in these matters.

"Absolutely, Mr. Whitley. I've got it covered," I say, and his eyes roll over me as if he's detected a hint of bullshit. So I throw him off the scent with a sweet, slightly Southern-sounding, "Now you go on and have a good night, sir."

The moment he passes, I'm off to the races again, finally flinging the door open to Fawn Douglas's office. "Olivia, I was just about to come get you. The reservation's at seven."

"Yeah, about that . . . How would you like to fly solo in this meeting?"

Now before you go thinking my evil plan is to schlep my responsibilities onto someone else, let me explain. Fawn and I are not that different. Except that she actually likes being an attorney. It's her dream. A dream she had to fight for when her hippie artist/ activist parents had a fit, convinced she was to become a cog in the capitalist machine. The only thing worse would've been if she told them she voted Republican. I too had to face a parental tribunal when I came out as a comic. So if I can support her dream by letting her shine at tonight's meeting while she helps me step into the spotlight in front of a brick wall, then all the better for both of us.

"Why?" Fawn's suspicious tone is unexpected.

"Okay, I don't have a lot of time so I'm just gonna level with you. I got an incredible opportunity to open for a—" I stumble, still unsure of whom I'm helping out tonight. "A super well-known comic at the same time as the Fenwick dinner. I wouldn't ask if I thought you really needed me tonight because you don't. You're a rock star and it's going to be a fabulous night because of you. What do you think?"

She shakes her head like she's taking it in. "Yeah, okay, I guess I can do it alone. But where should I say you are?"

"Tell him I had some bad potato salad at lunch."

"Potato salad?"

"You think I should class it up a little?" I ask, and she nods. "How about tuna salad?"

"Let's go with shrimp."

"Whatever you're in the mood for." I glance at my watch. T-minus twenty-four minutes. "Shit. I have to get downtown. Thanks a bunch. I owe you one."

"Your office does have a better view," she teases.

"I'll keep that in mind." I begin backing out the door as she calls out, "Have a good show!"

"Shh!" I hush her like a crotchety old librarian and mime zipping my lips. She whispers an apology and mirrors the gesture back at me. As long as Mr. Whitley doesn't come to Funnies tonight, I'll be in the clear. Lucky for me, my boss doesn't have a funny bone in his body.

Two

Outside, droves of people pass by as sweat beads on the bridge of my nose, causing my glasses to slide down a bit. If I'd known summer could be hotter in the city than the country, I might've considered Los Angeles. Now I have to contend with the heat and make that crucial decision all Manhattanites are faced with in a hurry—taxi or subway.

That's one thing I miss about Texas, my own transportation. Blasting Britney Spears while I cruise 158 with the windows down, dust blowing in the wind, is a far cry from stop-and-go cab rides or squeezing into a packed subway car and praying no one *accidentally* grazes my tits or ass.

According to my maps app, either option will get me there, but barely on time. Given the current circumstances, staying aboveground feels safer. So cab it is. I wag my arm, mustering my inner New Yorker. I've been here two years and I still ask myself, *Am I doing this right?*

A lit yellow Toyota pulls in front of me and I slide in. Guess that answers that. "Damn, it's hotter than Satan's asshole out there." I lean forward, letting the air conditioner blow some frosty air on my face.

"Where to?" the driver asks.

"Funnies on Eleventh and Third, please. I'm performing soon."

"Got it," he says. "What kinda accent is that?"

I like to pretend that I escaped West Texas with nothing but an optional twang (you know, for party tricks and such) but a real New Yorker can always spot a transplant.

Damn Yankees.

"Midland, Texas," I say.

"Never heard of it. Is that near Dallas?"

"Nope."

Out of the entire Lone Star State, I've found that most non-Texans are only familiar with the two major cities—Dallas and Houston, which apparently is pronounced *how-stun* in the city.

"Near Houston?"

See?

"It's about five hours from Dallas and eight hours from Houston. So no."

The only reason I know this is because growing up road trips were the only way we "vacationed." We also never left the state. How could we? You can drive ten hours and never cross a border. Good Lord, I hated how my dad had total control over the radio. A constant repeat of Boston, the Eagles, and the Steve Miller Band. All I wanted was a little "MMMbop."

My Texas trivia seems to shut the driver up and I pull my stage clothes from my bag. I manage to trade my button-down for a loose white V-neck without flashing a boob, and slide my pleather pants up beneath my pencil skirt. Yes, y'all, pleather! Maybe when I go pro, I'll graduate to real leather.

"Hey, Dallas, why don't you tell me a joke?" the driver asks. This is probably the most pervasive question any comedian is asked. Most of the time I make a sarcastic crack about coming to see my show, but today I've got one for him.

"Okay," I say, "I went to a taxi driver convention . . . Everyone showed up twenty minutes late."

"Ha. Ha." He offers a stilted laugh, clearly not my desired audience. "We're almost there. Don't get your Wranglers in a twist."

Did he just say *Wranglers?*

I double-knot my sneakers then read over my set, rehearsing it in my head as if I haven't been preparing these last two years for this moment. The clock strikes six forty-five and we're still four blocks away. "Would you mind speeding or running over a cyclist? I'm late."

"Speeding costs double. Murder is triple."

"You drive a hard bargain," I say, inwardly counting the seconds and street signs.

"Might I suggest leaving early next time?"

I roll my eyes. "Can you pull up here?" I ask when he approaches the corner, and toss an appropriate amount of bills his way. Clutching my bag, I dash toward the club, hell-bent for leather, muttering "Shit, shit, shit" every sharp exhale. Panting, I push my way into the front door at Funnies. "I'm here! I'm here!"

Ralph, the booker for the club, raises his brows. "Hey, slow down, Supergirl. Why are you so sweaty?"

"It's a million degrees out," I say, bent over, gripping my knees and gasping for breath. I take in Ralph's Gallagher mustache, '80s Larry David do, and plaid shirt with the sleeves rolled up. He's been at this club almost as long as I've been alive. "Quick question. Who's headlining tonight?"

"You don't know?" he asks.

"It's a long story."

"Well, why don't you go find out? He's in the greenroom."

"You're such a tease," I say.

"Takes one to know one," he snaps back in a singsong tone.

As much as I would love to continue this little banter session, I'm already late for . . . I still don't know. Though now I know he's a guy. No surprise there. Eighty-five percent of comedians in the U.S. are men. But I see more and more ladies take the mic every day so we're catching up, slaying that shitty rumor that women aren't funny. Still, I've come to learn firsthand that when you're a single female comedian in New York City trying to make a name for yourself, the odds are stacked higher than the Empire State Building. And not in your favor. I imagine it's about the same for female comedians in relationships too. Only their friends back home don't pity them as much.

I pass through the wood-paneled lobby and through the warm, red walls of the hallway. The deeper I go, the cooler and darker it gets, like a comedy cave. I'm sure most women my age find these sorts of places filthy but I find the drabness sort of romantic. Especially here at Funnies. This club is legendary.

When I first moved to New York, *this* is where I wanted to perform. So I took their workshop for new stand-ups. Best four hundred dollars I've ever spent. Got to know the staff and made a ton of connections. It's even where my agent, Bernie, found me. Now I perform here usually two nights a week, three if I'm lucky. Like so many who came before me.

I glide through the hall of fame. Framed headshots of some of the most famous comedians of all time—Chris Rock, Adam Sandler, Wanda Sykes, Eddie Murphy, Sarah Silverman, and of course Jerry Seinfeld. Standing here, staring at these icons is like being sprinkled with magical funny dust. I get to remind myself that before they were superstars, they were just like me. If these walls could talk, they could tell me what it was like for these guys to perform here for the first time. Did they bomb? Did they kill? Did they fall in love with the euphonious sound of laughter right here in this club?

I'm sure everyone feels a little thrill when they get a chuckle out of someone but comics are particularly compelled by it. We're sort of a special bunch. Not the extraordinary, revered kind of special. More like *bless your heart* kind of special. I'll never forget when I popped my Funnies cherry. It was one of those amazing moments when the world falls away and it's just you, the mic, and the audience. And there isn't a shadow of a doubt that you're exactly when and where you're meant to be. That's how I feel when I perform. That's why I ditched that dinner meeting.

Turning the corner for the greenroom, I hold my breath. Usually before a show, it's packed with comics and buddies—jokin', smokin', drinkin', havin' a good time. But tonight it's just a guy lounging in a chair, tapping his fingers on his chin like he's trying to remember why his wife sent him to the grocery store. Though I don't catch a glint of a wedding ring. He turns to me with a familiar face that I can't quite place.

"Are you Olivia Vincent?" he asks with a bold, smooth voice like a good bourbon—the kind that can be intoxicating.

"Yeah. And you're, um . . ." I speak slowly, buying myself time that neither of us has. The guy walks over. Pretty suave for a comedian in his black leather moto jacket (no, not like Andrew Dice Clay).

"I'm Nick Leto." And so the mystery of the headliner is finally solved. Nick's a pretty big name on the circuit, though I've never seen him perform. If I remember correctly, he spends most of his time touring venues up and down the East Coast. He slides his fingers back through his touchable, wavy hair and a tendril falls across his forehead. I straighten my glasses, getting a better look. Oh, yeah . . . he's got a Stamos-meets-Springsteen kinda vibe. And there's nothing wrong with that.

"You're late," he says.

"Hardly, and it's not like you're gonna start without me."

Nick smiles and two identical dimples reveal themselves beneath his two-day-old stubble. "I suppose that's true."

"Actually, I told my cab driver to take out any cyclist needed to get me here on time."

"That's very admirable of you."

"Thanks, but seriously, apologies. I just got the call and had to come from my office," I say.

"Well, I appreciate you coming last minute. What's your nine to five?" he asks.

"I'm a lawyer."

"My condolences. What kind of lawyer?"

"A funny one." This provokes a small laugh and Nick's dark brown eyes glimmer in the light.

"Well, if you don't mind, I'm going to finish preparing. You should be going on soon. Are you good?"

"I'm great. Thanks. I'll see you after the show."

I leave Nick to his preparatory process and find a cool corner in the hall for me to do the same. Studying scribbled notes is so much more fun than combing through contracts. I let out an easy breath, then hear the emcee over the mic. It's almost show-time. I set my phone to airplane mode and hit record on my voice memo app. Ever since I started recording my sets and playing them back, listening closely to what works and what doesn't, I've been able to improve exponentially. And maybe that's why Bernie called me tonight and not someone else—because there are so many of us champing at the bit for a slice of the comedy pie. The emcee gives me a short and sweet introduction ending with, "Now let's hear some noise for Olivia Vincent!"

That's my cue.

The crowd's applause welcomes me onstage. I take my place in front of the FUNNIES sign hung on the old brick wall and an upright piano on my left. It doesn't matter how much stage time I get, I'm always a bundle of nerves right before I go on. My heart, my mind, and my adrenaline race a mile a minute. But the moment I step out in the spotlight and feel the metal mic on my palm, my hands steady and I come to life. Eager for what I came for.

That gorgeous laughter.

Three

My time's almost up but I don't want it to end. If only I could stay up here all night. Or at least for another eighteen minutes, because that's about all the solid material I have. I pace myself, leading into my closing punchline, which I always want to rush for the simple fact that it's exciting. I hit my mark. Hard. A wave of laughter swells from the back of the room to the front and back again before crashing over me. Hot damn, that feels good.

The headlining Nick Leto is propped against the wall just offstage in the shadows. His pearly white teeth illume the darkness as he joins the audience in a jovial laugh. A thrilling jolt tickles my insides. I made him laugh. Genuinely.

Uh-oh. That's usually how crushes begin.

Not that I've had one in forever. Some women develop the warm and fuzzies only after they know the other person's into them. For me, those warm and fuzzies bloom when a man sincerely laughs at one of my jokes. I can't help but get all starry-eyed after that.

"That's my time, everyone. I'm Olivia Vincent. You've been great!" I gaze out over the crowd of grinning faces, capturing it in my mind as I do with all the best shows. The emcee retrieves the mic and I exit the stage toward Nick, who seems to be basking in the glow of a good laugh that I inspired. At least that's how he looks to me.

I smooth my dark hair back, gently tugging on my ponytail as I approach him. "I got 'em all warmed up for ya."

His eyebrow flicks, intrigued. "Now that's the kinda foreplay I like."

Oooh, did you hear that? It's the sound of my heart thumping against my chest, rumbling all the old cobwebs away. I take in a breath. Nick's Irish Spring scent with a hint of sweet, musky cologne enchants me further.

But you know your girl's got to play it cool. So I snap back playfully, "'Cause you didn't have to do any of the work?"

"That's funny." Nick's lips curl up, his dimples like a double feature act while his eyes headline the show. "So what kind of last name is Vincent?" he asks.

"A good one."

He chuckles. "No, I mean the origin."

I'm pretty sure this is a much subtler way of asking my ethnicity. I've gotten Italian, Spanish, part Brazilian or some other South American heritage. The truth is I don't really know. My mom's side is some European blend, while my dad's is a bit of a mystery wrapped up in his foster care childhood he wouldn't say much about. I haven't exactly gotten around to doing one of those DNA tests because I've never really been interested in the past. I'm all about the road ahead and who I'll become. Plus, Vincent is a stage name—which is a story for another time. So instead of briefing him on all the details, I simply answer, "It's Latin, I think. It means *to win*."

"*Are* you a winner?"

"I think that's pretty obvious." I like to think I have a healthy sense of hubris, which Imani often tells me is an oxymoron. But it works for me. Even if I have to fake it sometimes.

With the emcee onstage cracking an extra joke or two (comics like to ham it up), Nick's eyes remain fixed on me like I'm some kind of puzzle, wondering how the pieces fit. Or perhaps he's wondering if our pieces would fit.

"What? Why are you looking at me like that?" I ask.

"I'm trying to decide if your glasses are prescription or not."

I touch the edge of the plastic tortoiseshell frames. "Why? You think I'm wearing them just to make myself look smarter?"

"Maybe."

No joke, people do treat me differently when I wear my glasses. When I first moved to New York, I tried contacts for the first time. Neither my bosses nor my clients took me as seriously. So I went back to glasses and problem solved.

"They're prescription."

"Good." His shoulders fall like he's relieved. "I can't stand those poser hipster glasses. Is nothing sacred to millennials?"

"No," I say with a straight face. "I just bought a pair of couture crutches."

He drops his head in a snicker. "So you gonna hang out after the show?"

Hang out is the term comics use to refer to joshing around and drinking into the late-night hours, which could be considered networking time. I would love to . . . *hang out* with Nick but I have to decline.

"Wish I could but I've got more gigs later tonight," I say. Comedy comes first.

"Maybe I'll see you around then," he says, and I really want him to ask for my number, or follow me on social, or kiss me good night without a word. But he doesn't.

"Sure. Thanks again for the opportunity tonight. It was awesome."

"Thank Bernie. She was bragging on you, said I would do well to give you a chance. I think she was right."

"I appreciate that." I can practically hear the voice of an AI in my head saying, *Crush activation complete. Loading romantic pop playlist.*

"Well, Olivia Vincent, I owe you one." Nick pats the edge of my shoulder and looks past me at the stage as the emcee calls his name. "Wish me laughs."

In all the years I've been doing stand-up, I've never heard that expression—*Wish me laughs.* I kinda like it. Only I'm not sure what the appropriate response is so I just say, "Okay."

"Have a good night." With that he hikes up the stage and into the spotlight. The crowd roars for him like he's Richard Pryor or something. They love him. And at first glance, I can see why. But the real test is his act.

Moments later, Nick's bassy voice fills the room and the audience's response is palpable, a natural exchange of energy between comedian and crowd. Some stand-ups have that thing. And Nick might just be one of them. Some stand-ups should be called stand-stills because they hardly move about the stage, like

Janeane Garofalo or Nate Bargatze, while others walk back and forth like they're trying to get their ten thousand steps in like young Chris Rock or Whitney Cummings.

I'm somewhere in the middle, but Nick doesn't move any more than he has to. To me, it's a sign that the material stands on its own—it doesn't need anything more than timing to animate it. It's a special craft that doesn't work for everybody. He's got that wry, honest humor like George Carlin and Bill Hicks— clever comics with fresh, thought-provoking perspectives. I spit out a laugh as he slides in the punchline.

Nick's good. Really good.

No wonder he's a headliner.

Since I have some time before my next show, I wander over to the bar in the far corner of the club for a little refresher. Liza's bartending tonight. Before I even take a seat she sets my usual down on a cocktail napkin—an iced tea. Unsweet. Apparently there's a sugar shortage north of the Mason-Dixon Line.

"Well, look at you picking up a feature spot with Nick Leto," Liza says.

"How'd I do? Be honest," I say, clasping my hot hand against the chilled glass.

"Honestly, I laughed. It was really funny." Liza is my ideal audience member, so if she thinks it's funny, then I'm getting somewhere. She nods toward the stage. "This guy's hilarious."

The crowd roars with laughter again and Nick appears modestly satisfied—but doesn't seem to let it go to his head. "Yeah, this is the first time I've seen him."

"Really? I guess he *is* on the road a lot."

"That's what I hear." You know when you watch figure skaters move along the ice effortlessly even though it takes a lot of damn work to look that smooth? That's what it's like watching Nick. I know what goes into creating a worthwhile set. It's a lot of trial and error but Nick performs so naturally, like he came out of the womb with a mic in his hand, looked at his lengthy umbilical cord, and said—*Now that's what I'm talking about.* "He is good. What do you think his secret is?"

"Aside from doing this for a decade?" A decade—I guess there is something to that ten-thousand-hours rule. "He's candid. It's like what Charlie Chaplin said: 'To truly laugh, you must be able to take your pain, and play with it.' I've watched a lot of stand-ups from behind this bar and the best comics are the ones who have the courage to tell their story."

I don't want to discount Liza's wisdom or anything but I'm pretty sure success in comedy is about being funny, not telling your story. Save that for the memoir.

Four

Riding the high of my Funnies gig, I kill it at The Mic Stand across town. Then I head to the Upper West Side, where they'll surely put me in jail for life, because my set murders at Comedy Crypt. Finally, it's time to head home for the night.

Walking the streets of New York in pleather pants at the end of June feels a little swampy. Though after the night I've had, I'm practically floating home and less inclined to care about pit stains on my white tee. That's not to say I don't still have my wits about me. I always take the proper precautions on my commute by grasping a self-defense weapon until I'm safely inside my apartment. Fortunately for me, and anyone who dares to cross me, I've never had to use it. I know what you're thinking—I'm from the South so I must be packin' heat. But it's just pepper spray.

Still, don't mess with Texas.

It's just after eleven when I walk into my building. While the elevator climbs to the fourth floor, I check my GPS to see if Imani's home. She is, which means her date must've ended at a decent hour. Ten bucks says she's curled up in bed listening to some ASMR podcast. There's something nice about coming home when the building's quiet and everyone's retired to bed for the night. I approach our unit, punch in the pin code, and the lock clicks loose.

The door creeps open to a dark apartment. That's strange. Imani always leaves a light on for me. Gripping my pepper spray can a little tighter, I steady my glasses and step inside. A stark light spills out from the open refrigerator, and a chill sweeps over me. Huh? How could she have forgotten to—

I catch a foreboding glimpse and gasp. A broad-chested man in a black-and-white-striped shirt glares back at me with his big gray eyes. What the . . .

A burglar?

Are we being burgled?

Still armed, I aim my loaded can at the intruder. He gulps, face morphing to a panic-stricken gape. Good. I'm glad he's scared because I haven't exactly tested my weapon before (a terrible decision in hindsight). Dammit! Why isn't there a spray range with Ted Bundy cardboard targets, pepper-proof masks, and badass songs like "Heads Will Roll" blasting overhead?

My mind races as fast as my heart, and it's painfully obvious that I'm not at all prepared for this. I press on anyway. "Stay back or I'll spray the shit out of you!"

Yeah, Olivia. I'm sure he's shakin' in his boots now.

He steps away from the fridge, yelling back in some kind of guttural gibberish I can't understand.

"Now get out! Shoo!" I gesture with my free hand, getting the sense that I've been atrociously misinformed of how to deter a *cat* burglar.

He backs into the hall with no intention of escaping. "Oh. No. You. Don't!" I hit the trigger and a pitiful foamy spew sound emerges. Not the heart-stopping hiss I had expected.

Mother fu . . .

I shake the can and shoot again only to hear another measly squirt. My nose crinkles, stinging something fierce from the peppery stench. The intruder shouts incomprehensibly, shielding his face with the crook of his elbow.

"What in the hell?" Imani's voice cuts through the scene as she flips the light switch. With her fists balled at her hips, she stands firmly in her black nightgown and matching satin robe.

I screw up my eyes and rub my nose. "Imani, run! This guy's robbing us!"

He stomps her way, uttering that gobbledygook once again. This time with overly animated hand gestures. In the illuminated apartment, the man appears more human and less creature of the night. Wait a second . . . He's not speaking gibberish. It's German.

She raises a commanding hand. "Calm down. He's with me."

"Huh?" I guess the horny heels strike again. Still, I didn't expect her to bring anyone home. She prefers to love 'em and leave 'em at their place, keeping her bedding clean. So yeah, a robbery seemed more plausible.

"Yes, Olivia. Stand down." Her stare shifts to my still-aimed pepper spray. I lower my poor excuse for protection while Imani turns to her fine foreigner and speaks to him in his native tongue. What are they saying? After a moment, he shoots me a look and stomps back into her bedroom in a huff.

"You okay?" she asks.

With a hand on my heart, I could melt into a puddle of relief right about now. "Yeah." Gotta love a girl who's concerned for her friend even when said friend attempts to assault her date. But that's what we do. She's my penguin—a term of endearment we started using way before everyone started calling their besties *my person*. Why penguin? Well, they mate for life, and while we don't *mate*, we are forever mates.

We met in our junior year at Highland High. She was an army brat who spent half her life on a U.S. military base in Germany and the other half in the States. Her newly retired father took an oil job in Midland of all places. Since she knew no one, and I was desperate for any insight as to what life was like outside of Texas, we became fast friends. To avoid babysitting one of her younger siblings, she'd escape to my house, where we were free to scarf down stovetop quesadillas and watch as many *Chappelle's Show* reruns on DVR as we wanted. We followed each other to UT in Austin for undergrad. When it came time for law school, I stayed in the Berlin of Texas and Imani left for New York, which made my decision to move here that much easier.

Imani moseys over to the scene of the crime and grabs a glass from the cabinet. "I meant to text you that I had company but, um, I was a little busy."

"More like gettin' busy."

She does her best to hide a bashful smile but no dice.

I set my bag down, adjust my glasses, and toss the pepper spray can into the garbage. "So where did you pick up the Hamburglar?"

"Be nice, Liv."

"I'm just sayin'. With that shirt? It's like he just walked off the set of *Jailhouse Rock*."

She indulges me in a little laugh. I'll take it. "His name is Lukas. He's from the Frankfurt office."

"Makes sense." I lean on the cool stone breakfast bar between us, eager to get the rest of the details.

"We had a few drinks. One thing led to another . . ." Isn't that how it always happens? You're having a friendly drink and before you know it your bra's dangling from some guy's lampshade and you're screaming, *Ja, ja, JA!* (For those of you who don't know, that's *yes* in German—I picked up that much.)

"Ooh, you did the nasty with him," I tease, gyrating my body like we're back in eleventh grade.

"Girl, you don't even know." She widens her eyes as if she's about to spill the tea. "Boy can make my body talk!"

"In what language?" I ask, and she shoots me a sassy pursed-mouth stare. "Does he speak any English?"

"Only a few words, but they're all the right ones."

I roll my eyes, finally feeling the adrenaline rush of the evening simmer down. "Should I get a hotel?" I'd prefer not to hear my BFF enjoy her German boy toy all night.

She waves a carefree hand. "No, Liv, you're good. There's no way he can go again."

"How many times has it been?" I say out of the side of my mouth even though I know he's not listening to our conversation from the other room enough to understand it.

She lifts a finger for a count of one, then two, then three.

"Damn! For you or for him?"

She nods in the direction of the bedroom. "Him, for me it's been . . ." She holds up a full five-fingered hand. My jaw drops. "Try not to hate me."

"I never could." Though, I am envious of her orgasm extravaganza. I haven't had one since I came to New York. I'm not talking about a multiple-orgasm sexfest. I mean any orgasm. It's true. Whether I'm alone or with someone, it never shows up. But I'm busy. By the time I get home from my twelve-hour days, how can I expect my body to give any more? I'm sure things will bounce back when I have only one career to manage instead of two. At least I hope so.

"So how was the show?" she asks, and I immediately think of Nick's smile.

"So good. The crowd was awesome. Imani, I'm telling you. This is what I should be doing." I breathe out a sigh as my gaze wanders to the ceiling, imagining a scene I've thought of a million times—just me and a mic, onstage, thousands of people in the audience laughing as I land joke after joke after joke. I fantasize about seeing my name on a marquee and making friends with my comedic heroes. The ones who are still alive at least. Maybe I'd have time for an actual relationship with someone who gets it. Someone who gets me. Maybe someone with a face, and sense of humor, like Nick.

Imani's eyes soften. "Liv, that's great. You're like . . . glowing."

"Well, I sorta met a guy too," I say playfully.

"Really? Who?"

"He's another stand-up."

"Are you going to see him again?"

"I'm not sure. He's on the road all the time anyway." Unfortunately. "Well, you better get back to the Hamburglar."

"I just hope he doesn't snore."

"Yeah, all the good ones have sleep apnea."

She lets out one of those too-tired-to-laugh laughs. "G'night."

"Night. Sorry about the pepper spray."

"Don't be. You're my penguin." She lays her hand gently on mine and gives it a little squeeze, forgiving me for pepper-spraying her German sex-god guest.

Five

After a long hot shower, I emerge from our tiny white-tiled bathroom, steam spilling out into the hallway. My dark, damp hair is crimped from the towel-dry because it's too late to run the dryer. I never sleep well with the smell of comedy club lingering in the strands of my hair.

The sound of Imani's giggle seems to slip beneath the crack of her closed bedroom door as I pass it on the way to my bedroom. It echoes out into the apartment and I freeze. Muffled voices grow steady. There's movement too. So much for keeping it quiet.

Screeeeech.

Are they dragging the chair across the floor? Oh, Lord. There's only one reason to rearrange furniture at this hour. Good. For. Them. Welcome to New York roommate life, where everyone's listening to everyone's everything all the time. I roll my eyes, hurry to my room, and close the door. Imani might be my penguin but I can't listen to whatever sexual acrobatics she and the German Hamburglar are experimenting with now.

I yank my phone from the charger and dig in my nightstand for a pair of headphones. If I were smart, I'd pull up a meditation podcast and allow five minutes of deep breathing to lull me unconscious. But instead I'll indulge in my favorite pastime— stand-up comedy.

Curled up on one side, I prop up my phone on the nightstand next to my glasses, careful not to yank the headphone cable. A few feel-good jokes should release the right neurochemical cock-tail for rest and relaxation. My new favorite stand-up special begins. No matter how many times I've seen it, it never gets old. There's something comforting about watching a comedy special in the dark when everyone else is asleep, or busy, in Imani's case.

On my summer breaks as a teen, I'd stay up late in bed sipping on sweet tea, the fan blowing on my feet kicked out of the covers, and watching specials on The Comedy Channel or HBO. All while trying not to wake my dad with my laughter. My favorites were Margaret Cho, Wanda Sykes, Judy Gold, and Chris Rock. Little did I know it was the caffeine in the tea that was keeping me up. It was so much fun discovering comedians for myself and developing my own taste in stand-up.

I carried that tradition into my college years but by then the stand-ups weren't enough to keep me company. I longed for someone—a man to lie next to. Someone to laugh at all the same jokes with. It's a rare thing, you know, a shared sense of humor. Trust me, I've looked. For some reason I always ended up dating guys who liked stand-ups that just don't do it for me. But since I know the comedy grind, you won't catch me trashing anyone.

Now this special streaming on my phone totally does it for

me. Not to mention how inspiring it is to see a woman who's not much older than me produce her own hour-long special that no one can stop talking about. Hello, goals!

I try to fight my heavy lids with a laugh while Ali Wong cracks jokes about trapping her husband and mistaking hot homeless men for hipsters. Soon Ali's voice is in my head but my mind drifts beyond consciousness.

Sirens blare down the street, alerting me awake to a sun-filled room. I suck in a deep inhale, rub the crust out of my eyes, and attempt to wet my desert-dry mouth with my tongue.

Shit. What time is it?

With a plastic headphone stuck to the side of my face, I blink my eyes wide and pull the cable, reeling my phone over. Uh-oh. I was supposed to be at the office ten minutes ago. I sit straight up like I've just been administered a double shot of espresso intravenously. Patting around the nightstand for my glasses, I shoot off a panicked text to Imani and scramble out of bed.

OLIVIA: I overslept. Why didn't you wake me up?

Sometimes we act as each other's backup alarms. Her more than me since I'm the one always running on fewer hours of sleep.

IMANI: I left early. You want me to cover for you?

Since she's in a different department, there's not much she can do. Scrubbing my molars with a toothbrush in one hand, I tap out a response with my other.

OLIVIA: Thanks but I got it.

It's a good thing I started that food poisoning rumor. It'll make the perfect alibi for my tardiness. Besides, why is arriving at nine A.M. considered late? At the law firm of Whitley, Bauer, Carey, and Klein, come in past eight and the partners look at you like you're rolling in past noon with sneakers on. Maybe it's because I'm from *take your time* Texas but I don't understand what's so glamorous about the seventy-hour workweek grind. I don't care how many vitamin B–infused green juices you chug a day, we're not machines. I do it now only as a necessary evil.

I fly into work just after nine, carrying my nearly empty twenty-ounce travel mug. No time to stop for coffee, so I had to make it the old-fashioned way—at home. Passing through the halls to get to my office, I expect the usual *nice of you to finally join us* glares. Instead, no one makes eye contact with me. It's like they're giving me the silent treatment. Nah, it's probably in my head. I am the teensiest bit self-conscious since this is the fourth time I've been late in the past two weeks. But who's counting?

At my desk, files are stacked haphazardly in one corner, the slate-colored phone cord is tangled up in itself, and my company-issued laptop waits to be opened. Everything is exactly as I left it except for one small detail—a blinding, Day-Glo yellow Post-it stuck to my coffee-stained ceramic mug.

See me ASAP—W.

W. for Whitley, my boss. Uh-oh. His handwriting does not look happy.

Six

S hit," I mutter. Hope I'm not in trouble. Eh, it's not like I've monumentally screwed something up. Well, not to my knowledge. And there wasn't anything alarming when I read through my emails on the subway earlier. I snatch the note off my computer and crush it in my hands as I head for his office. The door's open, so I knock on the frame. Whatever this is about I'll smooth it over with a smile the way I always do. Plus everyone knows girls who wear glasses aren't troublemakers. At least not according to mainstream television.

"Good morning, Mr. Whitley. You wanted to see me?" Good, Olivia. Keep it cheery. Easy breezy does it.

Boss man looks up from his desk, straining to smile. Part of me wants to cheer him on like he's a baby pulling himself up for the first time—*Come on, Mr. Whitley, you can do it. Almost there!* "Yes, Olivia. Please come in. Take a seat."

I do as I'm asked, smoothing out my skirt before I plop down on one of the russet-colored leather chairs. He sets his silver fountain pen on his desk and leans forward, resting on his elbows like something bad happened. Maybe someone died and that's why it's so weird around here. Oh, no. Was it Fawn? Did she choke on a shrimp when she lied for me? No, that can't be it. I got a message from her this morning.

"You missed the Fenwick dinner last night," he says.

I smile, keeping my tone gentle. "Yes. I'm sure Fawn mentioned I had a terrible bout of food poisoning yesterday evening. But according to her, the meeting went perfectly well without me."

"Yes, I heard as much too."

"Great, then I'll follow up with Fenwick this morning."

"That won't be necessary," he says, like he's gladly removing something from my plate and encouraging me to relax, go on vacation. Not that I've had a chance to travel past the tristate area since I started working at this firm.

"Why is that?"

Mr. Whitley stares at me for a few seconds, but it feels like an eternity. What? What is it? Finally, he opens his mouth. "It's come to my attention that in the past several months you've been showing up late, leaving early, and, more concerning, missing deadlines."

C'mon, man. Like three deadlines. Surely, that's not so bad.

"With all due respect, Mr. Whitley, I primarily oversee commercial real estate contracts. It's not like we're litigating murder trials."

"See!" He points a firm finger at me. "That attitude right there. You're not taking this job seriously. You're not taking yourself seriously."

Sheez. What's with the hostility? All this over nothing.

"*I'm* not taking myself seriously?" I say.

"That's right. Now I understand that you're young and you have other . . . interests." Whitley has to be referring to stand-up. It's no secret around here that I'm a comedian. Hell, three P.M. at the coffee machine is basically my own personal open mic night. Not to mention, I got them to hire me as the entertainment for the holiday party last year. I wrote some killer jokes about the firm. Now, those were some big laughs. A pretty big paycheck too. My boss continues, "And it's hindering your work."

"Can you be more specific?" This is a little trick I learned in law school. It throws the ball right back at them and lets you listen out for any holes in their claim.

"Yes." He pauses as if quickly collecting his thoughts. "I don't think you're a good fit for Whitley, Bauer, Carey, and Klein." Can't argue with that. "I'm sorry, Olivia, but we have to let you go."

My face cracks into a smile and I spit out a chuckle. He's got to be setting up for a hilarious punchline. After a moment of his solid silence, his words begin to sink in. *We have to let you go.* I've been present for this entire conversation but he can't be serious. "You're kidding, right?" I ask.

"No, we're not all joke tellers."

Well, damn. Then this is really happening. My chest tightens and I struggle to breathe for a second. Me? No job? No boss? I shake my head, trying to reassemble the rattled pieces until they make sense. "Just to be clear, I'm being fired?"

"Yes."

"Huh," I utter, and attempt to sink into the chair but the stiff leather has no give. No more contracts. No more bullshit meetings. And no more trying to find an empty ladies' room for my post-coffee deuce.

"If you leave respectfully," Whitley continues, "you'll get a month's severance out of the deal."

That doesn't sound so bad. None of this sounds that bad. But I'm an adult with bills, student loan debt, and a company-sponsored health plan. It would be irresponsible to take this lying down, right? I must fight to save my shitty job! "And there's nothing I can do to change your mind?" I ask.

Yep, that's about as much fight as I can muster. (Let's call it an honorable attempt.)

"No."

So that's it. The chains of corporate America dissolve into a month's worth of pay. And just in time for summer. No, no, I should be freaking out right now. Panicked. Maybe even devastated. But the truth is I'm grateful Mr. Whitley has the balls to do what I couldn't. Because the way I see it, *fired* is just another word for *free*.

I give my thighs a satisfactory slap and hop to my feet. "I appreciate the opportunity, Mr. Whitley. Good luck to you."

"And to you." Wow, he actually looks relieved. I've never seen him without that jagged wrinkle down his forehead before.

I take in a deep breath and saunter out of his office. There's no point in collecting anything from my desk. Nothing there I care about. I didn't even bother to bring a personal photo.

On the way to the elevator, I pass by Fawn sitting alone in the conference room, files spread out in front of her like a hand of poker cards, though not nearly as fun. I pop my head in and she looks up, seeming totally at peace. I'm happy for her. She's where she should be, and now I will be too.

"Thanks for taking care of Fenwick last night."

"Glad to help."

"I gotta run but I want you to have my office. You can move in anytime."

"Really? Just like that?" What's that saying? Every time a comedian gets fired, an aspiring law partner gets a new office?

"That's right," I say. And just like that, Olivia has left the law firm.

After I wrap my head around the news, I ask Imani to meet me for an early lunch at Shake Shack. Because nothing says *I'm free to do what I want* quite like a hamburger. At least for me. Sitting at a bistro table outside the restaurant, Imani and I soak in the heat, cooling ourselves with our respective milkshakes—mine chocolate, hers strawberry. Cabs, cars, and buses stop and go along Broadway, while everyday New Yorkers take long strides hiking up and down the gray sidewalk.

Imani takes a break from hoovering her shake, leaving a burgundy lip stain on her straw. "Why does sugar have to be so bad when it tastes so good?"

"It's the devil's work." I toss a crinkled fry in my mouth. "So listen, I have something to tell you." Dusting salt off my hands, I straighten up in my metal-made seat. I really hope she gets on board with this.

She leans back, crossing her arms and legs. "Let me guess, you got fired?"

For a moment, it's like all of New York stops and stares at me, shaming me for being a naughty little lawyer. But I can't back down now.

"You knew? How?"

"I came by your office and Fawn Douglas was in there re-decorating the place. She said they let you go." By her tone, she's much more upset about this than I am.

"I got a month's severance out of it."

"Well, at least that'll tide you over until you get another job." Imani would say that. Sensible to her core, she clings to stability and certainty. Probably because she moved around a lot as a kid. That's what her therapist thinks anyway.

"Or, it'll tide me over while I pursue comedy full-time," I say with 100 percent confidence. Why not use this time to try? What's the worst that could happen?

She drops her head, rubbing her fingers into her forehead like she's got a splitting headache. "Oh, Livy, no." Livy? She never calls me that. It's Olivia, Liv, girl, or bitch (but only in the most affectionate way). "How are you planning to pay rent when you're making like thirty bucks a night?"

"Those are just the spots I have time for so far. If this is all I do, I'll have the freedom to go for bigger, better-paying gigs." It's true. I've turned down some great offers from Bernie due to my work restrictions. Opportunities don't come up all the time but I'm sure my new availability will move things along. Considering she called me last night, I must be on her mind.

"Even if that's true, you still have a six-figure student loan to pay down. How are you gonna manage that?" Damn that expensive-ass education.

"Imani," I say, wide eyed, "why are you grillin' me? You know more than anyone that I moved here for stand-up."

"The caveat being you need a lawyer's salary to pay your bills until your career takes off, remember? The Jim Gaffigan plan." Gaffigan must have a lot of patience. And kids.

"I know but I don't have a family like him. So this is the new plan. The Olivia Vincent Plan," I say, squirming some in my seat. Of all the people in my life, she's the one I count on to support my choices. I support hers—like, um, I don't know . . . when she got that lotus flower tattoo on her lower back. (You know—a tramp stamp.)

"Since when are we not family?" Imani snaps, totally using my point to argue against me.

"I mean a family who depends on me financially."

"Did you forget we're roommates?"

"I don't understand why you keep getting hung up on these minor details. Have I ever been late paying the landlord?"

Imani crosses her arms tighter, wrinkling her starched suit. "Olivia, you know I love you. And I really do think you're going to make it in stand-up *one day*. I just don't think it's wise to voluntarily leave your law career at this juncture. You need to be able to support yourself."

Her words, in whatever way she means them, trigger something in me. Something I'd like to believe I chucked out on the side of the road when I left mind-numbing Midland and never looked back. "You sound just like my dad," I snap back like a bitch, and *not* in an affectionate way.

Finally, her harsh glare melts, evaporating the hostility. She begins softly, "Your dad was just looking out for you, Liv. And so am I. I want to make sure you think this through."

"I have thought it through." Okay, I really don't have a thorough plan but I will, and in the meantime, I've made a few calls.

Besides, after a while you learn that sometimes when you make plans, God shits on them. My grandfather used to say that.

"Okay, then." She picks up one of my cheese-covered fries. "What's your first move?"

I lift my chin and smirk. "I have a meeting with Bernie this afternoon."

Seven

Let me tell you a little about Bernice Ludgate. More commonly known as Bernie. She's been representing comedic talent in New York City for the past twenty-five years. Having discovered some of the biggest names in the early days of their comedy careers, she's got an eye for hot new talent. Even plucked me out after a performance at Funnies and said in traditional showbiz fashion, "You got somethin', kid."

That was about a year ago.

It's only because of her I actually started making money from performing. Not that I'm raking in enough to make it rain—as Imani so kindly reminds me. With Bernie's help, I have no doubt I'll be able to land something substantial. And by substantial, I mean televised, streamed, or the like.

I march into her office ten minutes before our appointment at two P.M. As a gesture of good faith (and maybe to butter her up), I picked up a bagel schmeared with cream cheese from the best bakery in the five boroughs. You know, the *good* bagels. On the fourth floor of an old downtown building, Bernie's place of business is nothing more than a reception area the size of a closet, a private room with an exposed brick wall, and a slight view of the park. Well, *a* park. The reception chair is empty and Bernie's door is wide open so I slip in.

"Is that you, Olivia?" Bernie barks with that scratchy voice of hers, tossing someone's headshot on the mounding slush pile of photos and résumés on her desk.

"The one and only." I hold the bagel bag up near my face, a grin schmeared across it. "Special delivery."

She glances up over the rim of her glasses, a knowing glint in her eyes. "Is that for me?"

I nod and set the paper bag down in front of her and she peeks inside, keeping her expression vague. Bernie's not someone I would consider facially expressive. That is, unless she thinks something's really funny. "I'm surprised you were able to get away from the office long enough to come down here and stop for bagels."

I take a seat on the worn chair. "That's actually what I wanted to talk to you about."

"All right, the floor is yours."

I clear my throat and my heart starts pounding the same way it does right before I go onstage. If I had a mic in my hand and a spotlight on my face right now, this would be a bit easier. Bernie stares, waiting for my announcement. Why am I nervous? I'm simply about to tell my booking agent that my entire life currently rests in her professional hands. I gulp back my jitters and my mouth turns drier than the Chihuahuan Desert.

"Bernie, no one is better at spotting upcoming talent than you. And we both know that you only work with comedians you truly believe in, right?"

"Yes," she answers with that *where is this going?* tone. "Unless you count my brother's kid who couldn't make a group of kindergartners laugh slipping on a banana peel. But he's family so what can you do?" Bernie gestures for me to continue.

"Right, um." I shake my head and take a breath. "We both know that I have potential. And not just potential, I have drive. I hustle with the best of them. I write. I perform. And I consistently show up at the clubs night after night after night after putting in full days at the office because I really want this and I'm willing to do what it takes." She opens her mouth to speak but I barrel on. "So, I want to take the next step and throw myself into stand-up full-time, but I need your help. What do you think?"

She narrows her eyes, leaving me holding my breath. "Are you leaving your law firm?"

"Well, I kinda already left."

"Are you having one of those almost-thirty crises?"

Almost thirty? "I'm not having a crisis. I'm just ready."

"Are you sure?" she asks, like I'm pulling her leg.

I put on my *please, take me seriously* face. "Bernie, have I ever been at your office in the middle of the afternoon?"

"Good. Because I've got some things cookin' for ya."

Whew! "You do?"

"Yes." Finally, someone who's on board with the Olivia Vincent Plan. "In fact, the call just came in today. It's an audition. A big audition."

"I'm listening." I scoot to the edge of my seat with an eager grin. God, I hope it's something to pay the bills. Or *a* bill. "What's the spot?"

"Ever heard of *The Late Night Show*?" Her pitch falls for dramatic effect. A rhetorical question of course. Everyone knows the freaking *Late Night Show with Anderson Vanderson*. Though, I still can't believe that's his God-given name.

"Seriously?" A spot like that has the potential to catapult careers into full-blown stardom. We all saw what Johnny Carson's show did for Ellen DeGeneres. Well, technically I wasn't even a thought then but I've seen it many times online. (Gotta love a woman who rocks a mullet.) "That's amazing!"

"I know, because I'm amazing. Now try to show them you're amazing, would ya?"

"Yes, ma'am. Where's the audition?"

"Los Angeles. In two weeks."

"Oh," I say. "Not exactly a cab ride away, is it?" Using my next check toward airfare and a hotel isn't written into the new Olivia Vincent Plan. I hope I can afford the revision. Then again, I could make a case that I can't afford *not* to make it happen.

"Don't sweat it, kid. I know just how to get you there."

"How?" Please don't say *Hitch a ride on a cargo train then tuck and roll at the first sight of the Hollywood sign.*

"You've been offered a feature spot on a nationwide road tour by one of my comedians. Nine cities. Two weeks. Leaving the day after tomorrow." She hands me a printout with the dates and tour stops. "The last stop's L.A. Same day of the audition. You can fly home from there."

"Another one of your comedians offered me a spot?" Feature

on a road tour? Auditioning for *The Late Night Show*? All after getting fired from a job I hate. This is better than best-case scenario. "How is this even possible?"

"You must have a guardian angel or somethin'." Despite being from a very Jesus-loving town, I'm not very religious. With my past bad luck in life, it's difficult to imagine anyone watching over me. And I don't know any dead people that would take time away from eternal peace and happiness in order to orchestrate a way for me to succeed as a stand-up.

"Or maybe I'm just that good," I offer.

"I'll say. The original feature just booked a movie role and canceled a couple days ago. You were the obvious choice but I never thought you'd actually do it considering I've been trying to get you on the road for the past year."

It's true. Bernie makes money only if I make money, and one of the only real ways to make money in this business is to tour. That's never been much of an option for me when I've got only two weeks' paid vacation and it's basically frowned upon to take it. So I've been able to do only occasional regional events on weekends.

I glance over the itinerary—D.C., Atlanta, Nashville, Gulfport, New Orleans, Dallas, and El Paso, which means we'll be driving straight through my hometown. The place I ran from two years ago and haven't been back to since. "No way," I say.

"What's that?" she says.

"Nothing. I'll just be passing my hometown in Texas." The thought of going back there isn't helping my burger sit very well in my stomach.

"Dallas, right?"

"Midland."

"Is that near Dallas?"

Instead of giving a geography lesson, I settle for, "Yeah."

"So what d'you say? You ready to hit the road?" she asks.

Hit the road? Yes. Face my past? I don't think so. But I need the money, the experience, and Bernie's support, so what else can I say?

"Yes, I'm ready." There. I did it. And the rest, I'll figure out. "Thank you, Bernie. You have no idea how much this means to me."

"No sweat, kid." Bernie reaches inside the bag and pulls out a well-deserved bagel.

"Oh, wait," I say. "Who's the headlining comedian?"

With bread stuffed in her cheek like a chipmunk and cream cheese stuck to her lip, she manages to say, "Nick Leto. From last night."

"Wait a second. Nick Leto offered this?" This is way better than asking for my number. Me on the road with Nick for two weeks? Now there's a plot twist.

"Yeah." She stares at me a moment longer. "What's that look on your face?"

I drop the soft grin, dreamy-eyed gaze, and flushed cheeks immediately. "There's no look. This is just my face."

"Mm-hmm, I know that look." Bernie sets the bagel aside, swipes the cheese off her mouth, and points at me like she means business. "Now listen. This is a legit opportunity. I know Nick's a handsome, charming, funny guy with dimples you just wanna lick."

"You said it, not me."

"I'm serious. You don't want to go down that road. Keep it professional."

"Okay," I relent. She's right. I don't want to complicate things too much at the outset of the Olivia Vincent Plan. Even if his smile makes my knees weak.

"I mean it. No funny business."

Eight

t's the eve of the tour and I can't sleep. After tossing and turning endlessly, I flip on my light, slide on my glasses, and pull my oversized suitcase from underneath my bed. I don't think I've used this since I moved to the city. The dust bunnies are confirmation of that. I brush them away.

Huh? There's something stiff in the front pocket of the suitcase. Then, my heart sinks as I remember what it is. I unzip it and pull out Eddie Murphy's self-titled comedy album.

On vinyl.

The cover is slightly worn from being squeezed in between a collection of albums for thirty-some years. Photo strips of Eddie doing stand-up crisscross along the back. At least one of them is from Funnies. Which, looking at it now, carries new meaning for me. It was my father's favorite. He used to listen to this album shamelessly while making dinner on Sundays when I was young. I'd listen with him while I finished my homework at the kitchen table. He didn't even care that there were a lot of *bad words* in it.

Every now and then I'd look up and watch my dad laugh at a punchline. The context of which I couldn't wrap my head around. It wasn't until I was a teen that Murphy's material started to make more sense. The rest continued to elude me until I was old enough to vote. Listening to a good comedy special, whether it was Richard Pryor on vinyl or Sinbad on HBO, was the only time I'd see my dad really relax.

Looking back, I have to give him some credit. It couldn't have been easy being a single dad with a little girl. My mom took off when I was three. I can count on one hand how many times I've seen her since then. From what I understand she was a free-spirited dreamer, always chasing something. Something that wasn't us.

Since the circumstances with her were such a mess, I tried to make my dad's life a tad easier. Jokes brought him joy, so I learned to tell a few. They were no more clever than run-of-the-mill knock-knock jokes but he always laughed like they were really funny. I could tell because his nose would crinkle the way it would when he laughed at John Leguizamo's Super Latin Dad bit. It's the same way mine does when I watch Bo Burnham do his Kanye West–Chipotle bit in autotune.

And then there was that one moment. I must've been eight or so. We were sitting on the floor, sorting through a bag of Canel's chicles from Mexico. Each colorful wrapper printed with the name of their flavor in teeny-tiny letters. I didn't speak Spanish. Still don't, but I'd try to guess how to say each one and he'd inevitably correct my pronunciation. I picked up one called *anís*, flashed him the label, and said proudly in my innocence, "Anus!"

He lost it. Laughed like crazy. Nose crinkling. Wheezy laughter. Slapping his thigh. I had no idea what I had done but somehow I'd made my dad laugh the way Eddie Murphy did. When he finally got ahold of himself, he gently explained the meaning of the word *anus*—which I thought was totally gross. My expression became very serious, trying to make sense of it all. I held the gum between my fingers. "Are you telling me this chicle tastes like butt?"

Another belly laugh barreled out of him. This time he had tears coming out of his eyes. I wasn't sure I understood the joke but his laugh was so infectious I couldn't help but join in too.

"You're hilarious, Livy. You should be a comedian," he said.

I remember thinking that there was no way I could ever be a comedian since it seemed like a boy's job, but I liked that he thought I was funny enough. And so the seed was planted. Of course, no parent really dreams of their child growing up to use foul language in a punchline, performing for a bunch of strangers like little laugh whores. At least, I've never met any.

He never actually encouraged stand-up. Instead it was all— *Get good grades, Livy. Go to college, Livy. Get a good job, Livy.* All so I could have more luxuries than we could afford on his modest, manual-labor salary. So I did what I was told because *Livy's* a good little girl. And now every day, I vow never to let someone else dictate the terms of my life ever again. Not even him.

I slide my thumb inside the lower corner opening, pulling out a faded photo of my dad. Taken sometime in the early '80s, it's older than I am. He's standing on a small stage in front of that quintessential brick wall, holding a mic in his hands. There's a sign behind him of a white speech bubble that says THE HOOT in bold red lettering. The spotlight shines on his feathery dark hair and big, charismatic smile. He's rockin' brown corduroy bell-bottoms too.

Probably from the Vinnie Barbarino collection.

To think he played this album over and over, and I had no idea this vintage photo was hiding here the whole time. Not until I discovered it two years ago. Right after he kicked the bucket.

That's what he called it—*kick the bucket*. Said it sounded like something Charlie Chaplin would do.

It's sad, I know. The guy who taught me how to ride a bike and eat with chopsticks is gone. Poof! Show's over. But the thing is, I can't reconcile the man I knew with the one in this photograph. Yes, he loved comedy, but to think he actually performed stand-up. Didn't he think that was valuable information when I started performing in college while maintaining my GPA? Instead, he scolded me and said I was wasting my time, that I should focus on school, and that stand-up is nothing more than a pipe dream.

And you know what? I convinced myself that if he, a comedian lover, was talking shit about stand-up then maybe he was right. And so I stopped. Well, I stopped performing as much and I never said a word about doing it again. Not about the first time I got a laugh that seemed to raise the roof or the time before that when I bombed harder than a dive-bomber at Pearl Harbor.

Bad joke, I know. But now you know how epic it was.

I collected my degrees and piles of student debt and went on with my life. And while I was just beginning my life, his was about to end. That has to be the saddest part about losing a parent so young. Especially when you don't see it coming. You don't realize there won't be time to ask them the questions that really matter. And you never really get your answers. Let's face it, I got shortchanged. And now I'll never know the whole story—why did he stop performing? Did he perform once or was he a regular? Where's The Hoot? Why did he keep his stand-up days from me? And the question that haunts me the most: Why would he want to keep *me* from stand-up?

Nine

Less than two hours from now, Nick Leto and I will leave New York, heading south for our first stop. I'm still not packed. What's a woman like myself supposed to bring on a two-week cross-country comedy road tour anyway? The answer? Everything.

So I threw in most of my clothes, including several pairs of shoes, my leather jacket, hair dryer, flat iron, full bottles of shampoo and conditioner, everything on the bathroom sink, just-in-case tampons, laundry pods, my legal pad, laptop, and the tangled mess that is all of my chargers. But I couldn't close the damn suitcase. Now I'm down to the essentials and it's still stuffed. Let's see if the zipper and I are up for the challenge.

But before that, a sip of coffee.

Imani pops into my room. "You're really going through with this?"

"Yep." I flip the suitcase closed for emphasis.

Nick needed a replacement. If I hadn't said yes, someone else would've snatched it up fast as greased lightning. Was I hoping Nick had a tour bus all gassed up with a crew ready to head west? Yes. Too bad a midlevel headliner doesn't get rock star perks. Let's be real, being stuck in a car with a man who's managed to make a full-time living as a comedian, and is easy on the eyes, can't be a mistake. No matter how you slice it.

"But you don't even know this Nick guy," she says.

I know. I get that to her this is like the opening plot to an episode of *Unsolved Mysteries*. Imani's probably imagining Robert Stack walking a dark alleyway in his trench coat saying, *Olivia Vincent left New York on what was supposed to be a hilarious comedy tour. But when she didn't make it onstage that night, it turned out to be . . . no joke.*

"I know him enough," I say. Besides, Bernie wouldn't stick me with a psycho. How can she make money off my appearances if I don't make them, huh? This is essentially the argument I used with Imani when I came home the other night and told her all about it. She wasn't keen on it then and, with a hand on her hip like a mama itching to ground her teenage daughter, she's not keen on it now either.

Of course, this isn't about her approval. It's about landing the *Late Night Show* audition and changing the trajectory of my career. Correction: correcting the trajectory of my life. "Plus, look what I got yesterday." I whip out a fresh can of pepper spray and take a defensive stance. "Locked and loaded, baby! Even tested it in an alley. It's got a sharp spritz to it."

She looks more alarmed than relieved. "May want to keep that on you at all times."

"I will." I stick it in my backpack's side pocket.

"Fourth of July won't be the same without you." Every summer, our friends host a big party on their roof, where we can catch the fireworks over the East River. It's definitely a highlight.

"I know but I'll be in New Orleans. Hey, why don't you fly down for the day? Could be fun."

"That's a great idea in theory but I'm not sure I can make it happen."

"Just think about it."

"Speaking of visiting. Any chance you'll stop in Midland?"

The sound of the word *Midland* makes my stomach clench. Great idea in theory but I'm not sure I *want* to make that happen. With my dad gone, along with my grandparents, and my mother MIA, my connections back in Texas have been whittled down to a minuscule group. So I'll just pass through like a tumbleweed. I know Imani thinks a visit would do me good so I say, "Not sure yet. Depends if we have time."

"Are you positive you can't book shows here and fly to L.A. for the audition instead?" she asks for the second time in two days.

"I could but, to your practicality point, it would take away from what money I have left." The phrase *what little money I have left* is more accurate as a post–law school graduate millennial living in Manhattan. She already knows this. She's in the same boat. Still, it's better I don't supply her more ammo by emphasizing this aspect. So I steer away. "Plus, this tour is a great opportunity for me to get my name out there in a much bigger way. This is what pros do and I'm going pro." I can't wait to be a heavy hitter so I never have to endure this kind of scrutiny again.

Imani steps into my tiny room as I stuff my college hoodie in my luggage. "Well, I took the liberty of making some calls, and I think I found the perfect position for you."

I can't go back to law, which is exactly what she's been begging me to do. My messages are full of texts from her—links to job openings around the city with little comments like—this one has great benefits and this one is within walking distance. I know what she really wants to say is, this one will pay our bills so I don't get stuck with the whole rent. I zip up one side of my suitcase, wishing she would shut the employment hunting case.

"No more jobs, Imani—"

"Just hear me out. I have a contact at another firm. Simple contract review and it's part-time. It'll give you some cushion and you'll have more time for gigs."

"Speaking of cushion, would it be weird if I brought my pillow on tour?" I ask.

Take a hint, girl!

"So that's how you want to play it? Dumb?" Now here comes the sass, which is awesome when it's directed at anyone else but me.

"Yeah, maybe I do." With my tongue sticking out the side of my mouth, I use my body weight to drag the zipper around the corner.

Zip. Stop. *Zip.* Stop. *Zip.*

Almost there.

"Fine, but it feels like you're running away again."

"What do you mean, *again*?" I ask, wiping sweat from my upper lip.

"I know losing your dad was pretty sudden, but you just dropped your entire life to come here. And I get it. I'm sure I'd want to do the same thing. But you don't even really talk about it."

"Is this about going to therapy again? Because I'm good. Don't I seem good?"

She lets out an exasperated breath. "I just want to make sure you're being honest with yourself."

"Well, honestly, I came here to do comedy. A dream that was suffocating in Texas. And I'm not running away. I'm running toward my future success. And Imani"—I grunt, pulling the tiny zipper with all my might—"you're my best friend in the world. I really don't want to fight with you about this, especially when I'm leaving for two weeks." With one last heave-ho, the suitcase shuts and the momentum thunks me on my ass. I tumble back like a roly-poly, catching myself before my head hits the floor. "Ouch!"

"See, this is already a disaster."

My hair clings to my sweaty brow so I mop it away and rebalance my glasses. "No, it's not. I'm gonna be on *The Late Night Show*. You'll see." I get that she's trying to look out for me and as annoying as it is, I really do appreciate it. But she's wrong. My dad was wrong. And I'll be damned if I don't come back to this city as a winner.

"Lots of stand-ups audition for late-night TV. What are you gonna do if you don't get it the first time?"

I grab on to my bedsheets and pull myself up. "Why can't you just be my penguin and support me?"

"I am supporting you. I'm the voice of reason, protecting you from yourself."

I fill my lungs to capacity knowing I might need to put *what little money* I have where my mouth is. "I'll tell you what. If I don't land this audition, then the moment I get back to New York, I'll call the headhunter. Or anyone you want. And I'll get back on the Jim Gaffigan plan." There. That oughta pacify her.

"See! Now you're using your head." She taps her temple.

"But it's not nearly as fun as using my heart. Or my sense of humor." My nightstand clock signals me to go (as far away from this conversation as possible). So I slide the overstuffed suitcase off the bed and it slams down to the ground like an anchor on the sea floor. I hope Nick has a big trunk.

Boom, boom!

"Hey! Keep it down!" our downstairs neighbor yells, poking the ceiling, presumably with a broom handle. Okay . . . maybe I went a little overboard on the packing.

Imani winces. "You just had to go and wake the bear. Now I'm gonna have to tiptoe the rest of the day." I wish she were exaggerating but she's not.

"Sorry," I say, swinging my backpack over my shoulder and tucking my pillow beneath my arm. "I have to go."

"Okay." She throws her hands up. "If this is really what you want to do, I won't stand in your way."

"Is that why you're blocking the doorway?"

She shoots me a look and moves aside, making space for my luggage and me to pass by. I grab a clean garbage bag from under the sink and stick my pillow inside.

"Don't get too comfortable carrying your stuff in trash bags."

"Watch me make this the next hot trend," I say, piling it on top of my suitcase.

Imani rolls her eyes, then closes in on me with her arms open. "Just please keep your GPS locator on and text me when you get to D.C."

As much as she's been a pain in the ass, she's my penguin . . . in the ass. No, that doesn't really work, but you get it. I hold on to her tightly, feeling like this is goodbye. But it's not, it's just the beginning. "Don't get hit by a bus, okay?"

"I won't if you won't."

Ten

Brooklyn, where I'm meeting Nick, is two subway trains away. But, you know, I have to get some coffee for the road. I swing by my favorite local café, Roast 'N Grind. And by *swing* I mean *make an enemy of the door after it crushes my suitcase and knocks my garbage bag to the ground*. How the hell am I gonna get all this underground then back up again? Eh, I'll figure it out over a fresh brew.

"What's with all the commotion, Olivia?" Brenda, one of the baristas, asks, looking over the counter from behind her black frames. I'm pretty sure they're not prescription.

"I'm going on a cross-country tour and I need to fuel up. Can I have my regular over ice?"

"What? You're headlining now?" she asks, filling a cup with crushed cubes.

"I wish but this is one step closer."

"That's exciting! I'm surprised your boss let you off." I may gripe to Brenda about Whitley on occasion. Don't we all?

"He didn't. I left my job."

She makes one of those *yikes* faces and my chest tenses for a moment. "You got guts. I'll give you that." With the chilled coffee in my hands, my anticipation cools slightly.

"I'm auditioning for *The Late Night Show* too," I add, swiping my credit card.

"Well, good luck. Send Anderson Vanderson a wink for me."

"I will." I wave goodbye and head out, itching to get off the island where my usual allies are now looking at me like I'm off to join a nudist compound in the Everglades.

Of course there are no elevators at the nearest subway station. And since I have zero time to work out, I don't have the upper-body strength to carry the damn suitcase down the steep steps. So I drag it behind me and hope for the best. It smacks on each step. *Clunk-clunk-clunk.* A man shoots me a look so I smile and say, "I'm going on tour." He rolls his eyes and hurries ahead. Ta-ta, chivalry!

It's a good hour before I make it to my final stop. And despite my hundred-pound baggage, I'm feeling light and free. Goose bumps prickle my skin, though I'm not sure if it's from the cool morning breeze or the anticipation of this adventure. Finally, the headliner comes into view as I approach his building.

There he is. My road buddy.

Just a road buddy. Which is too bad because even from this distance, he looks good in the daylight. The bright morning sun reflects off his dark Wayfarer sunglasses. He stands coolly on the sidewalk, dressed in the same black leather jacket and jeans, sipping from a blue bodega coffee cup. His nearly black hair is tucked behind his ears. My stomach somersaults and I want to scream out with excitement—*This is really happening!*

I push my frames up with my index finger and squint in the light. "So we meet again."

Nick holds his stance for a moment, seeming to do a once-over behind his shades. Then, his mouth curls up in a cordial smile. "Well, if it isn't the winning comedienne." Just so you know, the term *comedienne* is antiquated. I'm sure he's saying it now only to break the ice. (Us *comedians* love to razz each other.) He shakes my hand with a palm that feels slightly worn—the way his tires will be when this is all over.

"So it's just you and me for two weeks, huh? I had a feeling you'd want to see me again." Oh, no. I'm flirting. Breaking the rules and we haven't even buckled up yet. I take a sip of what's left of my iced coffee, pretending it's a cold shower.

"That and I owed you one." I may have done him a solid the other night filling in at Funnies but I seriously doubt he'd let me join his tour if he didn't think I could actually work a crowd. "C'mon, let's hit the road." He waves me over toward the line of tightly packed cars parked along the curb.

I smile, my lip quivering slightly. Exactly like that moment right before I go onstage when all of my nerves dance around my body until they finally settle when I take the mic.

"There's not a ton of room but your suitcase should fit."

That's a relief.

Nick steps behind a black . . . Jeep Wrangler?

"*This* is our mode of transportation?" I ask.

"Oh, don't tell me you don't like Jeeps, Olivia?" he says like it's a deal breaker.

"Not at all. I grew up with a Jeep." Now this feels a little spooky. My dad drove his beloved 1981 Jeep Laredo until the very last moment of his life. Okay, *drive* is a little strong. Half the time, the thing would break down and he'd have to push it up the road wedged inside the door so he could steer it along the way. "Why don't you get a new Jeep, Dad?" I'd ask as a kid, embarrassed about being stuck on the side of a dusty road. Again. "It's my baby, Livy," he'd say. "Like you. Should I get a new daughter just because you whine sometimes?"

My dad was much more whine-averse than he was engine failure–averse. There were many moments over the years I'm sure we would have preferred to trade each other in for someone better. But he never gave up on that old Jeep. It was his most prized possession, aside from his vinyls, of course. Maybe it's a coincidence that I'll be riding in Nick's black Jeep on this comedy tour. A funny one (not the ha-ha kind).

"Good," he says. "I just got it. Bought it from a guy named Chris Rock."

My jaw drops. "Are you serious? You mean, Chris Rock, Chris Rock?"

"Um, same name. Different sense of humor."

"Okay, because for a second I thought maybe this Jeep belonged to Jon Voight."

Nick smirks, confirming he gets the reference. "*Seinfeld* fan?"

"A show about a stand-up living in New York? Of course I am." I walk halfway around the Jeep, admiring the bold black body. It's a soft top, which is great for summer but a terrible choice for our Northeast snow showers. And I don't even want to think about the fuel costs.

"She's a beauty, isn't she?" Nick asks.

"Yeah, she is. Not much of a city car though."

"Then it's a good thing we're leaving." He opens up the rear door. The back seats are folded and tucked in as much as possible, leaving a small space that's already filled with boxes piled on top of one another. His large black suitcase fits just enough for the door to close. By the looks of it, I'm not the only one who brought all my shit.

"What's with all the boxes?" I ask.

He glances at them for a moment and shrugs. "It's merch."

"You mean you sell T-shirts with your face on them?"

"With a face like mine, I'd be crazy not to."

I wasn't sure before but now I know Nick's one of those guys who knows how good-looking he is. Without a word, he scoops up my luggage with a grunt. "Jesus, what's in here? Bricks and mortar for your own stand-up set?"

I shrug innocently. "Home Depot was having a sale."

"Women and their sales," he says with a sigh like we've been married for thirty years and he's given up on me. I feel the urge to playfully smack his arm and say, "Hey!" with a giggle like I'm his girlfriend. But I resist, remembering Bernie's warning.

"This too," I say, holding up my garbage bag luggage.

"What are you, waste management?" he asks, letting his Brooklyn(ish)-Jersey accent fly.

"You don't think this is chic?" I stuff the poofy bag in between the luggage, the sound of the airy plastic making a mockery of me.

"As broke as everyone is these days, I'm sure it will be. What's in it?"

"What are you? TSA? It's my pillow," I say, trying to make it sound necessary.

He closes the back door and leans on the hanging spare tire. "Cute. You pack like a five-year-old going to a sleepover."

"You got jokes, huh? We'll see who's laughing when you're up all night, fluffing those lumpy hotel pillows."

"Ha, you're not gonna get any Marriott rewards on this trip." Nick swings the keys in his hand and heads for the driver's side door.

"A girl can dream. Especially with proper neck support," I say, climbing in the passenger seat. Faux new-car smell competes with stale-cigarette odor. I really hope that's left over from Chris Rock.

Nick turns the ignition and the rhythm of an '80s electric keyboard rises through the speakers. I know this one. Bon Jovi's "Runaway." Before I can comment on his choice of music, he clears his throat and turns to me like he's got something important to say. "Now listen, this Jeep is new. And it's special to me so I'll be the only one driving this tour, *capeesh*?"

"Did you just say *capeesh*?"

"Yeah, it means I'm serious."

Okay, now I'm so spooked I do a little shiver-shake. I haven't heard that word in years. Whenever I was being stubborn growing up, which I'll admit was a lot, my dad would always put his foot down and say *capeesh*. Something funny's definitely afoot.

"Got it. You control the wheel." For now.

"And the music."

"Sheez, dictate much!"

"Haven't you been on a road trip? Whoever drives gets to DJ," he says, defusing my warm fuzzies. Now there's an antiquated law that needs amending.

"So we have to listen to Bon Jovi for two weeks straight?" I snap.

"No. I've got a whole range of classic rock." Nonstop classic rock? Okay, Nick's really starting to sound like my dad. But I'm not going to take this lying down.

"Here's the thing, if this is all we listen to my head will be so clogged with guitar licks that I won't be able to remember my jokes. And that's bad for both of us. So how about this: you give me one veto and one song of my choice every hour. Seeing as we have three thousand miles to go, that's a bargain."

His mouth twists in consideration. "Fine. But you have to promise to play by the other rules." I'm not sure if he's referring to the no-driving thing or the no-funny-business thing but in any case, I agree.

Nick taps in an address on his phone and locks the device in place with a doohickey on his dashboard. Current ETA—2:17 P.M. Four hours and nine minutes until we get to D.C. Sounds long, but with our itinerary this is probably going to be one of our shorter commutes.

"Good! We've got lots of time," I say, strapping myself in with the seatbelt.

"Yeah, we'll see. Between the Jersey turnpike and D.C. traffic, that could change."

"Is that why we're leaving hella early?" I ask.

"People still say *hella*?"

I flash a tight-lipped smile. "Only really cool people."

"Get used to leaving *hella* early. Trust me, it's worth it." He turns up the volume and we're off.

I sit quietly, letting him focus on driving through the city and making his way to the bridge. As Nick picks up speed the road noise ramps up. The height of the Jeep makes me feel like we're towering over all the other drivers. I gaze over the little white peaks on the water as we cross into Staten Island. When we make it to I-95, Nick sets the cruise control and I watch him relax in his seat.

"So have you played Capital Comedy before?" I ask.

"Oh, yeah."

"Any pro tips?"

"Don't bomb."

"You're full of great advice, aren't you?"

He takes his eyes off the road for a split second. "That's the best advice I've ever gotten."

I roll my eyes with a slight chuckle. There's something about Nick that feels familiar. Maybe it's the Jeep, or that we're cut from the same stand-up cloth. Or maybe we both know we're going to be stuck together for a while so we might as well get used to it. No matter how it feels, the truth is we're still technically strangers, and I'd like to get to know him. Biblically. But I'll settle for something less naked.

"So, how long have you been touring?" I ask.

"On and off for about a decade. Mostly on." His words carry the weight of an exhausted sigh.

"Wow, I've only done shows in the tristate area."

"Really?" He sounds surprised and now I feel sheepish.

"Yeah."

"Well, buckle up because you're about to get a crash course on tour life." His tone echoes all the other comics that warned me the road isn't for everyone.

"What does that mean?"

"You'll see. I wouldn't want to spoil it for you." He flips his blinker and the ticking fills the space before he speaks again. "But I will say this. Be prepared for anything. And I mean anything. Because the road won't hesitate to show you what you're really made of."

I feel a twinge of something in my gut, and the urge to hug myself like I have a tummy ache. Instead, I roll my shoulders back and say, "Roger that. I'm fully prepared to kick this tour's ass."

"You think so?" he asks.

"Totally. This is like a dream scenario for me. Nothing can get me down." At least it better not. I've got too much riding on this.

Nick shakes his head. "Spoken like a true Vincent."

I look over at the sound of my name, wondering what he means, then remember we've established it's synonymous with *winner*.

With the city in the rearview, I look ahead toward my very bright future. It's so bright I reach into my bag and pull out my prescription sunglasses. Ahh, that's better. Time to sit back, relax, and enjoy the ride.

Dunk, dunk!

The sound of metal clanging beneath the undercarriage sends a jolt to my system, adrenaline surging in its wake. Nick grips both hands on the steering wheel as the metal object passes with no apparent damage. "What the hell was that?"

"Good question." He glances in the rearview, then back at his dashboard. "Shit."

"What?"

"Low tire pressure."

"A flat?"

You've got to be kidding me.

Eleven

Nick and I stand on the shoulder, staring down at the punctured, deflated tire. What's that he said? Be prepared for anything? Then I hear Imani's words in my mind like a haunting echo—*See, this is already a disaster.* I shrug the thought away and remind myself this isn't a big deal. It's not a sign or an omen or any of that. Flat tires happen. And like I said, nothing's gonna get me down.

Nick, on the other hand, looks a little deflated himself. He kicks the tire and his young Gary Gulman hair falls across his face. "I can't believe this. My brand-new Jeep!" I can hardly hear him over the cars whizzing by on the turnpike like a NASCAR track in the middle of a cup race.

"Talk about taking the air out of your tires," I say, channeling Rodney Dangerfield in an attempt to lighten the mood.

Nick raises an eyebrow over the rim of his Wayfarers. "I don't remember you being a corny one-liner comic."

"No, I'm more of an observational storyteller. Like *two come-dians are stuck on the side of the road* kinda girl."

"And?"

"One says to the other . . ." I look him square in the face. "Watch out for sharp objects."

"Ha. Ha," he says as inexpressive as Ben Stein in *Ferris Bueller's Day Off.*

I open my arms. "I'm here all week."

"*This* is why we have to leave early," he says, and I almost wonder if that conversation jinxed us.

"Duly noted. But this isn't a huge delay. You must get flat tires all the time on the road."

"Actually, I don't."

"Really? Then what was all that talk about *be prepared for any-thing*?" I ask as he lifts his phone to his ear. "Who are you calling, the tire fairy?"

"Roadside assistance."

"What do you need them for? You have a perfectly good spare right here." I gesture to the giant rubber donut hanging on the back of the Jeep. Nick lowers his eyes, pretending not to hear me. Wait a second. Oh . . . I see what's going on here. I step closer. "You don't know how to change a tire, do you?" I say low in his free ear like I'm trying to simultaneously tease and seduce him. I'm not sure which desire is stronger. Not to judge but how can anyone driving up and down the country on a reg-ular basis, like the headlining Nick Leto, not master this very basic skill?

"Hang on a second." He glances back at me with a hint of shame in his eyes before he begins calling out his insurance number in that stilted, annoyed way we address automated systems. "Zero. Zero. Four. Seven."

I step in front of him so he has to face me (and this situation). "Your keys, please."

"What? Why?"

"Because, the tire fairy's here."

He lowers the phone. "*You're* gonna change the tire?" And there he goes, throwing judgment right back at me. Like I haven't heard it before. You're *going to law school*? You're *moving to New York*? You're *a comedian*? I always feel like saying, *Yeah, I'm an intelligent, funny, self-sufficient woman and* you're *an ignorant prick*. Sometimes, I actually have the balls to say it. But given the circumstances, I let Nick off the hook.

Well, mostly.

"No, *you're* gonna change it," I say. "And I'm gonna show you how."

He doesn't look convinced, though who knows if he's now questioning my ability or his. But he complies with a click of the button on his keyless entry. I smirk. It's nice to be in a position of power for once. We make our way to the Jeep and begin removing our suitcases. He grunts, pulling out my luggage. "Seriously, what's in here?"

"I didn't know what to pack so I brought everything. You could say I'm prepared for anything."

This can't be Nick's dream scenario by any stretch but his lip curls up just enough for me to know that he's glad I'm here. "Here's the rest of your luggage," he says, handing over my trash bag. I take it and drag my suitcase safely inside the shoulder lane.

Nick grabs the jack and cross wrench from the tool compartment (at least he knows where that is) and looks at them the way a caveman would. "Now what?"

I place my hand on his shoulder and gently say, "Now you become a man." He frowns helplessly and I can't help but snicker at his expense. "Okay, okay. Go make sure the emergency brake's on. That's the one in the—"

"I know what it is." Nick hands me the tools and goes around to climb in the front seat. When he returns, he's lost the leather jacket (not that it has any place in this June heat). His sleeves are wrapped tightly around his bulging biceps. I didn't know those were hiding under that leather. What else is he hiding beneath his clothes?

Nick stands in front of me with his hands on his hips and the sun reflecting off his dark shades. "You sure about this?"

"Yes," I say, and hand him the cross wrench. "Now loosen the lug nuts." He points to the correct tire anatomy for assurance. And I nod.

Turning the first one, his arm flexes. "Damn, that's tight."

For a moment, I get lost again, thinking the same thing about his body. His rugged jaw clenches as he loosens the next one. Oh, man, it's gonna be a long trip if he keeps that up. Okay, Olivia, say something before he catches you ogling him. "You breakin' a sweat already?"

"It's hot out here."

He's what's hot. But seriously, the midmorning sun is really heating up the pavement. Plus this added humidity makes it extra steamy. And there's enough of that going on. I resist the urge to let my gaze roll down to his waist and keep my focus on the task at hand. But it's really hard not to notice his behind in those jeans when he squats down to rest the spare on the ground.

Stop looking at his ass, Olivia. "Heavy?" I tease.

He dusts his shirt off. "Nah, just *hella* bulky."

Back in Midland, I never had to teach a guy to change a tire. City boys are a totally different breed. Jeep tire changes can be tricky if you don't know what you're doing. But Nick's taking to it like a natural, following my instructions to a T.

I'm pretty proud of my protégé.

While Nick finishes up, I pull out my phone and begin texting Imani that I'm stuck on the turnpike with a guy who's having his first tire-changing lesson. As much as I'd like to share a good laugh about this, it'll only give her another reason to discourage touring. So I delete it.

When he's done, I scrutinize his work while he stands back, watching me. What are the chances he's telling himself not to look at my booty? "A-plus, Nick," I say, congratulating him.

"It's not complicated. Just a pain in the ass." He begins digging in his pocket.

"Not as much of a pain in the ass as waiting for roadside assistance." I push off the solid rubber tire to my feet and dust off my hands. When I glance up, he's sparking up a lighter in front of his face, covering the flame with his hand. I sneer. "You smoke?"

"Oh, yeah," he says as if he's saying *two packs a day*. He takes a long drag and releases a puff of smoke with each word. "You got a problem with smoking?"

I would love to list all the reasons why smoking is a huge problem for me, for him, and that baby from Indonesia, but it's too hot and too loud out here to get into it. The rising sun is beginning to burn my skin more than that bad habit's burning Nick's lungs. So I cross my arms and respond the same, "Oh, yeah."

"Sounds like you could use a cigarette." He flips open the little box of cancer sticks.

"Ugh. You really do live in the '80s." I'm tempted to snatch it away and chuck it out on the highway. But knowing smokers, that won't stop him.

"Please, I wish."

With an emphatic eye roll, I climb back in the Jeep and slam the door shut. Not that it matters now, or maybe ever, but it would've been nice to know I'd be traveling with a smoker. Even if said smoker is talented and gorgeous. After another minute, he gets in, squeezing the squished cigarette butt between his fingers. The stench of tobacco fills the cabin. He chucks the butt in his nearly empty bodega cup and secures the lid.

"Well, at least you're not a litterbug," I say.

"Hey, smokers are people too," he says in a sarcastically solemn tone. He probably thinks I'm one of those health snobs. Or worse, a vegan.

"I know," I say, reaching for the crank to roll my window down like I'm back in my dad's 1981 Laredo. But there's no handle. Just a set of automatic buttons that are supposed to make life so easy. The window lowers with a slight hum and soon road noise floods inside.

"I found a shop a few miles away so you can repair that puncture," I say. "Probably a good idea to have a spare, don't you think?"

Nick starts the engine. "Be prepared for anything, right?"

Twelve

t's been years since I've stepped foot in a mom-and-pop auto repair shop. A perk of being a carless New Yorker. I slowly inhale the unmistakable grease-rubber odor blend with hints of sweat and I note all of the common features. Like a nearly empty vending machine in the corner that looks like it was born in the Reagan years. A handful of faded burgundy tweed banquet chairs that were probably snagged from a church yard sale. An old tube TV screening *Judge Judy*. No volume, of course, just boxy subtitles across the screen. Then there's the guy behind the counter in his navy blue work shirt with a name patch above the pocket, listening to AC/DC's "Highway to Hell" low on the radio while a dusty oscillating fan breezes behind him.

I spent my childhood in a place just like this because my dad couldn't afford childcare. Doing my homework in the break room after school. Playing penny poker on the concrete floor with my surrogate uncles. And drinking as much Coke machine cola as I could stand (God, how I loved that thunking sound when the can dropped into the dispenser). It's a miracle I didn't end up with Jack Sparrow's mouth.

That part of my life is long gone. Some people like to cruise down memory lane; for me it's more like rush hour on "the 5" in Los Angeles—a nightmare. Or so I've heard. I take a deep breath but my throat grows thick. Maybe after all these years I've developed an allergy to auto shop fumes. "I think I'm gonna wait outside," I say.

"You mean you don't want to boss this guy around too?" Nick jokes.

I muster a tiny chuckle. "You're a big boy now. I think you can handle this one."

Outside, I breathe in the sweltering Jersey air. This is supposed to be a fresh start for me. Swear to God, this is the most I've thought about my dad since I left Texas. With all these freaking father reminders, it's like my past is coming back to haunt me. Good thing I don't believe in ghosts.

A few minutes later, Nick's voice sneaks up behind me. "Looks like we've got about an hour to kill. You want some lunch?"

"I could eat." If I'm being honest, I can always eat. Especially if it gets me away from this place. "I think I saw a Five Guys up the street."

He does a bro chin nod. "You a burger girl?"

"No," I say. "I am *the* burger girl."

While we wait in line, I lean against the checkered wall. "You're buying, right?"

"Why? You think we're on a date or something?" He rests his arm on the wall above me like we're flirting in front of my high school locker. Part of me wants to lean in. The other part is repulsed by the lingering smoke on his breath.

I step aside, pushing my glasses up the slope of my nose. "Is this a place you'd take a girl on a first date?"

"Maybe, if she was a burger girl." Now isn't that cute?

"Well, I did save you the roadside assistance fee and the time it would take for them to tow your car to the shop. Not to mention, I taught you how to change a tire."

"Is this a lawyer thing? Billing me for every little thing you do."

That's one way to look at it. The other is that I'm now in a lower tax bracket and have to save my pennies where I can. At least for a little while. "Please, a burger and fries are a fraction of my attorney fees."

Nick holds his hands up. "Whoa, whoa. Fries? Now you're just taking advantage of me."

I shrug. "Fair's fair, my friend."

"I'll tell you what, I'll get this one and you can get the next one." Mm-hmm, typical guy. He got what he wanted out of me and now he won't put out . . . the money, I mean.

"Throw in a milkshake and you've got yourself a deal," I say.

"Done." Nick offers his hand and, I swear, pulls me closer. Maybe an inch, but still. I think back to one of Imani's *don't go on tour* arguments—*Are you sure this guy isn't just trying to get in your pants?* My first thought was *What's wrong with that?* But instead I asked if she was implying that I'm not funny enough to feature on the road and of course she backpedaled from there. But seriously, Nick doesn't seem like the kind of guy who would have any trouble with the ladies (not like some of the other comics I know). So I put any malicious suspicion out of my mind.

While our burgers are on the grill and our fries are drowning in peanut oil, we find an empty table to wait. "I've never traveled with a feature before," he says. Based on what I know about road comics, our road trip is somewhat unorthodox. At least for his level. And now mine.

"Neither have I." I take a long sip of my chocolate milkshake. The chilled cream helps cool me down.

Nick stares out the window like he's looking for someone or something. "You know, being stuck in Jersey is my worst nightmare."

"Not a fan of the Garden State?" I ask.

"Nope, that's why I ran away to the city."

"Funny you should say that. My roommate thinks I'm running away on this tour." I'm not sure why I just said that so casually. It's like I've cracked open a door for him when there's nothing to see.

"Why's that?" Nick asks. And why wouldn't he?

"I'm not sure. I think it has something to do with the fact that I just left my job."

"Oh." Uh-oh, he's got that concerned expression like Imani and Barista Brenda. So much for escaping that look.

"Yeah, it's time for me to take the next step in my stand-up career. And so far, so good. I got this gig with you and an audition for *The Late Night Show*, which I'm sure will open a lot of doors for me. Don't you think?"

"Yeah, assuming you get it."

"Oh, I'm getting it," I say.

He stares at me for a moment like he's amused or maybe intrigued. "And what makes you so sure?"

"Because no one wants it as much as me." I flash him a playful toothy grin.

"And who's gonna say no to you."

"Exactly. Have you ever done *The Late Night Show*?"

"No." He shakes his head, tapping his fingers on the table to the beat of the song playing in the background. "But I have done other late-night television shows. I even have a thirty-minute special on The Comedy Channel."

Boom! My mind is blown. "Wow, really? What's it called?"

"*Born to Run*," he says.

"Why'd you call it that?"

"You'll have to watch it one day to find out," he says, toying with me. I've got to see this special. "Anyway, it was a while ago."

"That must have been an incredible experience."

Nick shrugs modestly or uncomfortably. I can't decide. At that moment, our food arrives at our table. The smell of Cajun fries tantalizes my nose. Mmm. I salivate like a dog about to chow down after waiting by the door for ten hours for someone to come home and feed him. I unwrap my burger and wet my lips before diving in. My teeth sink into the bread, through the tomato, onions, pickles, and cheese, down to the juicy beef patty. I manage to squeeze a hot fry in my mouth and let out a satisfactory moan. "Now we're even," I say.

He stuffs his face with a bite rivaling mine. "Oh, yeah?" For the minutes following, we don't say a word, just munch on our lunch. Finally, he comes up for air. "I always forget about this place. I'm partial to Shake Shack."

I nod, thinking of my last ShackBurger with Imani. "Shake Shack's pretty good."

"Pretty good? It's the best."

"Eh," I say with a mouth full of the sweet-and-salty combo of shake and fries. Now that's the best.

"Are you some kinda self-proclaimed burger aficionado?" he asks, and I take another big bite, smiling with stuffed cheeks. "You got a top pick?"

The first rule of being a burger aficionado is to know where to get the best burger. For me, there's no question. It's the only reason I'm looking forward to crossing the Texas border. I've already mapped out the locations near both comedy venues. "Definitely Whataburger."

He wipes his mouth with a flimsy, grease-stained napkin. "What the hell's a Whataburger?"

"Oh, you don't know about them Texas burgers?" I say, doused with Southern sass.

"Is that where you're from?" he asks, and I swallow hard, nodding. "Then how come you don't have a hee-haw accent?"

I nearly spit out my beef with a laugh. "Excuse me? Hee-haw?"

"Yeah, you know, *You dumbass Yankee, don't even know how to change a tire*," he says, a dead ringer for Blanche from *The Golden Girls*. Not bad. For a Yankee anyway.

"You said it, not me."

"Where'd you learn to change a tire anyway?"

My head must be flooded with dopamine from the free meal because without hesitation I spill a snippet from my past. "By-product of being a mechanic's daughter."

Thirteen

The steady hum of the road adds another raw quality to Nick's classic rock radio. He keeps inching up the volume. It's been about an hour since Nick and I picked up the spare tire after stuffing our faces with greasy fast food. With a full belly, I could really use a post-meal road nap. I'm talking *cheek suctioned to the window, string of drool dangling from the corner of my mouth* kinda nap. But I'm here to work. So I'll be a good little comedian and draft up some new material, which feels a little impossible with Def Leppard's "Photograph" blasting.

"No wonder you're a road comic. You have the musical taste of a truck driver," I holler over the guitar solo.

Even with his sunglasses, I can see him give me a sideways glance. "And I suppose you're a fan of who? Britney Spears?"

"And proud of it."

He smiles and lowers the volume. "You should listen up. They don't make music like this anymore."

"And there's probably a good reason for that." I don't actually mind '70s and '80s rock. I grew up on the stuff. Though I can't say I know anyone my age who swears by it. "Where are we anyway?" I ask, glancing at his GPS.

"Somewhere near Cherry Hill, I think." Nick yawns and I press my lips together, willing myself not to catch the contagious act. "Whatchu been doin' over there? Preparing a legal brief?"

I glance down at the half sentence scribbled on my yellow lined sheet with the curled corner edges. "Yeah, I'm planning to sue you for radio control inequality."

"Then you should've done a better job negotiating," he says. A valid point. So far I only got one play—Lady Gaga's "Bad Romance."

Nick takes his eyes off the road for a moment and glances at my nearly empty sheet. "Seriously. What are you working on?"

"*Work* is a little strong. I'm trying to write a new joke every day. You know, like Jerry Seinfeld."

"What are you talking about?" he asks.

"You've never heard that before? Every day Jerry would write a new joke and mark an *X* on his calendar, creating a never-ending chain. That's how he got so good. He never broke the chain." Seinfeld's a king of comedy. And legend has it, this little anecdote is his method of success. And that's something I could use right now.

"Oh, yeah, that's a myth. It's been debunked."

"Really?" My heart breaks a little, like the time I found out there's no Easter bunny. Not as devastating as learning there's no Santa, but still.

"Afraid so. And Jerry's not like us. He doesn't need to write every day to be good. He's just good. Same with Dave Chappelle. Good practice though." He pats my shoulder like an encouraging Little League coach. "Speaking of Seinfeld. I was thinking you and I might have a little Jerry-and-Elaine thing going."

"Because you're a headlining comedian and I'm a strong, independent, and hilariously funny woman?" I offer.

"That and I like you." Did he just say he likes me? Ohmigod. He *was* flirting with me at the burger place! "I think we can be buddies. For real." Buddies?

Womp, womp.

Nothing cools a crush like getting friend-zoned. A boner killer for sure.

"So you're not of the mind that men and women can't be friends?" I ask, as if giving him one last opportunity to admit he's attracted to me too.

His brow knits like he's not following the Billy Crystal reference. "No. Who said that?"

"Nora Ephron and Rob Reiner. You never saw *When Harry Met Sally*?"

"Is that the one with the fake orgasm scene at Katz's Deli?" he asks.

I wish I could have what she was having. "Yeah, that movie's nearly thirty years old and men still don't know when we're faking it."

Nick gasps. "Olivia, have you committed fraudulent orgasms?"

"Sure, when it's getting late and I just want to get some sleep." This poor guy doesn't know the half of it. And if we're just friends, then he never will. Oh, well . . .

"That's a quote from *Seinfeld*, right?" He spits out a chuckle. "Olivia, you're the Elaine of my dreams."

Well, that's something, I guess.

After a couple more hours of listening to Bon Jovi and Cheap Trick, we arrive at our nation's capital. Nick navigates us around the convoluted exits and loopy streets. We're not actually staying in D.C., but just outside of it in Arlington, Virginia.

He turns into an apartment complex of two-story brick buildings. I marvel at the tall shady trees, freshly cut turf, and row of shrubs beneath the first-floor windows. Growing up in the dusty plains of Texas and now living in a concrete jungle, I'm not used to seeing so much green.

He pulls the Jeep into a space and yanks up the parking brake. "Home sweet home."

I lean forward, gazing up at the building. "So this is a comedy condo, huh?"

"Yep."

Comedy condos are a notorious part of road-comic life. Or so I've heard. The clubs save money on motels by housing all their talent in an apartment. These condos have a remarkably seedy reputation but this place inspires a friendly feel, especially with the little squirrels chasing each other up a tree trunk. Perhaps this comedy condo is the exception to the rule. "It doesn't look so bad."

"You haven't been inside yet."

I gulp hard at his foreboding inflection, imagining something in the same vein as a frat house after a wild kegger. "Is it really filthy?"

"Eh," he utters, considering this. "It's not so much the filth you can see, it's more the filth you can't see."

My mind quickly goes to bedbugs—or as I like to call them, spawns of the devil. "Can you elaborate?"

"I'd rather not. But let's just say I wouldn't use a black light in there."

"Ugh." I cringe and consider sleeping in Nick's Jeep tonight. "Anything else I should know?"

"Yeah, don't eat the mayonnaise."

Nick gets out of the car and slams the door shut as I'm left to my own conclusions of what that could possibly mean. I let out a nervous breath and grab my phone, typing out the text I promised Imani when I arrived.

OLIVIA: Made it to D.C. safe and sound. It's going GREAT!

I'm not sure the trip here warrants all caps but the more she believes this is the right move, the better.

Nick unloads the luggage from the back with a cigarette hanging from his mouth. "I'm gonna need to charge you a handling fee. Your suitcase is ridiculous. You want this?" He holds out my puffy garbage bag, looking like a garbage man himself.

I take it and pull up the handle on my luggage. "How many of those do you smoke a day?"

"As many as I want."

Spoken like a true addict. I almost feel sorry for him. Almost. As we wheel our things over to the first-floor apartment, my stomach knots anticipating what's inside. Whatever it is, I have to take it. This is real comedy life. He finds a key under the flimsy doormat. Not a safety issue at all. "So I take it this apartment doesn't have Secret Service detail," I say.

"Relax, Olivia." Nick leads us into the dim and musty apartment. A puff of smoke rises into the air with a wheezy cough trailing behind it.

"Oh, hey, man," Nick says.

I push up my frames and peek around his shoulders. A guy wearing a pair of board shorts and a white tank top sits on a brown thrift store couch gripping on to a yellow bong. Who's this dude? I reach around my bag for my fresh pepper spray can. As a wise fellow Midlander once said, "Fool me once, shame on—shame on you . . . Fool me, I can't get fooled again."

Well said, George W.

The stoner looks up. "Hey-ey, Nick. What's up, man?" At the tone of their greeting and mention of Nick's name, I let my bag go and step around from behind Nick. The Cheech Marin wannabe catches a glimpse of me. "Well, helloooo." His gaze rolls over me like I'm a pleasant surprise then back to Nick. Maybe he's our Kramer. "Isn't it a little early to be bringing girls over?"

Nick lets out an uneasy chuckle. "She's not my girl. She's my feature, Olivia."

The stoner gives me a glazed, wide-eyed stare. "Ah, shit. My bad." He rises to his feet and stumbles over, offering me his hand. "Nice to meet you, Olivia. I'm Herb."

"Herb?" I say, spitting out a laugh and letting go of his lax handshake. "Your name is Herb?"

He tilts his head like a dog trying to understand English. "Yeah, why's that funny?"

Is he serious? I look to Nick for affirmation and he gives me a subtle headshake as if to stop me from going any further. I wait a beat, realizing they're both completely serious, then button my mouth. "Never mind. Who are you exactly?"

He sets his hand gently on my shoulder and looks into my eyes. "The question isn't who am I. The question is why am I?"

"That is *a* question." Now the better question is why am I here in this comedy condo? I wonder if I can squeeze a hotel stay out of my budget.

Nick clears his throat. "How long you been at it today, Herb?"

"No idea, bro," he says.

"Herb's a comedian. He's opening for us tonight."

"Is that a good idea?" I mutter to Nick out the side of my mouth.

"It's fine."

Herb smacks his head with his palm. "I'm sorry, guys. Did you want a hit? It's *Friiiiday*." He offers the bong. It's actually Saturday but maybe to Herb *Friiiiday* is more of a state of mind than a day of the week.

"Nah, I'm good, man," Nick says as I shake my head, leaning back. Call me a snob, but I prefer to keep my lungs as clear as possible.

"Cool."

Nick signals for me to follow him down the hall and I do so gingerly, dragging my heavy-ass suitcase behind me. He pushes each door open with the tips of his fingers. Who knows what other surprises there are—seen and unseen.

"Here," he says, standing in one of the doorways. "You can take this room."

I peek my head in, bracing myself for the worst. A futon bed, draped in slept-in linens (if you can call them that) and a double-drawer nightstand that I'm pretty sure my grandmother had in her bedroom. The window above is covered with partially torn mini-blinds and the carpet below is stained with spots of fruit-punch red and shit brown.

I slowly turn to face Nick. "Toto, I don't think we're on the Upper East Side anymore."

"Told you it wouldn't be the Four Seasons."

"I get that but what's with these sheets? They've clearly been slept in and who knows what else. It's unsanitary."

Nick rubs the back of his neck. "I recommend ripping them off and sleeping in your clothes. That's what I usually do. But if it really bothers you, I think this place has a washer and dryer."

"That's something, I guess." There's a tipped-over tissue box on the nightstand. I pull out the first sheet with my fingertips and chuck it to the ground before snagging the next "fresher" one. Using the coarse tissue paper to protect my fingers, I peel back the sheets from the so-called mattress. Fortunately, there's one of those vinyl covers. I inspect the surrounding area for anything creepy and crawly and breathe a sigh of relief.

"I need to catch some z's before the show. You might want to do the same." Nick pushes his way through the door next to mine and I feel myself panic a little. He's my comedy condo sherpa. I'm not sure if I'll be safe without him. "Oh, and Olivia." He looks back. "Welcome to the road."

Fourteen

Ha-hahahaha-hahaha!

You hear that? That's a comedian's favorite sound in the world. Well, favorite when it's the effect of our own killer joke. A strong start to the tour. Go, me!

After this very unusual day, I was champing at the bit to get to the club for our eight o'clock show. Capital Comedy is no amateur comedy club, or so I learned when I walked through its snazzy, brass-facade doors. Inside, pink and blue neon lights glisten off the many rows of round tabletops and giant posters of America's comedic heroes dress the walls. It's Saturday night and the room is bursting at the seams, which is perfect because every comedian knows the closer you pack them in, the more laughter you can create.

I can't wait to tell Imani about this later—like *Told ya so!*

Then just as I'm hitting my stride, the sound of my voice dims like a candle flame extinguished by a gust of wind. I continue but my mic has very obviously dropped. And not in the *uh, hell yeah* way. I tap the mic cage. "Hello. Hello. Is this thing on?" What I really want to say is, *What the hell is going on?*

I look over at Nick standing off in the corner. He's as confused as I am. I shade my eyes from the spotlight and catch a panicked expression on the audio tech's face.

Unbelievable.

Now everyone is staring at me like it's my fault the show stopped. Nick waves me to continue as the stage techs scurry around for a solution—at least I hope that's what they're doing. I continue with my last joke.

"So I know my relationships are over when my boyfriend starts a sentence with, 'My mother says—'"

"We can't hear you!" someone calls from the back with his hands cupped near his mouth.

"Oh." So I make my hands into a megaphone. "How 'bout now?"

"Louder!"

I step closer to the edge of the stage as if trying to get a better cell connection. "Can you hear me now?"

"Kinda."

Finally, someone taps me on the shoulder with another mic. I thank him and regain my power—sort of. "How's this?"

I catch Nick's eye again and he seems to be trying to send me a message telepathically like, *You got this, Olivia*, or maybe it's *Don't bomb, bitch!*

I clear my throat, take myself back to the moments before whatever electrical phenomenon that was, and pick up again. But I can't seem to recover the lost momentum. My cheeks grow hot. Sweat beads in my palms like it's rerouting moisture from my mouth. Every second of my remaining ten minutes is a losing battle despite how I'm working my ass off up here. Half of me is counting the seconds before it's over, and the other half will stop at nothing to win another laugh. So I give it one last-ditch effort with my final punchline. And guess what? On the Richter scale of laughs . . . it wouldn't even register.

"That's my time, everyone. I'm Olivia Vincent. You've been great!" A total lie.

Uh, I feel sick.

The emcee retrieves the mic, and I exit stage right and meet Nick. "Didn't get them as warmed up as you did last time, did ya?" he says.

I can't look him in the face but at least I have the courage to state the facts. "Nope, I totally bombed."

"Yes, you did."

This is the part where he's supposed to say something encouraging like, *You'll get 'em next time, slugger.* Instead, his crumpled expression reminds me that the stench of my stinky set hasn't dissipated. Great, now I have to come to my own defense. "I mean, it's not totally my fault. The mic stopped working. What the hell was that anyway?"

"I don't know. I've never seen anything like that before," Nick says.

With balled fists, I take a long breath as if to exhale the frustration. How can this happen to me? Sure, I've bombed before. We all have. But why tonight? I had them in the palm of my hand. One tiny malfunction and it just slips through my fingers. *A disaster*, just like Imani said . . .

"Hey, at least we've got another show after this," Nick finally offers, and the emcee calls him to the stage. "Wish me laughs."

There's that phrase from the other night at Funnies. Perhaps

If I'd said it before going onstage, I wouldn't feel like such a loser right now. "What exactly am I supposed to say to that?"

"Don't say anything. Just wish me laughs." He walks backward a few steps before turning toward the stage, swaggering over to the mic. And I mean *swagger*. It's like he's trying to cheer me up with his ass.

It helps a little.

I shake my head and shoulders, trying to shrug the whole thing off like a bad dream and move on.

Nick's rich voice booms over the sound system as he greets the audience. He hasn't even said anything and they're cheering like he's Kevin Hart. I need an iced tea. Sweet.

Our condo roomie Herb's already at the bar. "Sup, Olivia," he says with a chin nod, and I take the seat next to him. "That shit was wild."

"Tell me about it."

"It's like, who would want to silence you?"

"Um . . . I think it was a faulty mic, not a conspiracy." Like he said, who would do that?

He shakes his head. "I dunno, man. This is D.C. Haven't you read any Dan Brown books?"

"Why don't we watch the show," I suggest, turning my attention to Nick's crowd work. Some comics are brilliant at improv, which is tough since crowds can be unreliable. Sometimes the audience gives you nothing, and sometimes they provide the perfect fodder. Right now, Nick's experiencing the latter.

About halfway through, he starts a joke about being stuck on the road with a flat tire during a date with a woman. My ears perk up. Is this new material or is Nick more prone to flat tires than he let on? I really hope that's not it or it's going to be a long trip. I hang on his every word but as soon as he gets to the part where she changes the tire for him, I'm positive it's a spin on our morning. He finishes it with a slap-your-thigh kinda punchline. Waves of laughter barrel onstage and he's won the crowd. So effortless.

"He's fucking good, isn't he?" Herb taps me on the arm, leaning close. Still smells like herb. "Like a young Carlin."

"Yeah, he is. How does he do it?"

"I don't know but he's always prepared." True, Nick does take that quiet time to himself before the show. Maybe I should use this time to do the same instead of watching him in envy. "I'll be in the greenroom," I tell Herb.

"Did you say smoke some green?" He mimes smoking a joint.

"No." I shake my head and wag a finger to amplify my answer. Stoned onstage is not a good look for me.

Back in the empty greenroom, it's hard to focus on my legal sheet. Every time I try to concentrate, I relive the cringy, regrettable horror and smack my forehead. It's worse than if I flashed a boob. At least that would've kept their attention. So I set my things aside, head to the bathroom, and splash some water on my face. The cool cleanse feels good on my skin. I slide my glasses back on, get a good look at myself, and begin an internal pep talk.

This isn't a disaster. It's a dream. Don't let a little mic malfunction spoil the experience. Now buck up and get back to work!

Fifteen

O livia, wake up." Nick's voice calls me back to consciousness while he shakes my shoulder. I blink my eyes open.
"You fell asleep?"

I peel my head off the backstage couch cushion and wipe my
mouth with the back of my hand. "Not all of us got to take a
disco nap."

"I think people stopped calling them disco naps when Carter
was president."

"What time is it?" I ask with a yawn and peek at my watch.
12:05 A.M. How long was I asleep?

"Time to head back, Grampa Simpson."

After two back-to-back shows at the end of a very long, very
odd, very exhausting day, I decided to sneak back to the greenroom again after my last, slightly more successful and fully audible set.

"Did you get all those laughs I wished you?" I ask, reaching
for my glasses on the cushion next to me.

"Oh, yeah. That's why they pay me the big bucks." He smirks, wiping the sweat off his face with a plushy black towel.

"Careful, Nick. Your ego's showing," I tease, but his head's so inflated, he doesn't seem to care. "I noticed you stole my *two comedians are stuck on the side of the road* joke."

"What'd you think?" His brown eyes meet mine in a hopeful way that makes me think he not only wants to know but actually cares what I think. From bigheaded to humble in under fifteen seconds. I don't hate it.

"Not bad, adding the girlfriend-date part."

"It's funnier if we're dating."

Dating? What a charming idea. With freshly flushed cheeks, I swipe my finger across my bottom lip. Then Nick pops a cigarette in his mouth. Ugh. The sight of it burns away all the swoony feelings. It's probably good that his nasty habit can easily reset any mounting attraction back to zero.

"Want a souvenir?" He tosses a black T-shirt my way. It's his merch tee—an illustrated graphic of his head, dimples present, with the phrase *Buh-Bye* framing it.

Owning a shirt with Nick's face on it feels a little counterproductive at the moment. Of course, I don't want him to know that so I say, "Thanks, but my suitcase can't take any more."

"Fair enough," he says, retrieving the shirt.

We head outside where the sauna-like air is sticky and thick. Gravel crunches beneath my Converses as we make our way back to the Jeep.

"So listen, would you mind sitting in the back?" Nick asks, sparking up his cigarette. "I offered someone a ride."

"And where exactly do you expect me to sit?" I ask, seeing as

Nick's back seats are folded in to make room for his merch boxes and our luggage.

"I'll move things around. There'll be plenty of room."

"I'm supposed to sit on the floor and risk my life with no seatbelt while you drive around D.C.?"

"Relax. It's a fifteen-minute drive."

Relax? Did he not just wake me from a nap on the greenroom sofa? I am relaxed.

"Can't he sit in the back?" Like a gentleman.

"I'd rather she not."

"She?" Heat creeps up my clenched jaw. But I blame the D.C. heat.

He shrugs as if it's no big deal. "Yeah, she's a friend."

I narrow my eyes. "Why can't *your friend* sit in the back? Her legs broken?"

"Olivia, please," Nick begs. "Be a friend. My Elaine." He needs a wingwoman. No wonder he wanted to establish our buddy dynamic.

"No, you be a friend and get her an Uber, Mr. Chivalry," I say, doing my best to argue my way out of taking her with us, the same way Elton argued his way out of taking Tai home in *Clueless* after the party in the Valley. Sweat beads at my temples and under my arms. I wonder if *the Valley* gets this hot at night.

"She's coming home with me for a bit." Coming home with him? Then I remember Herb's sobering words when he first spotted me at the condo—*Isn't it a little early to be bringing girls over?* So Nick's one of *those* guys. Figures, with that face. Those biceps. That humor.

"Huh." I huff, taking a defensive stance.

A plume of smoke expels from his smirked mouth. "You're not jealous, are you?"

I flash him my best *as if* face. "Absolutely not. I just don't want to set a precedent that it's okay for you to shove my ass in the back every time you pick up some rando at a show."

"She's not a rando. I was with her the last time I was here."

"How romantic."

"So will you be cool?" he asks.

"That depends. What'll you give me for the seat?"

"You and your negotiations. How 'bout I buy you another burger on the way to Atlanta?"

I may have underestimated this one because that's a good offer, but I maintain my poker face. "That might work. But I get to pick the restaurant."

He offers his hand to seal the deal. "Done."

"Hey, Nicky!" The voice of someone not quite old enough to rent a car sings near us.

Nicky?

"Hey, you." He walks over to the young blonde. Oh, I see. She's one of the cocktail waitresses from the club. Nicky offers to take her backpack. A chauffer and a bellhop, huh?

She kisses his cheek, leaving a faded pink mark on his stubble. "Thank you."

Ugh.

Nick hands me the waitress's sack. "Stick this in the back with you, would ya?" Just for that, I'm adding bacon to my burger.

"Hey!" The waitress, whose name I still don't know because Nick isn't quite attentive enough to introduce us, waves to me.

"Hi!" It's hard not to offer her a phony smile and mimic her bright tone.

Nick opens the car door and she slides into the passenger seat like a princess. "Be cool," he says, passing me on his way around to the driver's side. I climb inside the back and squeeze in between the pile of boxes. When I scoot a stack off to the side, there's a clinking noise. That's funny, T-shirts don't clink. I bet it's filled with CDs he can sell in parts of the U.S. where people still use dial-up internet.

Finding a way to sit back here is like a game of Tetris. I try legs crossed facing the back. Knees up facing the front. Then settle on knees up facing the back with the waitress's bag near my feet. The Jeep backs out and my butt wobbles on the hard flooring. I should've negotiated a second burger.

"I liked your routine, Olivia," the woman says, easing my harsh judgment of the situation.

"Thank you."

"Too bad the mic went out on you the first time." Thanks for the sympathy. "It's always good to have women in the lineup. That's what I love about you, Nick. You're not afraid to share the stage with a woman." I can't see but she sounds like she's tracing her finger around his ear and down his neck with a starry-eyed gaze.

"He's quite the hero," I offer.

We ride along the highway, which is ridiculously crowded considering it's after midnight. My eyes wander around the loopy ramps, commercial buildings, and luxury apartment complexes right off the road. Then I see something I somehow missed on the way to the club. That notable piece of the capital's architecture.

"Hey, is that the Washington Monument?" I say, harking back to the moment I saw the Empire State Building in New York for the first time. The screen never quite does the structures justice. I guess some things are better live.

"Yeah, it's huge," Nick says.

"You're not jealous, are you?" I throw Nick's words back at him and, at the same time, feel certain that our white forefathers were trying to compensate for something. The waitress laughs at this, slowly winning me over.

"You know, the monument was the tallest structure in the world until the Eiffel Tower," she says, and I chuckle under my breath at the idea of the two countries having a *whose dick is bigger?* contest. Really makes you wonder what would happen if women ruled the world.

"How do you know that?" Nick asks.

"I remember it from a high school field trip."

"A recent one?" I ask, and she laughs again, not at all noticing (or minding) the dig. Not that it was meant for her as much as it was for a guy who is much closer to midlife than senior year. Perhaps this Jeep is a symptom of his crisis. And so is the waitress.

"No, I graduated like four years ago," she offers.

"Did you hear that, Nick?"

"Yes, Olivia," he drones.

"Clinton was president when she was born," I add.

He completely ignores me but I hear him say something to her. Something he wants to keep between them. I let it go and lean my head on the box next to me, watching the monument shrink in the distance.

My butt goes numb by the time we make it back to the comedy condo. Never thought I'd actually be relieved to be back at the shabby-ass apartment.

"You go ahead. We'll be right behind you," Nick calls back, probably wanting some privacy to whip out his Washington Monument.

Crawling on my knees, I reach for the latch and pop the door open. "You kids be safe," I say, then slam the door hard.

Inside the condo, it's quiet but still smells like Snoop Dogg's crib. I grab a bottle of water from the fridge (one of the few bottles left next to a jar of mystery mayonnaise). Stand-ups really are a special bunch. Strike that—*male* stand-ups are a special bunch. I wash the cap and head to my room for the night, making sure to lock the door.

By the time I slip on my pj's and into the double-washed sheets, voices rustle somewhere in the small apartment. The walls in this place don't provide much privacy. Something D.C. and NYC apartments have in common. My ears tingle at the sound of Nick's rough muffled voice followed by her giggle. Not like a response-to-a-joke giggle but more of the flirty, precoital variety. Exactly like the giggle Imani made the other night. Who knows how long it's been since one of those sounds slipped beyond my lips? Well, I know how long it's been but I'd rather not say because it's long enough that the most appropriate response would be—*Bless your heart.*

I sneer with an annoyed grumble, pulling the blanket up to my chin. I'm in no mood to listen to the two of them make the bed rock while the futon bar digs into my back.

After twenty minutes of trying to ignore the faint murmurs of their conversation or whatever they're doing, I hear the apartment door close. Must be Herb crashing their party. I sniff audibly. No sign of any fresh bud. The place goes quiet, and soon, a single set of footsteps slips past my locked door. The sound of another door closing follows.

Did the waitress leave? Did Nick send her home before things went too far? Hmm, maybe this night isn't a total disaster.

Sixteen

D*o-Dah-Lee-Do!*
I startle awake with a big gasp as if inhaling smelling salts.

Do-Dah-Le—! I silence the alarm and blink my eyes. Where the hell am I? Looks like a Salvation Army room display. I slide my glasses on.

Nope, just a comedy condo.

One day down, ten more to go. Throwing off the covers, I've got two things in mind—a shower and coffee. I grab my things before dragging myself out toward the bathroom. The hum of the exhaust fan drones behind the closed bathroom door. I knock. "Nick, are you in there?"

The door opens and a flood of steam pours out along with a waft of Irish Spring. Nick stands in nothing but a hunter green towel just barely wrapped around his waist. He smiles, humming Steve Miller Band's "The Joker" like he's in a very good mood. His wavy, wet hair drips on his shoulders, rolling down his defined chest. It'll be impossible to steal my gaze away from those pecs.

"Good morning," he says, breaking the bare-chest seduction spell.

"Morning," I murmur, trying to conceal my morning breath. Not to mention my bird's nest of a top bun (if that bird lived in a shantytown).

"Hope I left you enough hot water."

At the moment, a cold shower might be better. "Uh-huh," I mutter, and he slips past me. Before locking myself in the bathroom, I sneak one last peek at him. Of all the comics I could be on tour with, it had to be the one with the cutest butt. I bite my bottom lip then quickly wash away the dirty thought with a headshake. Time to get cleaned up.

All things considered, the shower looks pretty safe but I better not take any chances. So I slip out of my clothes and into a pair of five-dollar rubber flip-flops (because you know I packed 'em). The hot water is plentiful for the first few minutes before it dies out and gives me the cold shoulder. Literally. Icy water's just pelting my back. After I towel off my goose-pimpled skin and dress, I crack the door to get a little air circulating while I dab my face with concealer. These dark circles aren't going to hide themselves.

Nick knocks softly. "You decent?"

I grab a tube of lip gloss and swipe it on before he sees me. "Yeah, what's up?"

"We have to get on the road," he says, wedging his body in the door just close enough for me to breathe in his cologne, or deodorant, or whatever makes him smell so damn good.

I remind myself of Bernie's rule. This swooning has to stop. As much as I'd like to explore other possibilities, Nick's my road buddy, not my bed buddy. He's Jerry. I'm Elaine.

"What's the rush?" I ask. "We don't have a show until tomorrow. You got plans with another waitress tonight?" This is totally something Elaine would say to Jerry. Still, I find the idea more infuriating than funny. I wonder if she would too.

"Maybe," he says, and his double dimples (the kind you wanna lick) manifest once again, making this whole thing harder.

"What happened to your *friend* last night, anyway?"

"I never kiss and tell," he teases, and I roll my eyes inwardly. Or outwardly because then he asks, "Why?"

"Well, since you made me sit on the floor of the Jeep like a dog, I figured you'd be pouring her coffee right about now."

"It wasn't like that. Besides, we're out of coffee."

Uh, what was that?

"What do you mean, *out of coffee*? I can't get in that Jeep and drive for even one hour without at least one cup of coffee. I won't make it."

"We all have our vices, Olivia."

I knit my brow. "What's that supposed to mean?"

"It means you can get your fix at the gas station. Now c'mon, Miss Priss, you can finish your makeup later."

Over at the gas station under the canopy's shade, I scarf down a breakfast bagel sandwich while throwing back a swig of coffee, or in this case, the liquid of life.

"Better?" Nick asks.

"Yes."

He turns the ignition and that gorgeous Guns N' Roses guitar riff eases through the speakers like a breathtaking sunrise. "Sweet Child O' Mine." I haven't let myself listen to this in a long time.

"Veto!" I say, exercising my right for the first time this trip.

"What? Why?"

"Uh, because I can."

"This is a classic," he argues.

"Ugh, no. It's played out. Change it, please."

His expression turns sour but he complies and Tom Petty's "I Won't Back Down" takes over.

Whew, that was close.

"Where to next?" he asks himself, putting in the Atlanta address in his GPS.

I pull up the itinerary from my email to get the details for myself. "Not another condo, I hope."

"Nope. A motel."

"Is that better?"

"Eh, I guess we'll find out."

Moments later, we're off. Well, kind of. The roads are congested on the way to the highway, and it's hardly nine in the morning. "What is this? The church crowd?" Virginia is technically the edge of the Bible Belt states. I grab my makeup bag, flip down the visor mirror, and clamp my dark lashes in an eyelash curler.

"Whoa, what are you doing?" he says like I just aimed a can of pepper spray at him.

"What does it look like I'm doing?"

"Please don't do that while I'm driving. You're making me nervous," he says.

I turn with my lashes crimped in the curler. "Oh, this? This makes you nervous?" I tease, and he cringes. "I can drive and do this at the same time."

"Yeah, that don't make it a good fuckin' idea!" He does a Chris Rock impression and I let the curler go, laughing. Because I can't laugh and curl at the same time.

"*Bigger & Blacker*?" I ask.

"You know your stand-up."

"It's one of my all-time favorites."

"Hey, me too."

Right there, in stop-and-go traffic, we share a moment. Two comedy lovers stuck in a Jeep, one thinks of the other . . . *Why do you have to be so cute and funny?*

Then, he pulls a single cigarette from the pack hidden in the front console. Oh, yeah, how could I forget about that? So not cute. I shift the conversation. "What's with the crazy schedule? Is it always like this?"

"No. Not exactly." He steadies the stick behind his ear and sets his wrist on the twelve o'clock position on the wheel, keeping his eyes on the car in front of us.

"Then why are we touring like rock stars?"

"Because I always wanted to be one," he says, like he's sending me a wink behind his dark shades.

"That explains the leather, Billy Idol."

"Just trying to pack my gigs like your suitcase on the way to L.A."

"I can't wait to get to L.A." I let out a yawn and slink back in my seat.

"Tired?" he asks.

"Yeah, this caffeine isn't doing anything for me. Think I might catch a nap so if you want me to drive the second leg—"

"Uh-uh. We went over this." Nick shakes his head. "You're not driving my Jeep. A *capeesh* is a *capeesh*."

This is the second time he's said this but now he knows that I know my way around a Jeep better than he does. "I can change a tire on your Jeep but I can't drive it?"

"You didn't change the tire. I did."

"Because I showed you how."

He smirks. "It's not personal. I'm just not ready to let someone else drive it."

Why is he so protective over his Jeep? It's just a Jeep. Even my dad let me drive his eventually. Maybe by Georgia, Nick'll warm up to the idea. Then, a familiar '80s synth beat rolls through the speakers. I know this song! I like this song. Bobbing my head to the beat, I crank up the volume. It's got the perfect message for my possessive driver. "You know what I think, Nick? You gotta . . . *RELAX! Don't dooo iit!*" I sing along with Frankie Goes to Hollywood.

"Are you serious right now?" Nick spits out a slight chuckle.

"No, you're the serious one," I say. "Sing with me."

"I guess that coffee's kicked in," he says, and joins me. After all, it's his music.

"*When you wanna come . . .*" The sound of our voices singing those lyrics in unison feels like we're having vocal sex and sends a tingle down my spine. So I lower the volume.

"I forgot how dirty this song is," I say.

"I know, I like it." Nick and I share a look. It lingers long enough for me to wonder if Nick's any good in bed. I have a sneaking suspicion he is.

No, Olivia. Don't go down that road.

I swat the idea away like a damn horsefly in the house and turn my attention to the traffic ahead as it finally begins to clear.

"So what's your story?" he asks.

"My life story?" Isn't it a little too early in the tour for this one? Maybe we should wait another five hundred miles.

"No, like do you have a boyfriend back in New York?" Was he just thinking what I was thinking? Is that why he's asking me now?

"You first," I say.

"No, I don't have a boyfriend. I'm single and ready to mingle. Now you?"

"Me neither," I say, feeling my body tense beneath the seatbelt.

"Girlfriend?"

"I don't have one of those either. My life isn't exactly conducive to dating at the moment."

"And why's that?" He sounds genuinely interested. But my answer shouldn't surprise him. It shouldn't surprise anyone who's tried to make their way in New York City.

"I work like thirteen-hour days most of the time and I do shows on the weekend too. I barely have time to eat, let alone be in a relationship."

"Yeah, it's tough building a career and a life. Especially when our job requires us to be out most nights." And just when I think he's gonna leave it at that, he says, "But you do make time for sex, right?"

My cheeks flush at the word *sex* like I'm twelve years old. When it comes to Nick, I guess sexual tension's okay, but a candid conversation about the deed? Not so much. "Why are you asking me that?"

"I'm not trying to be skeezy. Just making conversation. Getting to know you. Jerry and Elaine talked about sex all the time."

"I don't know if they talked about it *all* the time." I hold a pregnant pause. Not that there's any chance I could be pregnant (because, well, you know why). Sure, everyone thinks the moment a single woman moves to Manhattan, her life becomes an episode of *Sex and the City* season one. But my show would be called *Busy in the City*. And yeah, I wear that busyness like a badge of honor just like everyone else in my generation. At the same time, I don't want Nick thinking I'm in the slow-sex group. Or worse—a twenty-eight-year-old virgin (No offense, Tina Fey— love you!). Nick nudges me with a look, so I say, "Yes, of course I have sex."

"Really?" He sounds unconvinced. "Then when was the last time?"

I take a second, skipping days and weeks, and begin calculating months.

"That long, huh?" Nick says.

"Give me a second."

"If you need a second, you're not doing it enough."

"Whatever." I push my seatbelt over and reach in the back for my pillow, the one tucked in my garbage bag. I need at least another REM before I can handle this conversation. "I'm not here to debate my sex life with you."

"What sex life?"

"Ha. Ha." I settle my pillow against the sun-streaked window and curl in. Nick takes the hint and doesn't say another word. I sneak a sideways glance his way. What's he thinking? And why do I care so much? I close my eyes, willing myself to conk out for a nap. But his words resound in my head—*If you need a second, you're not doing it enough.*

Yes, my schedule's packed but maybe that's not the reason for my lack of sexual adventure. I have no desire to fake it for some guy I hardly care about. Maybe that's the problem. I just haven't found the man I don't have to fake it with.

Seventeen

The sun beats on my face when I open my eyes. My nostrils are accosted by a waft of Nick's bad habit. Wind whips through the Jeep as he drives eighty miles an hour down the two-lane highway who knows where while Tom Petty's "American Girl" blasts through the speakers. How long have I been out?

I blink my eyes a few times and catch a glimpse of the clock on the dash when I slide my glasses back on. 1:56 P.M.!

"Have a good nap?" Nick asks, extinguishing his cigarette and rolling up the window.

"Yeah," I say, slightly disoriented and attempting to bring moisture back to my dry mouth by chugging every last ounce from my water bottle. When I come up for air, I look ahead for any local signs. "Where are we?"

"We crossed the North Carolina border about forty minutes ago." So it's official. I'm back in the South. "You know you sleep with your mouth open, right?"

Was he watching me sleep? From any other strange guy that'd be creepy. But when it's Nick, it's kinda cute.

"All these trees make me stuffy." The truth is, trees or no trees, I'm a straight-up mouth breather. And now Nick knows two intimate details about me—dry mouth and dry . . . you know.

"Is that why you snore too?" he teases.

I make a dismissive clicking noise with my tongue. "I do *not* snore." Do I?

"Oh, yeah?" He taps around the screen on his phone that's secured to the dash, keeping his eyes primarily on the road. "Look at this." He lifts the device from its place and flashes the screen my way. A video of me completely unconscious, mouth open while the sound of my piglet snores plays through the sound system. Heat slinks up my cheeks. "You're cute when you snore."

I take it in stride, feeling more embarrassed than violated. We're jokesters after all. Still, my heart flutters when he calls me cute. "Recording me while I sleep, huh? Classy."

"Classy is the mustache I drew over your peach fuzz."

"What?" I cover my upper lip and flip down the sun visor, horrified. But my face is clean, save for the smudged mascara carefully hidden behind my lenses.

He chuckles. "I'm kidding, Olivia. What kinda guy do you think I am?"

"The kind you can't trust while you're sleeping."

"Touché."

We come up on a highway sign checkered with logos of nearby restaurants, and one of them is a burger joint I haven't been to in years. One with real beef. "Remember that deal we made last night?"

"Yeah."

"Well, it's time to cash in. Take the next exit."

When we walk into the restaurant, I delight in the vinyl-covered booths and the Lady Liberty statue with her burger-covered torch. "I haven't been to a Red Robin in years," I say, my stomach grumbling. The last time I set foot in one of these I was living in Austin. The best part of law school was spreading my books out over the glossed table, studying contract law while I dipped steak fries in a pile of ketchup. Oh, yeah, this is gonna be good.

As hungry as we are, Nick and I seem to have only one thing on our minds. The only thing you can after a four-hour drive.

The bathroom.

When Nick still isn't back, I slide into our booth and pull out my set notes from last night. On a fresh sheet of yellow paper, I draft up the set changes for tomorrow's show. I'm so engrossed with what I'm doing that I don't even notice the figure hovering over me.

"Hey, buddy," Nick says, startling me. "You write like a crazy person." He's either referring to my scribbly, mismatched handwriting (some all caps, some sentence case) or the fact that I write sideways in the margins.

"Creativity has no bounds."

"I know, I've written jokes on a box of condoms." There he goes, subtly mentioning sex. But at least we're not talking about me.

"I guess that's better than writing it on some woman's ass during sex."

Nick slides into his seat and fans out his menu. "No. Men can't think like that during sex. Not even stand-ups."

"Well, it's good to know we have y'all's attention." I set my notes aside and unravel the flatware from a paper napkin. "What took you so long? I'm starving."

"Had to grab a smoke."

Why a man his age, who grew up with printed warning labels on the side of cigarette boxes, would smoke is completely beyond my comprehension. "You know, you'll be dead in your forties if you keep that up."

"You sound like my mother," he says. Must be nice to have one of those around.

Before I can quip back, our waitress appears with glowing, sun-kissed skin and a perfectly contoured face like one of those MAC counter girls. "How y'all doin' today?" she asks with a sweet Carolina drawl.

"Thank God you're here," Nick says, somewhat dramatically. "This woman is in desperate need of a hamburger."

She grins and locks her gaze with his. It's the second time I feel like I'm intruding on his moment with a waitress. "Well, you've come to the right place. What can I get you?" The woman turns her body toward me but keeps her gaze on Nick. I order a bacon cheeseburger with fries and a tea. Sweet, of course. My burger buddy kindly asks the waitress what she recommends.

"Can I see your menu?" she asks, and leans over the table, flipping it open. Nick's eyes trail up her face and down her chest as she reads off a few recommendations. I wish he would stop.

"Her eyes are up there, *Nicky*," I remind him.

Nick's face flushes and he rubs the back of his neck, meeting her gaze. "Which one's your favorite?"

"I'm a fan of the double," she says, but her waist tells a different story.

"A woman who likes her beef. I'll take it."

He did not just say that to her.

I watch the look in her eyes change from intrigued to insatiable. "I'll get this right in for you." He hands over the menu with an air of satisfaction and watches her walk away.

"Looks like you made another *friend*," I say, snapping him out of his trance.

"Mmm, I do love to make new friends." He finally looks back at me and narrows his eyes like he's got a burning question—a really intrusive one. I brace myself. "If you could have a burger with any comedian, dead or alive, who would it be?" Whew, not nearly as meddlesome as I thought. Let's see . . . the list of comedians I dream of meeting is incredibly long. They're all so different and meeting each of them would be meaningful in its own unique way. But I'll have to go with: "Margaret Cho."

He nods. "Not a bad choice. Why her?"

I let my mind drift back to the mid-'90s. "Well, when I was like nine my dad would let me stay up and watch stand-up with him. As long as I promised to never repeat swear words at school, of course. All of my friends had to be in bed by ten on Saturdays, and I felt like such a rebel." I smirk. "Anyway, it was one of HBO's half-hour specials and Margaret Cho was the star. It was the first time I'd seen a woman do stand-up. It blew my mind. I really thought comedy was a masculine thing."

"Really, why?" he asks.

"I don't know. I guess because I thought it wasn't *ladylike*. People always praised me for being a sweet little girl. But when

I started making sarcastic remarks and cracking jokes, it felt like the opposite of sugar and spice, you know? Sometimes I hated that about myself."

"What? Having a sense of humor?"

"Yeah, like I couldn't be funny and a girl at the same time. Can you believe that? As late as the '90s I believed that. But after watching Margaret Cho onstage, I couldn't sleep. So I stayed up in my room, using a hairbrush as a mic and trying to make up jokes about celebrities like Michael Jackson and Madonna." I watch the corners of Nick's mouth turn up. "I might've gotten into stand-up regardless but watching her let me know it was possible to be funny and female."

Man, I haven't thought about that in so long. That was back when I was small enough to lie on the love seat and fit. "So what about you? Who would you have a burger with?"

"Our buddy Jerry Seinfeld, of course. Same reason as you."

"You mean he proved men could be funny?" I joke.

"He was the first example of someone making a living doing stand-up. I wanted to be like him on the show—get into oddball adventures with my friends—"

"Date a lot of beautiful women."

"Exactly."

Hmm, maybe we really are Jerry and Elaine. I always did have the sense Elaine had a thing for Jerry. A thing that could've destroyed a perfectly sound friendship.

"So, are you living the dream?" I ask.

He seems to give this a moment of thoughtful consideration. "Eh, more or less. You got a favorite *Seinfeld* episode?"

"No contest, 'The Contest' was hilarious."

"The one where they see who can go the longest without masturbating?" He nods like he's reading into my answer more than he should. "You feel like making a bet?"

"*You* feel like making a bet? Because that is not a contest you would win."

He leans back in the booth, taking up the entire space. "Really? So you don't take time to masturbate either?" Oh, Lord, this again?

"Shh!" I scold him. "Keep your voice down. This is the South. God frowns on masturbation down here."

"Here's your drinks, y'all." The waitress slides our chilled plastic tumblers on the table.

"Thanks," I say, grabbing mine. "I'm so thirsty."

"That's an understatement," Nick mutters.

He has no idea.

Eighteen

Watching the ETA on the GPS fluctuate from 8:17 P.M. to 8:42 P.M. then down to 8:23 P.M. feels as obnoxious as someone hovering their finger near your face saying, *I'm not touching you. I'm not touching you!* Who knew sitting on your ass could be so exhausting? It's been over four hours since we left the burger place. I spent at least half that time working on material, setting up gigs back in the city, and checking in with Imani—keeping the details of the tour light and breezy.

I glance at the dash again. Not to seem ungrateful for the free ride and opportunity, but if I hear Mötley Crüe's "Girls, Girls, Girls" one more time I'm gonna toss his phone out the damn window. All I want is to climb in bed with a set of Reese's cups from the vending machine and fall asleep watching reruns of *Friends*—something I haven't had time for in a while.

Nick rolls the back of his head on the headrest and wiggles in the seat. "Oh my god, are we there yet?" The guy's been so chill with his *this is how we road* attitude that I was beginning to think he legitimately enjoys driving for hours on end.

Relief spills over me. "You're sick of the road too? I thought it was just me."

"No, I'm over it."

My ears perk up. "Over it enough to let me drive?"

He turns to me with an *in your dreams* glare. "As tempting as that sounds . . . no." So much for changing his mind in a weak moment.

"Maybe we should pull over and stretch our legs."

"No, we already lost forty-five minutes because your bladder's the size of a lentil."

"Hey, that's bladder shaming." I huff.

"Yeah, well, I think we need to limit your coffee intake," he says, rolling his shoulders.

I stretch my arms out and rub my face, checking the ETA again. 8:24 P.M. "You know what, we need a rally." I grab his phone and find a song better suited for a much-needed pick-me-up.

"Has it been an hour since you made me listen to Taylor Swift already?"

"Yep, but don't worry. I'll play something from your favorite decade." The song trickles in with feel-good beats and electronic hand claps. I roll up the volume dial so we can breathe in Whitney's mighty voice. Soon I'm singing the verse and dancing in my seat, using my fist as a mic. This is the song Imani and I used to blast in my dad's Jeep when I would drive us to the mall where we'd cool off in the summer, eating Dippin' Dots ice cream.

Nick's body stiffens, reluctant to join the party. "What is this, *Carpool Karaoke*?"

"Yeah, don't be such a hard-ass. Sing with me!" It'll get him eventually. I'm pretty sure this is one of those songs even metal lovers can't resist. At least, I've seen a couple at my dad's auto shop mouth the lyrics when they thought no one was looking. "*Dance with somebod-ay!*" I belt and my voice cracks at the top. "C'mon Nick!"

"*With somebody who loves me,*" he sings, flat as his tire yesterday.

The ETA on the navigation hasn't changed but I'm having a lot more fun than I was a few minutes ago. My buddy isn't enjoying himself as much as I hoped (even with me asking, "*Don'tcha wanna dance? Say ya wanna dance!*"). But he hasn't stopped me yet.

After nearly five minutes, the song begins to fade and Nick rescues his phone. "Okay, my turn." A moment later, a familiar piano-and-bass hook dances out of the speakers and Steve Perry's unmistakable voice croons on about a small-town girl.

Yeah, even hard-core pop lovers can get into this one.

"'Don't Stop Believin',' huh?"

Without an answer, he gazes past the steering wheel to the road ahead, singing along like he's alone in the shower. It's way out of his range but that doesn't hold him back. He's kind of adorable when he sings. That catchy-as-hell pre-chorus starts and soon both of us belt out, "*Straanngers. Waaaaitin'.*" Nick keeps the beat on the steering wheel while I pick up air bass. We make a good band.

"Now this is carpool karaoke," he says.

Another handful of songs later, we pull into the motel parking lot in the heart of Atlanta. I practically leap out of the Jeep. I didn't want to say anything after Nick clowned my bladder, but

I've had to pee for the last twenty minutes. With the sun far behind the buildings, the sky is a twinkling twilight blue. A steamy mist in the air settles on my skin, fogging up my glasses and frizzing up my hair.

"Ah, home sweet home," Nick says, unloading the luggage. Is he going to say that about every stop?

"Come here often?"

"Oh, yeah, Atlanta's a fun city. Sometimes too much fun." His words invoke an image of Nick escorting two waitresses back to his room instead of just one, and a sliver of jealousy creeps up. Then he pops a cigarette in his mouth. I wait for it to spook my attraction but it's not having the same effect as before.

Uh-oh. Those ciggies were my feelings fail-safe.

It's fine. Soon I'll be in a room all by myself. I just bet he's in a room by himself too.

"You go ahead. I'll be right behind you," he says.

"No rush." I wave goodbye and escape into the air-conditioned lobby and find the facilities. When I make it back to the front desk, Nick still hasn't come inside.

The clerk greets me and I give him my name for the reservation. After a few clicks on his keyboard, a wrinkle forms between his eyebrows. "I'm sorry, ma'am, but we don't have a reservation under the name Olivia Vincent."

"What was that?" I'm pretty sure I misheard with all the "Don't Stop Believin'" lyrics resounding in my mind. Lord knows that song will be stuck in my head for hours.

"No reservation."

Now my ears are fully engaged and I get that sinking feeling in my gut. You know, the one that tells you you're screwed. The automatic doors open and I get a whiff of Nick's Tobacco for Idiots cologne followed by him whistling Journey.

"What's up?" he asks without a care in the world.

"Apparently, they don't have my reservation."

"Hmm." He thinks for a moment. "Maybe it's under my name."

The clerk checks for our missing reservation and his face relaxes. "Yes, here it is. See, it was under your husband's name all along."

"He's not my husband," I say at the same time Nick says, "I'm not her husband." It's as if we're declaring the other has cooties.

"Oh." The clerk looks confused. "Well, that explains the double beds."

"Double beds? You mean double rooms?" I ask.

"The reservation's for one double room. Correct?"

One room. Did he just say the only reservation we have is for one room?

Nick clarifies with two fingers in the air. "We should have two separate rooms."

"I'm sorry, sir, but I only have the one."

My road buddy and I trade glances. "Then we're gonna need another room, please," I say.

Without hesitation or hint of regret, the clerk simply says, "Unfortunately, we're all booked this evening."

Uh-oh, I really hope he's joking. "Don't take this the wrong way but how can this place be fully booked?"

"It's a holiday week." Why anyone would want to spend Fourth of July week at a motel in the middle of Atlanta is beyond me. "Perhaps you can stay with your not-husband."

My gaze wanders over to Nick—a man I've gotten to know for only a day (day and a half, tops). A man who tells smart jokes onstage, looks great in leather, and makes girls giggle. Giggle! I can't stay in the same room with him. Not if I want to keep my end of the bargain with Bernie.

"Maybe I should find another motel." I pull out my phone and attempt a nearby search.

Nick nudges my arm. "Just bunk with me."

"What is this? Summer camp?" If it were, I'd totally sneak out in the middle of the night to make out with him while the mosquitoes eat us alive.

"It's just a couple nights."

I totally forgot. We don't leave until Tuesday. That's just great. The only thing worse than resisting temptation for one night is resisting it for two. The guy already knows I'm a mouth breather. After a couple nights, what else will he know about me?

Of course I can't exactly express these concerns. So I say, "Sure, for you it's no big deal. You bring home women you hardly know. And how do I know you won't kick me out when your Atlanta friend comes over? Or worse—invite me in on a threesome?"

Nick smirks at this idea. "Well, if you're open to it."

No way. If I was ever with Nick, hypothetically speaking, I'd want him all to myself.

"In your dreams, Fonzie," I tease.

"You think I wanna listen to you snore all night after driving for ten hours? No. But that's the road. And look at it this way: if we split a room, we can save the cash. Which means more money in your pocket. And trust me, if this is now your full-time gig, you're gonna want to cut all the costs you can." A valid point my budget can't argue with. "Didn't I tell you to be prepared for anything?"

"Yes."

"Like it or not, Olivia, we're in this together." He holds up three honorable fingers like a Boy Scout. "And I promise, no funny business."

Nineteen

So here we are in our little room together. Or rather, I'm locked in the bathroom, taking advantage of all this hot water despite the post–summer solstice heat. Meanwhile, Nick's out there, probably flipping through the local TV stations and wondering why in the hell I've been in here so long.

I take my time, washing the journey off my face and out of my hair, then hang out a little longer for a blow-dry. Finally, clean, dry, and dressed, I emerge back into the chilled room, the gusty hum of the AC blowing in the background.

"There she is." Nick's settled on one of the beds with his bare feet propped up, aiming the remote at the television as I suspected, but his gaze is aimed at me. "Wow, look at you," he says, staring at me like I'm brand-new. Like maybe I can be more than his Elaine.

"What?" I ask, pulling at the edge of my oversized T-shirt—the one that felt more like a sexual buffer than my skimpier summer jammies. If my goal was to get Nick in my bed, booty shorts would be part of my strategy.

"Your hair's all . . ." He waves his hand around his own head like he can't find the words. "It looks nice."

"Oh. Thanks." I run my fingers through my soft strands and pull them back into a ponytail, securing it with a hair tie from my wrist.

"Feel better?"

I exhale, feeling the most refreshed I've felt since we left New York. "I do."

"Good, 'cause I've got somethin' for ya." He holds the neck of a Blue Moon beer, swinging it in his hands. "You said you like this kind, right?" It was one of the things that came up on the 85 when he asked me if girls from Texas drink beer.

"When did you get this?" I take the bottle and spot the half-empty one on the nightstand between the two beds.

"While you were in the shower. I got some Doritos too." He holds up a family-sized bag. Between the junk food and sitting on my bum all day, I'll be ten pounds heavier before we reach Los Angeles. But how can I resist him? I mean the beer and chips.

He grabs his bottle and tilts it my way. "Wanna throw these back and watch some *Seinfeld*? I hooked up my media player."

"Sure, but I don't know if I remember how to relax and watch a show anymore."

"It's easy. Just watch me. I'll show you how to do it." He relaxes back onto his pillow and smacks his lips, letting out a super satisfactory sigh. "See?"

I giggle at his little demonstration, then grab my garbage bag pillow and mimic his position on my own bed. "Like this?"

He raises his beer. "You got it." There's nothing remotely sexy about this situation—I might as well be wearing my retainer. But lounging on a bed so close to Nick, even if it's not the same bed, is alarmingly arousing. So I swallow the sensation with a swig of beer (because I'm sure drinking an inhibition-dulling substance will help the situation). "I'll load up your favorite episode."

"'The Contest'?" Good idea. Watching that episode will only reinforce the idea of sexual deprivation.

"Yep." He clicks the remote and that unforgettable bass-slapping *Seinfeld* score begins. Ten minutes in, we're cringing and cackling at all the classic moments, nursing our beers, and crunching tortilla chips—our respective beds are littered with Cool Ranch crumbs. When Nick laughs, he really laughs. The sound is deep and warm and he doesn't try to hamper it with a hand over his mouth. His eyes crinkle at the corners. His Adam's apple dances. We seem to find humor in all the same things so our laughter's perfectly in sync.

In some ways, this might even be better than sex.

Nick catches me looking at him and I gulp back my beer, turning my attention to the show. "You wanna watch another one?" he asks.

"Yes, please." I set my drink down and settle under the covers with the blankets pulled up to my chin, then peek my foot out of the corner, only to tuck it back in again from the chilly air. "Hey, Nick, would you mind turning down the AC? It's really cold," I ask, wondering how a room in Atlanta in the middle of summer could get this frosty.

"What?" he says with his hand digging in the Doritos bag. "I didn't hear what you said because I was eating a chip."

I chuckle. "I said can you turn down the AC?"

"You mean turn it up?"

"No, turning it up means making it colder. I want it warmer."

"If you want it warmer, I have to turn it up. Higher temperatures are warmer than lower temperatures. Don't they teach you this stuff in college?"

Right when I was getting all relaxed, he wants to razz me. "We're not all trade school graduates, Nick, and I didn't say turn the temperature down, I said turn the AC down."

"What's the difference?"

"Never mind. I'll do it myself." I throw the covers off and march over to the unit beneath the window next to his bed.

He lays propped up on his elbow, watching me with my erect finger hovering over the controls. "See that red arrow pointing up? Press that one."

Hahahahaha! Seinfeld's live studio audience chimes in.

I shoot him a sideways glance and reluctantly press the up button. "I stand by my phrasing."

Later that night, I wake up, shivering beneath my covers so much you'd think I was in one of those sleazy-motel vibrating beds. I slip on my glasses. It's after midnight. Nick left the light on but he's nowhere in sight. Where'd he go?

"Nick?" No answer. Did he turn the AC down (I mean up) just to screw with me while he snuck out with some *friend*? "No funny business, my ass," I say, teeth chattering like one of those windup toys.

I shuffle over to the AC and hit the off switch. Like a zombie, the damn thing doesn't die. "You gotta be kidding me." I try again, on and off, on and off, but it blows on. Great. Of all the motels in downtown Atlanta, we've got the one with the AC ghost.

Then, the door swings open and I catch a glimpse of something white floating just above the carpet in my peripheral.

What in the . . .

"Ahh!" I scream, jolting back on my butt, clutching the drapes.

"Ahh!" A horror-filled man-scream echoes back. Where's the damn pepper spray when you need it? I blink and take in the spine-chilling stranger.

Oh, *hahahaha*, it's just Nick.

"Why are you draped in a blanket?" I ask, yanking myself up.

The door slams shut behind him. "I just spent the last twenty minutes at the front desk trying to get them to do something about this piece-of-shit AC."

"And?"

"They just gave me a couple extra blankets and said good luck." He plops a folded blanket on my bed and swaddles himself tighter.

"Can't we open a window or something?" I rub my shoulders briskly, tottering over to my suitcase for a pair of warm socks and my hooded sweatshirt—which was a total afterthought.

He flops back into bed and rolls himself in the blankets like a burrito. "Nope, they're just for show."

"Figures," I say, dressing my feet. I never sleep in socks. Not even when there's snow on the ground.

"Is that where you went to college?" Nick asks, and I glance down at the UT logo.

"Yep. Hook 'em horns." I flash him the Longhorns sign, just long enough to perform my obligatory alumni duty, then huddle under layers of blankets.

"Football fan, huh?" he asks.

"Of course. It's part of a Texan's DNA."

"Right . . . you think we can sue the motel?"

"For what? Meat lockering?"

He chuckles through chattering teeth. "But seriously, can it get any colder in here?"

The answer to that is yes. By two in the morning, the two of us are out of bed again. *Desperate* for warmth, we've gathered anything that resembles fabric from around the room and now we're on to the curtains.

No joke.

Nick's balancing on the wheeled desk chair wearing his leather jacket while I hold it steady. "How in the hell do I unclip these?"

"Who cares? Just rip 'em down!" So much for a good night's rest.

"You know, we could stay warmer if we slept in the same bed."

I slowly turn my head to see if he's serious. I think he is. Me, Nick, one bed? Sounds amazing, but it's way too risky. Especially after I catch a glimpse of his abs when he stretches up for the curtain rod. "Probably better not to share anything tonight except an oddball road story."

"I'm not trying to get you between the sheets, but I feel like Leo in *The Revenant* with his frosty-ass beard and frostbitten mouth. What if we get hypothermia?"

I want to tell him that he's being dramatic, but my fingers and toes are now numb. "Curtains first."

So here we are, bundled beneath every blanket, towel, and pillow we can find, topped off with the damn blackout drapes from the window. Nearly an hour later, I'm shivering too much to sleep. Maybe my eyelids are frozen too. I can't hear Nick breathing, which means either he already froze to death or he can't sleep either. I shut my eyes tight for a moment, praying I don't regret this.

"Psst! Nick."

Twenty

"A re you awake?" I whisper at his horizontal back, gripping the blanket to my chin.

"Yeah, I'm awake," he says like he's been lying with his eyes open the whole time.

I swallow hard. "I think you were right about hypothermia." We both know this isn't actually possible given that it's only about fifty-something degrees in here, but I'm hoping he'll make this easy on me and take the bait so I don't have to come out and ask.

"So . . ."

I wait for him to say more but he doesn't. "So, should we . . ."

"Should we what?"

Does he really not know or is he screwing with me? I try again. "Maybe it's a good idea that we, you know?"

"Ooh, I see. You're down to snuggle now." Oh, yeah, he's screwing with me. Too bad we can't solve this issue with an old-fashioned screw.

I swallow my desires and say, "No, I'm not *down* to snuggle. But I'm . . ."

"You're what?"

You see, a gentleman wouldn't make me say it. But Nick's a comedian. "I'm up for sharing the bed. Just because I can't feel my face."

He rises from his mattress, gathering all the miscellaneous linens and shuffling over like a big, dopey blanket monster. Apparently the cuddly type. He freezes over me. Not literally, of course, but I feel it's necessary to clarify. "Do I have your consent?" he asks.

"Consent for what?" What does he think is happening here?

"Do I have your permission to lie down next to you?"

"Obviously."

"No, not obviously. A man in my position should get consent."

"Oh my god." I don't think he's joking. And while I appreciate that he's trying to be respectful, I prefer that he shut up, get in this bed, and radiate some damn body heat my way so I can get some shut-eye. "Yes, you have permission to lie next to me."

"Since you're an attorney, can you say, 'I, Olivia Vincent, Esquire, hereby grant—'"

"Nick! Stop screwing around and get in the bed. I'm freezing my ass off!"

"Okay, I'll allow it." He throws his blankets, towels, and curtain on top of mine. The weight of it all is already an improvement. Still, the tiny hairs on my skin stand up at attention when he climbs in next to me, settling on his back. "I totally get killing horses now," he says.

Huh? What kinda psycho-slaughter-babble is this? "Okay, I changed my mind. Go back to your own bed."

"No, I'm talking about sleeping in a carcass for warmth. You know, cowboy style. Don't you do that in Texas?"

I roll my eyes, too cold to laugh. "Believe me, if I had a horse right now, we would *not* be sharing a bed."

He scoots himself a little closer, and the tip of his pinky finger just barely touches my knee, but it's enough to send my heart racing to a steady gallop. "Am I too close?" he whispers gently. I'm far closer to Nick than I should ever allow. The heat of his body warms the space between us, and all I want to do is close that space. Maybe even lie beneath him for just a little while. For survival, I mean.

"No, you're fine," I say.

"Okay, good, because your body's hot."

"What?" I feel myself warm up in a way I haven't for so long, and bite my bottom lip.

"I mean your body heat is helping."

"Oh." His clarification does little to stamp out this fire that's beginning to blaze inside me. Every inch of my body is responding to him. The way his breath moves slowly in and slowly out. The leftover scent of his sweet cologne. There's a whirling in my belly as my breath grows heavier.

"Good night, Olivia," he utters softly.

I close my eyes and fill my lungs with the chilled air. "Good night."

It's not long before I finally drift off. And with Nick keeping my bed warm, I sleep soundly until the sun comes up. The AC drones on, pushing out arctic air. When I open my eyes, Nick's snoozing next to me—snug as a man in a motel curtain. And oh so dreamy . . .

He stirs and his eyes peek open like he can sense I'm awake. "Are you watching me?" His accusation is enough to jolt me out of this snuggly sleepover.

"Don't flatter yourself. I just woke up." If it weren't so warm next to him, I'd hop out of bed and march as far away from him as I could.

He takes in a deep morning inhale and rubs his face. "I actually slept pretty good, considering your snoring."

I have no defense so I say, "Same."

He turns to me, taking in my morning look, and I pull the sheet up over my chin and mouth. "I didn't want to say this last night, but you fart in your sleep too."

That's it. My face is now officially the hottest thing in the room. I gasp and shove him away. "I do not!"

He laughs, blocking my playful blows. "If you say so."

"Don't be gross," I say, silently praying it's not true. But if it is, it's probably for the best. The more barriers between Nick and me, the better.

Nick presses his lips together, stifling his laughter. "I'm just bustin' your chops. And anyway, my ears were too frozen to hear anything."

Whew! Now that's a relief (and not the audible kind). Too bad having this conversation in this context first thing in the morning is uber embarrassing. You know how hard it is to humiliate a stand-up? "Just for that I'm never sleeping next to you again. I don't care how cold it is." Or how hot he is, for that matter.

"Were you planning on sleeping with me again?" he asks.

I sit up, the motel curtain draping my chest. The room is like a cold pool that I'm slowly making my way into, inch by inch

"Let's get something straight. We didn't sleep together. We slept in the same bed. There's a big difference. *Capeesh?*" Don't be fooled. I'm saying this for my benefit. Not his.

"That's too bad for you," he says, climbing out from under the sheets and stretching his arms wide.

I find my glasses on the nightstand and watch Nick slowly peel one of the towels from the bed. "Why?"

He looks me right in the eye. "Because I'm really good at sex."

And it's like the mic drops. Or is that my jaw? I don't know because I can't think or breathe. That's it. I don't care. Screw the rules. Screw my better judgment. I want to screw him—

Clunk. Clink.

The AC unit makes a crinkly sound and craps out. Nick and I freeze then whip our heads toward it. Not a breath of air comes out.

"Is it?" I toss the covers off me and we give it a few more seconds.

"It is."

Nick and I grin like we've just won the battle with the AC beast. We cheer at a decibel that will definitely wake the neighbors. But who cares? The damn thing is dead! With our arms flung open, I leap into his for a victory hug. He spins me around, our noses just inches from each other's as we celebrate. That's when I realize that *this* is the closest I've ever been to Nick, and by the look in his eyes, he's feeling it too. I could. He could. What's stopping us?

We drop each other instantly and he walks away.

"I'm gonna take a shower," he says, trying to sound casual. But we both know what just happened even if nothing happened.

"Okay," I call in a pitch that's way too high for seven in the morning. The bathroom door closes behind him, and I glance back at my bed with its piles of covers.

Oh, boy.

Twenty-One

've been tapping my pen on my yellow legal pad for the last thirty-four minutes. I was hoping to get a little writing in but I've just been sitting here trying to convince myself that everything that happened between Nick and me in the last eight hours is totally normal. I throw my head back, downing the rest of the lobby coffee.

That's where I've been since Nick locked himself in the bathroom—the lobby. And in case you've never been in a motel lobby, it's extremely . . . underwhelming. There are no real chairs. Just a couple of stools against a tiny bar in an alcove next to a couple of old vending machines. The smell of ammonia battles with one of those air freshener sprays with a name like Garden Spring or Fresh Linen—but there's nothing fresh about it.

"I thought I might find you here." Nick's voice startles me and he tosses a fast-food breakfast sandwich on my legal pad.

"What's this for?" I ask, averting my eyes.

"It's for eating, Olivia. Didn't think I'd need to explain that one to you." He takes the stool next to mine and unwraps his greasy sausage biscuit. I peel back the crinkly wrapping, melted cheese sticking to it, and my gut grumbles eagerly. "I know how much you like bacon," he says with a full mouth.

"Thanks." I finally look over at him chewing away. His hair seems softer this morning for some reason. Everything about him feels softer. Would it be wrong to crawl back in bed and cuddle with him right now?

My mind's telling me no, but oh, my body . . .

I try to picture him with a cigarette in his mouth but it's not working.

"You're welcome. I've never met a woman who loves greasy fast food as much as I do."

"They call it SAD but I love the standard American diet."

"Land of the free, home of the morbidly obese." He holds his half-eaten, processed biscuit high, and my bacon sandwich–holding hand meets his in a toast. The moment our knuckles meet, there's a tingling in my belly and it's not from the trans fats. Our eyes lock for a split second, just long enough to feel visually penetrated. That's it, I can't touch him again for the rest of the trip.

Not without consequences anyway.

He swallows his big bite, completely unaware of the battle that's brewing in my mind. "So last night was bizarre."

I laugh nervously and feel a strong vibration in my pants.

Oh, *hahahaha*. It's just my phone.

I pull it out of my back pocket, holding my breath for a moment before I send it to voicemail. I'll call her later. "It's Imani," I say, setting the phone aside.

"You should take it. I was about to go outside anyway." Nick crushes the sandwich wrap.

"It's okay. I don't want to talk to her right now."

"Why? Is she obnoxious?" Nick asks.

"Not usually but she's been up my ass about getting another real job. I keep trying to tell her that comedy is a real job."

"Is it though?"

"Yeah . . . I mean, I think so. Don't you?"

"I used to think it was." To hear Nick somewhat side with Imani on this is like a smack in the mouth. It stings.

"You know, seeing as I just left a steady job to go on a comedy tour with you, you're not exactly inspiring a ton of confidence right now."

"Let me tell you somethin', if you're looking for someone else to validate your choice, you'll never make it in this business."

His words feel like another smack. Only this one is so hard that it knocks the wind out of me. After a moment, his statement settles and I can breathe again. I'm a ball of confidence, ready to roll over any naysayers (or ignore their calls). I don't need anyone to validate my choice to be a comic. Not even Nick.

"Excuse me." A motel clerk approaches, a gold watch shining on his wrist while his plastic name tag reads *Fredrick Hudson— Manager.* "Are you the couple staying in room 137?"

"We're not a couple," we blurt in unison. Nick steps away from me, reinforcing the idea.

Fredrick raises an eyebrow. "But you are staying in room 137, right? With the broke PTAC unit?"

"Yeah," Nick says.

"Well, we just sent someone over to look at it and there ain't no way we're gonna get it fixed by tonight." Uh-oh. With this heat, sleeping in the Jeep is hardly an option. "We've gotta move you to another room. One will be available this afternoon."

"Only one?" I ask.

"Yes, ma'am. It's a king room." King room? As in one king bed with plenty of room for Nick and me to roll around in? "Wait a second." Fredrick narrows his eyes at Nick. "You look familiar. What's your name again?"

"Nick Leto."

"Hold up, I've seen you on The Comedy Channel? You're a comedian, right?"

Nick welcomes this semi–celeb sighting with open arms. "Yes, I am."

The clerk offers his hand. "Oh, man, you're a funny dude. You're playing Cedric's club tonight?"

"You know Cedric?" Nick asks.

Who's Cedric?

"Yeah, that's my big brother."

"Oh, I see, Fredrick and Cedric," Nick says. "You got another brother named Hedrick too?"

"Actually, yeah. It's like our dad's Dr. Seuss or some shit." Nick and Fredrick share a laugh but I still can't get past the one-room—one-bed—one-night issue. "I'll tell you what, I'll comp your whole stay for the AC inconvenience but y'all gotta come out and have a drink after the show with us. It's Cedric's birthday."

"Hey, thanks, man. I really appreciate that. We'll be there." Nick offers Fredrick one of those slick handshakes like the two are old buddies, and the motel manager heads off. When he's out of earshot, Nick turns to me. "Did you hear that? Free stay and he thinks I'm hilarious."

"He said you were funny. Not hilarious," I say. "So you're sleeping on a cot tonight, right?"

"What's the matter, not in the mood to cuddle anymore?"

I want so much more than cuddling, which is the problem. "No, it's weird. I feel like Charlie Bucket's grandparents all smushed in one bed."

"Okay, if you're not comfortable sharing a bed, maybe I'll find somewhere else to sleep." He doesn't say so but I know he's referring to a lady friend. Being beneath the sheets with him is a terrible idea but I don't want him under someone else's sheets either.

Twenty-Two

Ohe of the things I love about the stage is having the mic. It's like being the most powerful person in the room. All eyes on me and all ears open for my next joke. Ask any comedian. Every time they have to hand the mic over, they're whining like a third grader on the inside—*One more joke, please! Just one more!*

Tonight, however, is not at all like that. In fact, the emcee is welcome to come out anytime and rescue me from my atomic bombing. Okay, maybe I'm exaggerating a little but it's not good. The spots I typically get in the city are half or less of the time I have up here now. Beads of sweat drip from my hairline into my eyes. The combo of heat and moisture is fogging my glasses. I actually stretch the collar on my shirt and say, "Is it hot in here?" like I'm a female Dangerfield. Totally effing regrettable. My tongue keeps sticking to the roof of my mouth and my lips to my gums because it's drier than a Christian wedding on a Sunday. Oh, Lord, take me now!

How can this happen to me again? I blame listening to my set from D.C. Hearing the whole mic fiasco again might've wigged me out a little. Still, it's like I don't know how to do stand-up outside of New York. God, I hope that's not the case, or this tour really will be a disaster.

No, it can't be that. I made plenty of people laugh in Texas. So what's different? If anything, I should be better since I'm finally free to just be a stand-up comedian for once. This is my dream. So why is it beginning to feel like my worst nightmare?

When it's over, I gladly give the mic back and drag my feet offstage. I can't look at Nick as I pass him. This time, I have no excuse. No electrical failure to blame.

"Olivia," Nick calls after me like he's about to ground me and take away what I hold most dear. The mic.

I slowly turn toward him, using the time to force my lips into an innocent smile. "Yes, Nick?"

His expression is even sterner than I imagined, and the doe-eyed stare I'm darting his way does nothing to soften it. "We need to talk after the show."

Uh-oh. Does that mean? Of course it does. He's taken a chance on me and somehow I've managed to blow it. One week since I left law and now I might seriously have to go back. Imani's words resound in my head over and over like a skipping vinyl. *Disaster, disaster, disaster . . .*

I grit my grin and swallow hard. If I pretend there's nothing to fear then maybe he'll reconsider. "Sure!" The emcee calls him to the stage but he keeps his stare on me. "You better go. Wish you laughs!" I wave my hand as if urging him to head up and simultaneously flinging fairy dust his way. If I had magical powers right now, I'd make him see that even though I've had a couple bad nights, I'm not a bad stand-up. I'm good. And if I can keep this going then maybe one day I'll be great.

Nick turns without a word and I let out a contentious breath. I'm safe for now but I think I need something to take the edge off.

Cedric, the club's owner and Fredrick's (motel manager) brother, hangs out behind the bar. He gives me a disappointed-yet-pitying look. "What's your poison?" he asks, sliding over a bowl of tortilla chips with spinach dip.

"Got anything that'll take me back to thirty minutes ago?"

"No, but I can get you something that'll make you forget it ever happened."

"Close enough." A moment later, there's a tall tumbler of what looks like iced tea in front of me. "What's this?" I ask, then promptly take a sip.

"A bourbon sweet tea."

I make a face. It tastes like equal parts bourbon and sugar. I'm definitely in the South now. Cedric leans on the bar, staring at me like he wants to ask me why the hell I came to his club to bomb. So I steer the conversation away. "I hear it's your birthday."

"Yes, ma'am." I haven't been called ma'am this much since I left Midland. Southern gentlemen, God love 'em.

"Well, happy birthday!" I raise my glass and he toasts me with his lowball. "So where are we celebrating tonight?" I ask, thinking back to the deal we made with Fredrick for the free stay.

"There's a place a few blocks from here called Wild Peacock."

I take another sip of my bourbon sweet tea. The alcohol burns my chest, numbing my insides. I better pace myself. "Wild Peacock? Is that where Channing Tatum strips?"

He shakes his head. "No, it's not some Magic Mike shit. But I'm sure you can find some dude to grind up on you if that's what you're into."

My mind drifts to an image of Nick and me dancing to some '90s R and B song, his arm around my waist and my waist against his . . . Even under the circumstances, I don't hate the idea. Then again, if we get that close, we'll have to talk.

That's it!

I need to make it impossible for us to talk. And I know exactly how to do it. I slide my drink aside. If I want to survive the night, I'll need to keep my wits about me.

Nick takes the mic and opens strong. The birthday bartender watches him, eyes lit up, laughing at every punchline. "That dude's funny."

Yeah, yeah. What else is new?

By the end of the show, I'm hiding from Nick at the bar while he's busy posing for photos with his adoring fans, handing over those Buh-Bye shirts left and right. Sneaking glances at his sexy smile from across the room makes the thought of leaving this tour even more unbearable.

After the fan mob dies down, he comes my way. Ooh, there goes those stomach knots. Relax, Olivia. Just act like you're having a great time. Like you've met your two-drink minimum.

"Hahahaha!" I throw my head back in a laugh and my new friends at the bar shoot me a look.

"What's so funny?" Nick asks.

"Oh, nothing. Have you tried one of these? It's so good. I'm on my second one." I raise my bourbon sweet tea, playing the role of fun, tipsy comedienne, and he raises an eyebrow.

"Can't say that I have. Can we go talk in the greenroom?"

My heart thumps against my chest. "Later—we have to get to the club for Cedric's birthday, remember? He's already headed over there. C'mon!" I hop off my barstool and motion for him to follow me out of the club.

"Wait, Olivia," he says, not far behind me.

"What's the matter? You don't dance like Elaine, do you, Jerry?" I imitate the character's infamous dance, jerkin' around with major hitchhiker thumbs.

"Are you drunk?" he asks, laying his hand on the small of my back and leading me to the Jeep like a gentleman. I'm stark sober but I stumble a little. His touch is intoxicating. My body loosens up, eager to lean into his hand. Into him.

"Maybe," I say, hoping he'll buy it and keep his talk to himself awhile longer. "Let's go dance it off." I tap him on the nose with a "boop" and he smiles, opening the passenger door. I think it's working.

As he walks around to the driver's side, I scramble to connect his auxiliary cable to my phone. My song's locked and loaded with the volume on high by the time he opens the door.

"You sure you're okay?" he asks.

"I'm uh-mazing."

He turns the ignition and Bruno Mars's voice steals the speakers. I pump my fist to the beat, singing along to the first verse of "Uptown Funk." Can't talk over this jam.

"Olivia," he calls, but doesn't look too mad that I hijacked his stereo.

"*I'm too hot!*" I sing as he pulls out and heads down the street. Dancing around as much as my seatbelt will allow, I get the party going. No way he'd want to have a serious conversation now. The song isn't even over by the time Nick pulls up to the valet. "Whoohoo! We're here!" I shout.

"Maybe we should get you some food."

"Later. Let's party!" I play up plastered girl and practically skip into the club. A Drake track blasts overhead as I whip out cash for the cover. The sooner I get on the dance floor, the better. I hardly make it into Wild Peacock with its blue, purple, and green uplights before Nick takes my hand. Another rush comes over me.

"C'mon, we gotta go make an appearance," he says, no doubt referring to finding Motel Manager Fredrick.

"Let's go dance first," I beg, stealing my hand back.

"We need to make good on our promise."

I relent, following several paces behind him to the VIP section. Fredrick and Cedric and a few others sit at one of the roped-off booths and lay eyes on Nick and me. "Oh, hey." Fredrick grins and waves us over. "You made it. Come have a drink."

Good idea. That oughta loosen Nick up.

"Okay!" I climb over the ropes and slide into the booth. A tall bottle of whiskey sits on the table surrounded by empty glasses, mixers, and lime wedges. Bottle service, huh? I grab the bottle and look to the birthday boy. "May I?" I ask, and he gives me the okay.

"Maybe you've had enough," Nick says, gently stopping me from pouring any more.

"It's not for me. It's for you, you fuddy-duddy." I hand him the glass, pour some soda for me, and we all toast to Cedric's birthday.

Nick takes a tiny sip, then leans in. "Maybe we shouldn't stay long. I really want to talk to you."

Damn! This drunk act is failing me. Plan B.

"What? I can't hear you! I'm gonna go dance," I yell over the music, and slide away from the booth before he can say anything. The DJ plays "Lose Control," a throwback from Missy Elliott, and I groove to the beat, getting lost in the crowd. What are the chances a classic rock–obsessed comedian like Nick will follow me?

As the DJ seamlessly segues the dance track into another, Nick glides up, head boppin' and hips poppin'. I may have misjudged this one.

"Hey," he calls.

"Hey!" I say, making sure there's plenty of distance between us. I turn away from him, hoping he won't attempt any conversation. And there are definitely worse things than his becoming mesmerized by my bouncing booty. Staying light on his feet, almost bobbing and weaving, he makes his way around to face me once again. I do another half spin, then another. Each time he follows me. Here I am, afraid he wants to get rid of me when I can't seem to get rid of him.

"Wanna get out of here?" he yells clearly over the music.

"What?" I cup a hand over my ear like I can't hear him.

Finally, he steps close to me, puts his hand on my waist and his mouth to my ear. "Wanna go back to the motel?"

His eyes meet mine in an intense gaze and my pulse goes haywire. Only I'm not sure if it's the fear of being fired for the second time in a week or the rush of excitement that comes from thinking of going home with him. I turn slightly and shout over the music. "I'm having a good time!"

The song shifts again, this time to something slower. And

somehow it seems quieter too. I don't know what to do so I just stand there frozen, looking at Nick looking at me.

"Why are you avoiding me?" he asks, and this time there's nowhere to run. I have to face him.

"Because I bombed again and I don't want you to kick me off the tour over some subpar sets."

He wrinkles his brow. "What? I'm not kicking you off the tour."

"You're not?"

"No, you've had some rough nights but I know you're a good comic. You have a lot of potential. A lesser comedian would've given up a long time ago."

"Then what did you want to talk to me about?"

"Well, like you said, you've had some subpar sets. It's the tour. The first time you go on the road it can be intimidating. We're comics. We're all a little neurotic. But if you want things to go better, you have to get out of your head. So tomorrow in Nashville, try to relax. Go up there like you would at Funnies. Same jokes, different crowd. I know you can do this, Olivia. I believe in you."

"You do?" I ask, feeling a rush from his acceptance. At least one person sees me the way I want to be seen.

"Yeah, I wouldn't have asked you on this tour if I didn't. Besides, I like having you around," he says, but the way he's looking at me, I'm almost sure what he means is that he likes *me*.

"I like having you around too," I say, holding his gaze. Then his eyes fall to my mouth and my lips part. Nick reaches for my waist at the same time I reach for his leather lapel. Without a word, Nick and I crash into each other, our lips locked in a hot kiss. His hands crawl up my back as my palms scrape his stubbly cheeks, and I caress his soft hair with my fingertips. It's like he's been wanting this since we met too.

I know we're not supposed to but now I see something Nick and I have in common.

A slight disregard for the rules.

Twenty-Three

Stumbling inside our king room, we hang on to each other for balance. Totally drunk on each other's kiss. The lyrics from "Paradise City" still playing in my head from the drive back to the motel—*please take me home!* His mouth comes for mine again but then stops short.

"What?" I say, nearly breathless.

"Are you sure you want to do this?" he asks, and his momentary hesitation actually makes me want him more.

"Yes," I say.

"But you're drunk."

"No, I'm not. I was just pretending to make it harder for you to talk to me."

"You really did make it hard for me," Nick says low in my ear, and kisses my neck. I surrender to his touch, my eyes rolling back. "I thought you didn't want to share a bed tonight." Last night, I needed him in my bed for survival. And tonight is no different.

I smirk, tugging my lip with my teeth. "You know, for a guy who's about to get laid, you have a lot of objections."

"We're on tour. What kind of guy would I be if I didn't ask?"

"Even Jerry and Elaine had sex sometimes. Now shut up and kiss me," I say, tearing off my glasses. Let's see if Nick's as good in bed as he is onstage. My body's in desperate need of a pro. And I get the feeling I won't have to fake anything.

Without hesitation this time, Nick takes my face into his hands and pulls me in for a good one. The kind you imprint in your memory and replay on a cold, lonely night. In the warm hotel light, we wrestle with each other's clothes, flinging them from one side of the room to the other, as if we're competing for who can toss the farthest. All the while making sure our lips don't separate for more than a second. Damn, it feels good to touch a man's bare back. Nick really is hard in all the right places.

Soon, we're fully prepared beneath the sheets. Two comedians intertwined. My body calls to him and he responds well . . . at first. The moment I relax, feeling like he speaks my body's cryptic language, my sexual buzz begins to wane. I close my eyes and kiss him again, reminding myself of how much I've wanted him. How turned on I got when he simply lay next to me.

A small peak of pleasure emerges but fizzles out like a single tiny firework. This makes no sense. I've been deprived of intimacy for so long. And Nick is so sexy and funny. I really like him. Why am I not getting off like gangbusters? I let out a decent moan to encourage myself and him.

Leaving a trail of kisses along my neck, he whispers, "Are you close?"

"Uhh, maybe," I say, trying to make it sound like a yes. He

seems to take the hint and switches positions, getting his hands involved now. Okay, here we go. I think I can get into this.

"How's that?" he asks, staring down at my naked body.

"Good," I say, but it's quickly downgraded to *pretty good*. All right, let's be real, I've never actually gotten there on the bottom and this doesn't seem very promising. I push him down onto the mattress and climb on top.

"There's my little cowgirl," he says with that sexy smile spread across his face. *Yeehaw!*

Our hips find a common rhythm and it's good. Really good. Just not good enough. Is it him or is it me? Is it us?

"Hold still," I say, trying to salvage it. Who am I kidding? I haven't been able to get there in years. This is as futile as looking for the ocean in the middle of the desert. So much for Nick being the one who could change that. It pains me to say it, so I won't. Instead, I'll have to fake it.

Rolling out a finale of cries and moans, I give a performance Meg Ryan would be proud of.

Twenty-Four

Ring-a-ling-a-ding! Ring-a-ling-a-ding!

I suck in a deep inhale as if resuscitating myself from the dead. You know the feeling—waking from a dead sleep to a chime-chimey alarm. Only this alarm isn't my usual one. In fact, it's not even my phone. I blink my eyes wide, taking in my surroundings. Nick's snoozing, shirtless and sprawled out next to me. I nudge him awake. "Hey, your alarm."

He startles alert. "What?"

"Turn your alarm off."

He reaches for his phone on the nightstand and holds it an inch from his nose. "It's not my alarm. It's Bernie," he grumbles.

"Huh?"

"Bernie's calling me." Uh-oh, I promised her no funny business. Does she somehow know we slept together last night?

Oh my god. We slept together last night.

"Hey, Bernie, what's up?" Nick says, propped up on his el-

bows. I cover my mouth, worried she might hear me breathing.
"Uhh, yeah, she's right here. I'll put you on speaker."

With panic-stricken eyes, I mouth, "What are you doing?"
Nick mutters, "It's fine. Say hi."

"Hi, Bernie!" I say, trying to sound like I'm fueled by a second cup of coffee. "Nick and I were just . . . about to grab some
breakfast before we head to Nashville."

"Are you sure you're not having breakfast in bed?" she asks in
her gruff accent.

I throw my head back in a big laugh. "Oh, Bernie. Don't be
ridiculous." I glare at Nick and mouth, "She knows what we did.
Did you tell her?"

Nick screws up his face like I'm bonkers then speaks into the
phone. "What's going on, Bernie?"

"There's been a change of plans." Nick and I share puzzled
expressions. "You're not playing Nashville tonight."

"Wait, what happened?" Now Nick sounds panicked.

"I got you a better gig in Memphis. It's at Graceland."

Okay, now we're really confused. "Graceland? As in Elvis
Presley's house?" Nick asks.

"That's right. It's Elvis Week and their stand-up duo canceled
at the last minute. Their loss, our gain. And, you'll get to stay at
the hotel on-site. Probably better than the shitholes you've been
sleeping in." I like the sound of that.

"See, told you to be prepared for anything," Nick whispers
my way.

"Think they booked us two rooms?" I whisper back.

"What was that?" Bernie asks.

"I was just saying that's great," I say. "But do you think a
bunch of guys in faux pompadours will get my jokes?"

"I'm sure it'll translate. Just do your corporate act." Corporate shows have been my only real paychecks since I've been performing. It's probably the best way to make some cash while climbing the comedy ladder. As an attorney, I usually had an in on the local or nearby corporate functions. Bernie would hook up the rest.

"What's the pay?" Nick asks, popping a cigarette in his mouth, and I practice my Elvis impression with a snarled lip.

"It's triple the Nashville show."

I gasp. Triple! "You're kidding?" More money. Better lodging. Now this is starting to sound like a proper tour.

"I haven't told you the best part," she continues.

"Wait, it gets better?" My stomach tightens in anticipation. I could really use some more good news.

"They're gonna dress Nick in a full-on Elvis costume."

It does get better!

His jaw drops and the cigarette tumbles out of his mouth. I can see it now, Nick trading in his black Wayfarers for an elaborate gold pair. I start snickering at his mounting humiliation. That's going to be hilarious.

"You think that's funny, huh?" Nick asks.

"You in a bell-bottom spandex jumpsuit? Please, that takes the comedy cake!"

He wags a finger at me. "Just so you know, Andy Kaufman and Eddie Murphy did Elvis impressions."

I don't know about Andy Kaufman, but how could I forget Eddie Murphy's Elvis bit from *Delirious*? "That's right! Eddie's was spot on."

"There's something else you should know about tonight," Bernie says.

"Let me guess. Nick has to end every joke with, 'Thank yooooou, thank ya very much.' " I break out my Elvis timbre, feeling it all the way down to my pelvis. Had my inner Elvis made an appearance last night, I wouldn't have had to put on a show.

"Sorry, kid," Bernie continues, "but *you* have to dress up like Priscilla."

Bless my heart.

I should've seen it coming. Nick snorts a laugh and I roll my eyes. "Thank you, Bernie."

"I emailed you the details. Good luck."

Nick ends the call and we stare at each other, our cheeks a little too pink for first thing in the morning. I look at him, wondering if my crush is still alive or if the sex smothered it. He smiles and runs his fingers through his hair, his bare abs popping as he lets out a satisfied exhale.

Yeah, it's still alive.

"So," he begins. "How you doing?"

"Good," I say, hugging my knees to my chest.

"Good, because I want you to know I don't usually sleep with comics I tour with." Does that mean he sleeps with stand-ups he doesn't tour with? Not that it should matter, the deed is done.

"I haven't slept with any comics," I say.

"Really? Never?" he asks.

I shake my head. "It's not like a hard-and-fast rule or anything but I figured it's better not to complicate my comedy career with sex." Saying those words sends a chill down my spine. Yes, I like Nick. Who wouldn't? But did I just make a rookie mistake the very moment I'm trying to go pro?

"I suppose that's smart. Maybe it's better we stay out of each other's pants for the rest of the tour. Go back to being Jerry and Elaine."

No sex the rest of the tour, huh? Is he trying to respect an appropriate boundary or is he done with me? I don't know and I can't bring myself to ask if last night meant anything to him. I'm not even sure what it meant to me. And until I do, keeping things professional sounds like a plan.

"Good idea," I say, wringing my hands.

Nick's phone rings again. But this time I don't think it's Bernie. He silences it. "I'm gonna get some air." He slides on his jeans and shoes, and I watch him leave the room.

After I wash last night off my skin and out of my hair, I wrap myself in a rough, bleach-scented terry towel, clear the misty mirror with my hand, and wipe the smudges off my lenses with a washcloth. That's when I notice a small green speck of something stuck in my teeth. Upon closer inspection, I conclude it's leftover spinach dip from the club.

"Yuck." I cringe with freshly flushed cheeks. That was there since last night? When we were kissing? Did Nick see it? Of course he did. He must've told himself to totally ignore it and keep going. According to Patrice O'Neal's stand-up, when it comes to men and sex, the bar is relatively low. Damn little horndogs.

Like any self-respecting woman, I first try to weed the spinach out with my nail. When that doesn't work, I scrub the clogged nook with my toothbrush. Still stuck. And of course, of all the things I packed, dental floss wasn't one of them (try not to judge me). I glance around the sink for some kind of helpful apparatus. Any chance the cleaning staff left some floss next to the bar of soap? Nope, this is not The Plaza.

Nick's black toiletry bag sits zipped up in the far corner. I crack open the bathroom door. "Hey, Nick!" I call, but there's no answer. He's probably still outside. He wouldn't mind me borrowing a little waxy string, would he? Doubt it. I carefully unzip his bag and begin pulling things out, one at a time. A razor, earplugs in a plastic case, Trojans (boy, did those come in handy), loose Q-tips, a lighter, and . . . a white gold wedding band?

What the . . .

Is he married?

I examine it, enamored like it's the ring that rules them all. But it doesn't seem to be ruling Nick one bit.

Oh, no. I slept with a married man. I think I'm gonna be sick.

"Hey!" Nick calls, banging at the door, and I gasp.

The ring slips through my fingers and drops against the porcelain. *Clink, clink*—bouncing off the bowl. Frozen, I watch the ring circle the drain. And down it goes.

"Shit," I whisper.

"You almost done?" Nick asks. "We need to get on the road soon and I need a shower." Yeah, so he can wash the filthy affair off him. Oh, Lord. This is bad.

"Just a second," I call, digging desperately at the sink, sweat beading on my brow. "Fuck, fuck, fuck," I mutter under my breath, scrambling to put everything else back. And fuck him too. Playing the nice guy just so he can get in my pants. I try to swallow but anger clogs my throat. What am I gonna do?

Just tell him the truth. Spinach, floss, ring. It's not like I'm the worst person in this scenario. Or am I?

Forget it.

I can't tell him.

But I also can't be the one responsible for losing his wedding ring, even if *he* doesn't seem to care about it. I take a deep breath, settle my trembling hands on the knob, and yank it open like ripping off a Band-Aid. "Hey," I say, feeling both guilty and indignant.

"Can I get in there now?"

"No, I need a little more time. I'm not feeling well," I say, hugging my stomach.

Nick observes me for a moment, then his expression shifts— like a lightbulb going on. "Oh, did you just get your period?"

Why are periods always the go-to thing with men? Something's wrong, it must be the menses! I don't want to give him the satisfaction but at the same time, it seems like a reason he'll accept long enough for me to rescue the ring. "Yeah, and it's really bad." If I have to buck up through mind-numbing cramps, it's only fair that I be able to cry Bloody Mary every now and again (like you've never lied about your period to get out of something).

"Do you need me to get you something for your, um . . ." He signals to his crotch. Jesus, my condolences to his wife.

"No, thanks. I'm all set with my supersized tampons!" I slam the door in his face. Fucking philanderer. I look back at the sink, annoyed. Almost hormonal. Maybe I should've told him the truth and made him fish it out.

"Okay, you son of a bitch," I mutter, and squat down in front of the open cabinet. Luckily, I know all about fishing shit out of pipes. Growing up my dad got sick of my hair clumps clogging the bathroom sink, so dismantling the plumbing and flushing them out became one of my regular chores. I set the garbage bin beneath the sink and unscrew the trap loose. The stench of rotten eggs mixed with sewage spills from the drain. *Ugh.* I gag and dunk whatever's in there in the can. Pinching my nose with one hand and fishing around for the ring with the other bare hand, my imagination runs wild.

What am I touching? And whose is it? Gross!

It's true what they say. Karma's a bitch. I'm never going through Nick's things again. And I still have spinach in my teeth. Then through the sludge, I feel that small band of gold.

Got it.

I repair the drain and wash all the gunk off the ring, then slip it back into his toiletry bag. And it's like the whole thing never happened.

Except it did.

Twenty-Five

The infectious rhythm of Elvis's "All Shook Up" plays in the distance. I'm still pretty shook up myself after this morning. Throughout this entire six-hour drive, I haven't been able to look Nick in the face. I've kept quiet, busying myself with writing and rewriting jokes, listening back to successful recordings from New York, and drafting long texts to Imani about the whole ordeal only to think twice and delete them.

I also priced out car rentals so I can make the rest of the trip on my own. His infidelity is infuriating. Do you know how hard it's been not to scream out, *You're married!* this entire trip? I should've screamed it a million times by now but I find myself waiting for the right moment and using my one song an hour to play hits like "Before He Cheats" and "Womanizer." To think I really liked him, that he might be someone I could trust. Now I want nothing to do with him.

Nick steers us down Elvis Presley Boulevard. Crowds of tourists mosey around the grounds. A variety of Elvis wannabes are sprinkled throughout. Seventy-year-old Elvises, short Elvises, Elvis on stilts, lady Elvises, and even pompadours on three-year-olds. The guy kicked the bucket nearly forty years ago but I guess it's viva Elvis Presley.

"Have mercy!" Nick says, gawking at the Presley pack. Figures he'd break out a Stamos impression.

"That's Uncle Jesse, not Elvis." I bite back the end of my sentence—*you cheating bastard.*

He knits his eyebrows. "Are you sure?"

"Yes." What I'm not sure of is how we're gonna perform in those ridiculous costumes. My stomach tightens. When not seething with anger and planning my escape, I obsessed over photos of Priscilla Presley—her gorgeous dark hair, alabaster skin, striking blue eyes, and perfectly arched brows. Will I be dressed like the more modest, newlywed 1960s Mrs. Presley or the vivacious, go-go-style 1970s Priscilla?

He lowers the music and asks, "Are you sure you're okay?"

"Yeah, fine," I say, and crank up the volume as Vince Neil sings "Girls, Girls, Girls" for the hundredth time this tour.

We arrive at the back of the soundstage, where we were asked to meet one of the event coordinators. After wandering around for a few more minutes, we find her.

"I'm Nick Leto. This is Olivia Vincent. We're your stand-ups," Nick says, introducing us.

She doesn't bother to drop her tablet and shake our hands. "You're the husband-and-wife duo?" I'm not sure what's giving her that impression but the mention of Nick's wife, even if incorrectly referring to me, makes my skin crawl.

"No, we're not married," Nick clarifies, seeming pretty tense for a guy who's *single and ready to mingle*. Ugh, that phrase should've been my first clue.

"I see." She stares at us over the rim of her glasses, shifting her eyes back and forth between us. "Well, thanks for coming on such short notice. I'm Jane. Follow me." Jane heads farther backstage, her short legs carrying her quickly. We hurry close behind. "You need to get to hair and makeup right away. You got your material, right?"

Nick and I share a look—the first since we got the call. "Material? What material?" he asks.

"For cryin' out loud." Jane does not seem pleased and presses a button on the side of her headset, turning the corner. "Lindsey, I need a copy of the Elvis-and-Priscilla stand-up act in makeup ASAP."

"What is she talking about?" I mutter to Nick but by the bewildered look on his face he's got no clue either. Jane waves us to follow her into a room with a long, well-lit vanity punctuated with four makeup chairs. One of which is occupied with a black-leather Elvis, his matching black hair getting a full-on Aqua Net attack.

They still make that?

"So here's the deal," Jane begins. "You're not doing *your* act tonight. You're doing ours."

"Excuse me?" Nick panics. Now so do I.

"This isn't a corporate retreat. It's Elvis Week. We need Elvis-related material for the guests," she says, then a woman, presumably Lindsey, rushes into the room with a couple of scripts and hands them over to Bad News Jane. "Priscilla, you'll do this ten-minute routine, and Elvis, you've got twenty minutes." She shoves our respective material at us. "You go on before the grand-opening show. You've got two hours to get familiar with the material."

"Two hours!" I blurt. How am I going to memorize a whole new set with the right timing and inflections in only two hours?

Jane raises an eyebrow. "Is that a problem?"

"No, it's no problem. Right, Olivia?" Nick says through a clenched jaw. Is he getting the gravity of the situation?

Still, I'm a professional. And a professional performer needs to be able to adapt quickly. "Right," I say.

"Good." Jane doesn't crack a smile. "Lucky for you two we'll have a teleprompter but I'd prefer you not rely on it. Got it?"

"Yes, ma'am," I say.

"Good luck. Don't screw it up." She leaves without another word, and Nick and I stare after her like dogs left at the pound. Then I remember, Nick is a dog.

"Bernie didn't mention anything about this," I say in a hostile whisper. That word pops up in my head again. You know, the one that's been haunting me this whole trip—*disaster*. This is more than a disaster. This is just more karmic retribution for hoppin' in the sack with Nick—a total cad. "How am I gonna pull this off in two hours?"

"Hey, I've got twice as much material as you." That's probably because he lied twice as much—deceived two of us at the same time. "At least you don't have to risk bombing your own material tonight."

That's it. I'm after Nick's blood now. And I'm taking the Jeep when I get away with it.

"Just remember," he continues, "triple pay, free hotel."

I take in a deep *so help me God* breath. "Triple pay, free hotel.

Triple pay, free hotel," I say, simultaneously chanting in my mind—*Nick's gonna get it. Nick's gonna get it.*

"Are y'all the comedians?" a woman asks with a Tennessee twang. She reminds me of one of the Designing Women with a big, feathery '80s do held together with copious amounts of hairspray. We nod. "Good. My name's Millie and I'll be gettin' y'all ready. Now go on there and take a seat." Nick and I gingerly make our way to the makeup chairs and Millie pats Leather Elvis on the shoulder. "You're all set, baby. Have a good show." The guy gives us a nod, dragging with him an obnoxious trail of cologne as he passes by.

I cover my crinkled nose. "Ugh, he smells like Rico Suave."

"Close, honey. It's Paco Rabanne," Millie offers.

"That's still legal?" I ask, spotting a set of long fake lashes on the counter. Those will definitely get smooshed behind my lenses.

"Yes, young lady. I got a whole case of it in the back."

"Hey, Millie, does my costume look like that?" Nick asks.

She smirks, looking him up and down like she knows his type. "Oh, we've got somethin' extra special for you."

"You know what that means," I say out of the side of my mouth, then begin looking at my material.

Nick seems just as engrossed in his Elvis set study. "Listen to this one. 'You know, Elvis was a red-meat guy. Boy, did he love his steaks. That's why he wrote . . .'" Then Nick sings, "*Loooove meat tender. Love meat true.*"

I roll my eyes so hard that my head rolls back with them. "Those are the kind of jokes we're doing? We have to sing?" I frantically flip through my pages.

Don't be cruel, Elvis Week.

Millie hovers near me. "Now, you got some contacts you can put in or somethin'? Or are those glasses just for show?"

"No. They're very necessary." Especially since I will likely be relying on that teleprompter.

"Well, I'm not sure they're gonna work for this look. Priscilla never wore glasses. You know the saying, *Elvis don't make passes at girls that wear glasses*." Millie's completely serious and my cheeks grow resentfully hot. This is definitely punishment.

"Triple pay, free hotel," Nick says, reminding me this time.

I grit my teeth and remove my glasses, thankful I can't see my own reflection in the mirror. Fortunately for me, I'm near-sighted so I focus on studying my material while she contours my cheeks and swipes my spidery fake lashes with mascara. Finally, she fashions a giant bouffant wig to my head. I don't need 20/20 vision to see that it gives me a good eight inches. "Good Lord, this is extra."

"Just be grateful you don't have to dance in it," Millie says, and spritzes me with an Elizabeth Taylor perfume.

"Really? Because I feel like a go-go dancer."

"You look great. Now let me get your costumes." Ms. Millie runs out of the room. I slide on my glasses to get a proper look at myself. Nick shifts his eyes my way in our mirrored reflections.

"You look like a knockoff Danny Zuko," I say.

"And you look like a goth Dolly Parton."

"Hey." I point a stern finger his way. "Leave Dolly out of this. We're at Graceland."

"Here we are!" Millie sings, returning to the makeup room holding the famous white Elvis jumpsuit, a white dress . . . and a wedding veil? Can this get any worse?

"Have mercy," Nick says, staring down at his.

"That's not Elvis, honey. That's Uncle Jesse," Millie says, handing him the costumed hanger. Finally, something we agree on.

"See," I add, then turn my attention to the dress and veil I'm now holding. Of course, I sleep with a married man and now I have to dress up like a Halloween bride. Why doesn't she just spray a scarlet *A* on my chest with the perfume or scribble *whore* on my back with the mascara wand and call it a day? I can't put this thing on. "Exactly what kind of costume is this?"

"Priscilla's weddin' dress, of course."

"Where's the rest of it?" I look over the so-called wedding gown that could use another ten inches of length.

"Well, it's been modernized, I guess."

"So Nick gets to be the famous rock star and Priscilla's reduced to a sexy bride? And God forbid she wear glasses to see all those Elvis wannabes objectify her. And me." For a woman on her pretend period, it certainly seems like I have PMS.

"Oh, don't get your panties all in a twist," she says. "I swear you millennials don't know how to relax and have some harmless fun."

"Yeah, Olivia. You'll make a beautiful bride with that wig," Nick chimes in with a laugh. Beautiful bride my ass. I've never even been invited to be a bridesmaid. It's like brides don't make passes at friends that wear glasses.

We take our respective costumes into the changing area, following her instructions to avoid getting any makeup stains on the white garments. After a good five minutes, Nick's privacy curtain whooshes open. I stare at the makeshift bride in the mirror. I hate this. But if I want the money, I'll brave the stage.

"What do you think?" Nick says with a snarled lip and an Elvis baritone. "Am I just a hunk, a hunk of burnin' love?" Nick does a few pelvis thrusts, and I'm reminded of the moves he used on me last night.

"I am so embarrassed for you."

He points to the center of his partially exposed chest. "Me? Look at you!"

I scoff. "Whatever."

"Why are you being so weird today? Is this about last night? Because I thought it was great."

"Oh, really? It was great?"

"Yeah." Nick knows he's missing something. How has he not figured it out by now?

"Well, I faked it. Fake, fake, fake!" I confess, hoping the admission will hurt as much as his lie hurt his wife and me.

Ripping off his gold shades, he says, "You faked it?"

"Oh, don't act all innocent. I'm not the only one here who's faking it."

"What are you even talking about?" He thinks he's got the wool over my eyes but he's got another think coming.

"What am I talking about? This!" I gesture to my getup—veil and all. "Does this remind you of anything?"

"Only a really bad night in Vegas."

That's it! Not even a can of Aqua Net can hold me down. "You're unbelievable. Do you have any respect for the sanctity of marriage?"

"Hey, I get that you're cruising through PMS City right now but you're kinda being a bitch."

He did not just say that to me. "I'm not a bitch. *You're* an asshole."

"What is your problem?" he yells back.

"My problem is that you used me. You lied to me."

"Lie? What lie?" Man, he's good. It's almost like he's con-vinced himself of his own bullshit.

"I know you're married, Nick! I found your wedding band in your bag this morning."

"Wha . . . you went through my stuff?" Who knew a man wearing polyester bell-bottoms could look so angry? But I'm sure my wig isn't doing me any favors either.

"I wasn't going through *your stuff*. I was looking for dental floss. And don't try to turn this around on me. You're the one who's shamelessly cheating on your wife. What kind of husband are you?" And more important, what kind of man is he?

"I'm not anyone's husband, Olivia!" His voice booms through-out the dressing room. "I'm divorced."

Wait, what?

"Divorced?"

"Yeah . . . for eleven months." Nick's tone drops, still trem-bling with anger. "The next time you go snooping through my shit, make sure you have the facts before you go making accusa-tions."

Oh, no. How did I read this whole thing so wrong?

Without another word, he storms out. Patent leather shoes stomping. Bedazzled cape flapping behind him.

Nick Leto has left the building.

Twenty-Six

I t's after nine P.M. when the *Elvis Extravaganza Stage Show* concludes. I haven't seen Nick since he exited stage left while I waited in the wings stage right. I jetted after him as fast as these heels and hair would allow, but I couldn't catch him. And he won't answer his phone for me either.

Now all of the performers are heading over to the after-party in another area of the soundstage. A different Elvis cover band fills the room with those Gibson guitar strums and warm, familiar harmonies. Elvis sure could write a catchy tune. Still, the music doesn't distract me from my mission—find Nick.

After any other show, this would be a piece of cake. Just find the leather-clad funny guy. But I'm swimming in a current of Presley Ocean. There are way too many white caped jumpsuits and pompadours to count. I walk the perimeter of the darkened banquet room for a good twenty minutes and follow my nose more than my eyes. If someone smells like they've been doused in a bath of Spanish cologne, I follow them.

Wait, I think I see him. "Nick!" I call over the music, but he doesn't turn around. Still mad, I see. I rush over and grab him by the shoulder. "Hey, Nick!"

A clean-shaven man with pouty lips faces me. Definitely not Nick. Wrong Elvis slides his shades down the bridge of his nose. "Hello, baaaaby," he says like the Big Bopper.

"Uh . . . sorry, thought you were someone else." I back away. Not fast enough because he grabs me by the waist and pulls me in so close I can feel his pelvis.

Ugh, what a creep.

"I can be whoever you want me to be, beautiful." This guy smells more like he bathed in a barrel of Tennessee whiskey.

"Then be a gentleman and get your grubby hands off me." I shove him away but he's strong for a drunk and doesn't let up. My heart begins to race because even though we're surrounded by people, it's dark and loud and I can't see as well with these damn lashes stuck to my eyelids.

"I never seen a Priscilla in glasses as pretty as you before." He opens his mouth, his big sloppy tongue hanging out. I dig my elbows into him with every ounce of strength I have.

"Stop it, you douchebag!" The *one* time I don't have any pepper spray on me.

"C'mon, Priscilla." He kisses the air and I shake my head back and forth but still catch one on the nose.

"Get off her!" a man growls, bolting in, and I'm released from Creeper Elvis's grip. I catch my breath and squint in the dark at Hero Elvis.

It's Nick.

"You okay?" he asks, but before I can answer Creeper Elvis strikes back with a roar, swinging at Nick. He misses.

"Hey, you son of a bitch!" Millie appears out of nowhere, spraying the offender only inches from his eyes with mace.

No, wait.

With Paco Rabanne!

He howls, clawing at his eyes and stumbling around. The crowd begins to circle the commotion. Nick and I trade wigged-out glances then I turn to Millie, who pats her teased hairdo. A couple security guys arrive on the scene and drag Creeper Elvis away.

"You all right, honey?" Millie asks.

I nod, still reeling. What in the hell just happened? "Thanks, Millie."

"Anytime." She slides the small cologne bottle back into her pocket and proceeds through the crowd without a drop of sweat on her brow. They break for her, cheering as she passes. Still a little stunned myself, I slide my glasses back up my nose and dust off my dress. Nick stands by my side, and now I really owe the guy something.

"Hey, thanks for pushing that guy off."

"You're welcome." His words sound forced. I guess now that the perpetrator's gone, he's back to being pissed at me. I hate this part—*I was wrong. I'm sorry.* It would be nice to just move past it.

"What do you say we grab a couple burgers after this? My treat," I offer.

"No thanks." He scoffs and turns away, so I yank his ornate cape.

"C'mon, Nick. It was an honest mistake. Can't you just accept my apology?"

"Apology?" Nick whips around. "I didn't hear any apology."

"Hey, y'all doin' okay?" A man with a burnt-red tan and wrin-

kled forehead asks. A woman, presumably his wife (though assumptions seem pretty unreliable now), is by his side gazing at
us with a maternal concern.

I send them a polite smile. "We're fine, sir. Thank you."

"That was quite a scene," the man adds. "Hey, wait a second.
Were y'all the comedians at the show?" Nick and I nod, watching
their grins grow wider. "You two were so funny. That TCB joke
was hilarious," he laughs, referring to one of Nick's Elvis jokes
that went completely over my head.

"Thanks," Nick says with a modest smile. Definitely not his
usual chipper self.

"I'm Ed and this is my wife, Pamela. We're in town from
Knoxville." We greet them with friendly handshakes, hoping
this is the end of the interruption.

"I'm Nick and this is Olivia."

"Well, you make a beautiful couple," Pamela says. "I bet y'all
make each other laugh all the time. You know that's so important in marriage."

"We're not married," I say. When can I take off this veil?

"Oh," Pamela says. "Well, you must be close otherwise." Not
at the moment, ma'am.

Ed elbows Nick in the ribs. "She's already in the white dress,
might want to marry her now before someone else does."

Oh, Lord. This is a very awkward exchange under our normal
circumstances but with the marital miscommunication conflict
at hand, it's worse.

The music slows to a lullaby and the mood of the entire room
shifts instantly. It's an Elvis hit I recognize only from UB40—"Can't
Help Falling in Love."

"All right now, we're gonna slow it down for a beat," Stage

Elvis says into the mic. "All you Elvises out there, go on and grab your Priscilla sweetheart and let her know how ya feel." Then he croons, "*Wise men say . . .*"

"Go on, ask her to dance," our fan encourages us, giving Nick a gentle push.

"It's okay," I say, my knees locked. "We don't dance."

"Oh, c'mon. We wanna see you dance." Ed says it so loud that now others are staring. "Dance with her. Dance with her," he chants.

Uh-oh.

Then two, four, and ten others join in—*Dance with her. Dance with her.*

Ooh, shit, what do we do? Nick seems to feel the pressure because he relents and takes my hand.

"If it'll get 'em to shut up," he says low near my ear.

Our little fan club cheers us on. The rational part of me knows this is just a show for the fans. But the moment his fingers are wrapped around mine and his breath tickles my ear, that little bud of a crush (the one I thought was finished after the ring) begins to bloom inside me. Nick's hand slides above my waist and I rest mine lightly on his shoulder as we begin to sway to the romantic melody. I keep my gaze lowered and muscles stiff. He obviously doesn't want to be here with me. How much longer before this feeling (and song) is over?

I slowly look up his stubbled chin enough to know he's staring off somewhere else. There's only one way to fix this. And it's all up to me. "I'm sorry," I start. "About the ring. I shouldn't have been in your things. And I definitely shouldn't have made assumptions about you. Especially after last night."

"No, you shouldn't have."

I'm not even sure if I should say what I'm about to, because there's only one reason someone keeps that token of love after the big *D*. "And I'm sorry about your divorce. I had no idea."

I watch him swallow something back before he looks at me—the Priscilla version. "I should've mentioned it before."

"Why didn't you?"

Nick knits his brow like he doesn't know why. "I don't like to talk about it. So I don't."

"I get that."

"You do?" Nick stares at me as if he's trying to see past the lenses and the lashes and the makeup. And I do get it. There are many things I refuse to verbally acknowledge because when you voice something, it's real and you can't take it back.

"Yeah." Maybe Nick and I have more in common than I realized. I'm not hiding a divorce but there are painful things in my past that I prefer not to address with anyone, not even myself.

"So, can I buy you a burger? Any kind you want," I ask.

"Sure. As long as I can get out of this jumpsuit first."

"What's the rush? You can totally pull it off."

"Really? Because I feel like Liberace's nephew," he says, and I laugh—grateful for the joke. "You look pretty though."

My face feels warm and tingly at his words. "I do?"

"Yeah, in a drunk '60s housewife kinda way."

"Oh, that's so sweet."

Twenty-Seven

Triple pay, free hotel makes for a very good night of sleep (alone—in case you were wondering). After our continental breakfast, we get our second cups of joe to go and soon we're cruising south down I-55 toward Mississippi. Gray clouds cover the sky but so far no rain. So we ride with the windows down, Boston's "Peace of Mind" playing on the radio. I attempt to craft some new jokes on my legal pad—something about macing a man with Paco Rabanne has to have a good punchline in there somewhere.

"Question time." Nick shifts in his seat then looks to me. "If you could have a burger tonight with any comedian, dead or alive, who would it be?"

"Is this our version of punch buggy?" I blow a bubble with my cherry-flavored gum that lost its flavor ten minutes post-unwrapping.

"Yeah, not a lot of Volkswagens in these parts."

I gaze out at the long stretch of road, flipping through my

mental catalog of favorite comedians. One legendary stand-up, who more recently kicked the bucket, comes to mind. "I'm gonna have to go with Joan Rivers."

"Why Joan Rivers?" he asks.

"Well, aside from being a pioneer, she's the only comedian who's performed in as much makeup as I did last night."

"Very true."

"You know she was making single-girl jokes in the '60s on *The Ed Sullivan Show*? And they were hilarious!" I have to imagine my comedic heroes as young girls, sitting on the floor in front of the family television, watching Joan Rivers, opening their minds to roles they never thought possible—the single female stand-up comedian.

"So what about you?" I ask.

"I'm in a classic-comedian mood too, so I'll say Lenny Bruce."

Oh, Lenny Bruce. The original icon of every rebellious stand-up. "You two could certainly have a smoke together."

"Yes, we could." Nick pats around the center compartments for his cigarettes and flips the top of the box open, slinking out a stick.

"He was only forty when he overdosed," I say.

Nick drops the smoke back in the box. "It's too bad. A lot of great comedians die young—Chris Farley, Bill Hicks, Mitch Hedberg, Andy Kaufman—"

"Patrice O'Neal," I add.

"His last special had me rolling on the floor," Nick says, glancing my way.

"Me too!"

"You have to hear this song Bob Dylan wrote about Lenny Bruce." Nick grabs his phone and with a few swipes, a soft, simple piano melody begins. It's not the only song that mentions the trailblazing comedian.

"You think Lenny Bruce ever thought so many people would memorialize him in their music?" I ask.

"I doubt it. I doubt he knew how much he meant to people. How much he was loved. It's a special thing, when a comic puts you, or a moment with you, in a joke, or a writer in a book, or a singer in a song."

I think back to Nick's joke about the flat tire. Who knows, maybe one day he'll be this world-famous stand-up, playing Madison Square Garden, and talking about the girl who changed the tire for him. That would be pretty cool. I sit quietly for a moment, taking in more of Dylan's lyrics. "You really like music, huh?"

"Yeah. Before you it was my only road companion." He smiles. We may be talking about comedians from the past, but I can see by the look on his face we've moved on from yesterday. "A good song is like a good set."

"Yeah, except music is rarely ever funny."

"Yes, but a good joke and a good song require the same ingredient."

"What's that?"

"Pain. The kind that connects with the audience on a deeper level. It's like that quote, 'To truly laugh, you must be able to take your pain, and play with it.'"

"Liza from Funnies said that to me last week. Charlie Chaplin, right?"

"That's right. Tapping into that is what makes a song memorable. It's what gets the punchline a real laugh. And isn't that why we got into this business? For real laughs."

I sit back and close my eyes for a moment, and if I give myself just a second, I can almost hear my audience's laugh. I let that audible memory wash over me. "What is it about laughs that are so . . . so . . ."

"Delicious?"

"Yes, that's the perfect word."

"I don't know. I think we're just born craving them," Nick says.

"Mm-hmm. Bless our hearts."

Dylan's song concludes with the piano melody outro and then the Jeep is silent. For the first time since we've been on the road, nothing's playing on the radio and neither of us does anything about it.

"Can I ask you something personal?" I say.

"Only if I can ask you something personal too."

Of course this is a quid-pro-quo situation. "All right," I say. "But me first. If you believe our job is to tap into our pain, then how come you never talk about your divorce onstage?"

He lets out a sigh and settles his wrist at twelve o'clock on the steering wheel. "You know how we comedians find humor in everything?"

"Yeah." It's true. When you're a comedian everything is funny ha-ha, even really inappropriate things. Humor provides us humans a way to cope with hard things. Comedians are just experts at it.

"Well," he continues, "I haven't exactly been able to find the humor in the ending of my marriage."

His confession makes me wonder if that's why I never make jokes about my dad kicking the bucket. How funny can death be anyway? Then again, I've seen George Carlin pull it off so . . .

"That's understandable," I say. "How long were you married?"

"Five years."

"Wow!" I jerk back in my seat.

"What?"

"Don't take this the wrong way, but I don't really see you as the commitment type."

"That's because I'm not . . . anymore." Of course. All the hot ones are commitment-phobes.

"Do you miss her?" I ask, then realize it's a stupid question. Of course he misses her. Why else would he keep his wedding ring with him?

"I don't know if I miss her as much as I miss what we had. When it was good anyway."

"Is that why you keep your wedding ring?" I ask, gripping the edge of my seat. Why did I ask that? Of course I want to know (I'm sure you do too), but I don't ever actually ask these kinds of questions. Now it's too late to take it back.

He looks my way like he's surprised I'm *this* nosy after everything that's happened. "No," he says, and I feel the door of that subject close, lock, and nail shut. "Enough about me," he says, breaking the silence. "Let's talk about you."

"Me? I've never been married. Never even been a bridesmaid."

"You sound bitter about that," he says.

"You try spending your adolescence watching '90s romcoms. I just want to see what all the fuss is about."

Nick chuckles at me, shaking his head. He'd probably advise me to skip it. "I have a question for you now." I brace myself for whatever intrusive inquiry is coming. "Did you really fake it the other night or did you just say that because you thought I made you the other woman?"

Why did I not see this coming?

"No, I really faked it," I admit.

"Oh, did I do something wrong?" The poor guy sounds discouraged.

"Try not to take it personally. I just can't get there." This is a painful truth. Wonder if it'd make a good joke.

"You mean during sex?"

"I mean at all."

He takes his eyes off the road completely. "Wait a sec—you've never had an orgasm?"

"God no, of course I have!"

"Oh, whew!" He mimes wiping the sweat from his brow.

"I just haven't been able to for a while. It's like when I moved to the city, I misplaced it somewhere between Fifth and Madison Avenue. No idea why. I even had a very humiliating conversation with my doctor and she said to be patient, that it's probably stress-related. Everything is stress-related these days. But this is the least stressed I've been, and after you said you were so good, I thought maybe I'd find it again. But . . . yeah, still a no-show."

"Oh." I bet he's regretting his question right about now.

"See, that look on your face. That's why we fake it. It's just cleaner. Simpler."

We sit in silence for a moment too long. Like it or not, there's nothing clean and simple about this tour anymore. Maybe Bernie was right.

Twenty-Eight

We've been cruising down a two-lane highway lined with trees for almost an hour listening to Cheap Trick. Nick follows the GPS off the main highway. Having just traveled from major cities like New York, D.C., Atlanta, and Memphis, this place really sticks out. Because it's the sticks. Even Midland looks like a metropolis in comparison.

"What exactly is this place? I thought we were going to Gulfport." I survey the gas station on the side of the road, catching a Wendy's up ahead.

"No idea. We're just outside of it."

"Are you sure this place even has a comedy club?"

"Yep, it's new. Just opened up."

I like the idea of a small town like this in the middle of Mississippi opening a comedy club. It must mean they have a good sense of humor down here. At least I hope they do. "So Bernie booked this for you?" That woman never ceases to surprise me.

"Actually, they called me directly," he says. "I guess someone special-requested me. And it fit perfectly between Tennessee and Louisiana so I figured why not."

"Aw, *Nicky*." I bat my lashes. "You have a fan." He shoots me a sideways glare. If his merch sales are any indication, he has many fans. Now it's only a matter of time before someone special-requests me (even in a podunk town like this).

A couple hours later, after getting settled at our motel, we arrive at The Comedy Club—both its name and function. It sits in the middle of a quaint main street area of some little town in Mississippi that I keep forgetting the name of. The moment we walk in, my nose crinkles from the stench.

What the . . . the place smells like an ashtray—the old-car kind that can't close because it's jammed with sticky tar. The farther we get inside the club the more I see why. Sooty old ashtrays litter each tabletop. Either the city hasn't gotten the smoke-free memo or they just don't give a damn.

"Ugh. People actually smoke in here?" I ask.

"Oh, hell yeah! I love this club." Nick whips out a cigarette and pops it in his mouth.

Gross. "How is this even legal?"

"Why don't you chill and have a smoke." He offers his open pack for the second time this trip. I didn't take it then and I sure as hell ain't takin' it now.

I swat his hand away the way they taught us in the D.A.R.E. program. "What about *smoking kills* do you, and the patrons of this club, not get?"

My tour buddy puts his arms around me, an unlit cigarette resting on his lip—Slash-style. "Let me share some wisdom with you." I glance up at him. "Nonsmokers die . . . every day. That's a fact."

"It's also a Bill Hicks joke. You gonna steal any more of his routine tonight?"

"Nah," he says. "But I will enjoy one of these onstage like him. I really missed out on the '90s comedy scene."

Nick gets his wish because The Comedy Club in Sometown, Mississippi, is like living in a '90s time warp. The moment I step out in the spotlight, cigarette sparks flicker throughout the room and smoke billows out from the audience. I let out a rough cough. It's like Philip Morris's wet dream in here.

When I take the mic, some dickwad whines, "Oh, man, not a woman." I don't know what idiot started the rumor that women aren't funny but I'd like to chop his balls off so he knows what not-funny really looks like. (C'mon, like you've never threatened a man's scrotum before?)

I don't let his misogyny throw me. Instead, I hold my head high so all the ladies in the audience know that we don't back down. This time, I'm ready. Besides, Nick has fans here tonight and I want some too. So I lean into my Texas twang as I deliver my first punchline. It lands better than expected. Good. I keep truckin'.

Then, thick clouds of cigarette smoke barrel onstage in what feels like a deadly assault. I wave my hand to clear the air but the smog sticks to me like a spiderweb. Stay calm, Olivia. Don't let it get to you. Even smokers deserve to laugh. Assuming they can do it without wheezing.

As I set up my next joke, my muscles stiffen as if the smoke is coiling around me like a boa constrictor. The mic trembles in my hand. What's happening? I gasp for air but I can't breathe.

Oh my god, I can't breathe. Am I dying? I think I'm dying.

I can see the headline now—*Unknown Comedian Olivia Vincent Drops Dead During Stand-Up Routine.*

That can't be my story. I have to get out of here.

My foot miraculously breaks free from this death spell and I take a step, leaving the mic in my place. After two steps, my blood surges with adrenaline and I run out of the club. I run until I reach the black Jeep and grab the door handle. It's locked. Still gasping for air but not dead yet, I manage to climb on the hood and lie back, staring at the dusky sky.

My shallow breaths grow deeper and the tingling feeling in my feet and mouth subsides. I slap two fingers on my neck and feel a thumping pulse. Is it normal?

What the hell just happened?

I peel my back off the hood of the Jeep and rub my eyes beneath my lenses. Did I really just have some kind of weird panic attack and run offstage? That's never happened before. Why is it happening now? The only difference is I'm away from New York. That, and stand-up's all I have at the moment. Why isn't this working? Why is it . . . why is it such a disaster?

I dig inside my pocket for my phone and dial Imani. It rings. And rings. And rings until it reaches her voicemail—*Hello, you've reached Imani Turner. I'm unavailable to take your call at the moment. Please leave a detailed message or text message, and I'll respond as soon as I am able.* The one time this tour I actually need her and she's not there.

Part of me wants to cry and the other part wants to scream in light of the possible truth. Was Imani right? Was my dad right? But I'm not leaving that on her voicemail. So I lean against the windshield, pull my knees close, and fake a smile.

"Hey, Imani. Just calling to see how you are . . ." I want to tell her that I miss her and I could really use an evening of fuzzy socks and white wine with her. But I'm afraid if I say it, I'll lose it. So I end with: "Hope your week's good. Call me later."

Sitting in silence for the next hour, I try to decide if I can somehow redeem myself on this comedy road tour. Or will staying only make it worse? Guess what the evidence suggests?

"There you are." Nick appears from behind the Jeep. "I was worried about you. What happened?"

"I don't know. I was telling jokes one minute, then the next I felt like I couldn't breathe."

"Are you okay? Do you need to see a doctor?" he asks.

"No, but . . ." I start.

"But what?"

I slide a hand down my face, wishing I didn't have to say this out loud. "Ugh. I think maybe it's time to admit that this isn't working."

"What's not working?"

"Me on this tour. I think I should go back to New York, where everything makes sense. I can just fly in for my audition and pray I don't bomb there too."

"What? No, Olivia. I'm not letting you leave."

"Why? Because I make you look so good after I die onstage?"

He folds his arms in a firm stance. "No, because I thought you were a winner, Olivia *Vincent*. Weren't you the one who said you were going to kick this tour's ass?" Nick asks, and I shoot him a look. "I know what you're thinking—the road sucks. And you're right. But it's also where you'll learn to be great. I don't care if you bomb every night the rest of this tour, I'm not letting you give up, *capeesh*?"

I look into his eyes, biding my time as I search my soul for a valid rebuttal. But I can't find one. "Yeah, *capeesh*," I say.

"No, Olivia, say it like you mean it. Say it like you're headed to perform at a sold-out stadium show like the big dogs."

"Capeesh!"

"That's the spirit."

Nick is the last person in my life I'd expect to support the Olivia Vincent Plan. "You're like my guardian angel, you know that?"

His mouth twists. "I've been called a lot of things but an angel isn't one of them."

I chuckle as I slide off the edge of the Jeep and my feet hit the ground. I guess I'm here to stay.

"Hey, Nick Leto, wait up!" some guy with a Mississippi drawl calls behind us. It's a man in a white T-shirt, snug around his midsection—kinda like a young Louis C.K. type but without the receding red hair. A petite blond woman follows close behind him.

"What's up?" Nick says, pulling a cigarette from his pocket.

"Hey, I'm Jordan and this is my wife, Kelly." He extends a hand to Nick.

"Nice to meet you guys. What can I do for you?"

"My brother . . . Jeremiah was supposed to be here at the show tonight. Actually, he's the one who requested that you come. You see, you're his favorite comedian." Jordan rocks on his heels with his hands in his pockets, and his wife stares at Nick all wide-eyed like he's a movie star. "He even traveled to Tallahassee to see you once."

"You played Tallahassee?" I ask out of the side of my mouth, and he nudges my side, silencing me.

"Well, please tell your brother I really appreciate his support." Nick swings his keys in his hands, just as ready to go as I am.

"That's the thing, I . . . I can't tell him." Jordan's voice cracks and Nick and I trade glances. "Jeremiah died this week."

"Oh, shit." My jaw drops. I did not mean to say that aloud.

Nick must be gaping too because his cigarette goes toppling to his feet. Right where it belongs. "What happened?"

Jordan sniffles back tears. The poor guy just lost his brother. And Nick just lost his number one fan. "It was a firework mishap."

"Firework mishap," I repeat bluntly. You'd think after losing a close loved one myself I could be a smidge more sensitive. Who *was* this Jeremiah?

"I'm sorry for your loss, man." Nick's tone turns gentle, handling this whole thing with grace.

"Thank you. That means a lot." Jordan lowers his head. "Anyway, I came here to ask you, since you're in town and all, if you'd be willing to come to his funeral tomorrow and . . . perform."

Kelly, his doe-eyed wife, steps in. "It would mean the world to him."

What. Is. Happening.

"You—you want me to tell jokes at your brother's funeral?" Nick asks.

Jordan nods. "Yes, sir."

"Uhh." Nick and I trade unsure glances. "I'm not sure that's the best venue for my material. I wouldn't want to offend any of his friends or family."

Jordan throws out one of those *don't be silly* looks. "Oh, no, sir. It'd be just fine. Help lighten the mood. And I know Jeremiah would want it that way. He was your biggest fan."

"What time is the funeral?" Nick asks, like he's actually considering it. He wouldn't. He couldn't.

"It's at eleven thirty."

"Hey, Nick." I squeeze in between their conversation, tapping my watch. "We have to be in New Orleans tomorrow for a show. And with the Fourth of July holiday traffic, we both know how important it is to leave extra early."

"New Orleans is only a couple hours south, one if you drive right. You'll be back on the road by one o'clock, tops," Jordan offers.

"The show doesn't start until seven thirty. Even with traffic, we'll get there in plenty of time," Nick adds.

Has he lost his damn mind? "I don't know, Nick. Remember what happened last time?"

"Can you excuse us for a moment?" Nick smiles politely and pulls me out of earshot of the bereaved couple.

"What are you doing?" I ask in a hostile whisper.

"What are *you* doing? This Jeremiah guy is the reason we got this gig and he's my biggest fan!" Nick whispers back.

"It's. A. Funeral!" I mouth.

"So what? They're not asking you to perform. What's the big deal?"

"Nick, do you really want to risk humiliating yourself over someone's grave?"

"The guy died, Olivia," he says, like it's a compelling reason. I get that people die. It doesn't mean you turn the funeral into a Netflix stand-up special.

"In a firework accident. And you didn't even know him."

"It doesn't matter. He knew me. He liked me enough to bring me to this tiny town so he could see me live. It's people like him that allow people like us the privilege to do what we do. The least I can do is pay my respects and bring a little joy to his surviving friends and family. Wouldn't you want the same thing if it were your brother?"

I hold a stubborn stance but consider his question. If Eddie Murphy or Richard Pryor or Pablo Francisco were in Midland the night before my dad's funeral, I might've done the same thing—no matter how inappropriate the material.

Nick continues. "Besides, it's good karma. If I perform for my biggest fan, then maybe Jerry Seinfeld will do a set at my funeral."

"You really think Jerry Seinfeld would come to your funeral?" No one's karma is that good.

He shrugs. "Why not? And if you come, maybe Carrot Top will perform at yours."

I suppose it wouldn't kill me to be supportive. I owe him that much. Even if I still think this is a terrible idea.

Twenty-Nine

Knock, knock.

Morning light spills into my darkened motel room when I open the door. Nick's clean-shaven face and tamed hair are almost unrecognizable. Not to mention the getup—a tailored dark gray suit and light blue tie. I'm partial to tousled-hair, scruffy-beard Nick. But I could get used to this look on him. Hell, with those dimples and that body, he could probably make anything look good.

"Did you rent that outfit this morning?" I ask.

"No, it's mine." He dusts the lapel. "I clean up nice, don't I?"

"You brought a suit and tie on tour? You really are a Jerry, aren't you?"

"If I were, this blazer would have shoulder pads."

"Or an emblem. Remember that episode?" I ask, and Nick snickers. "But seriously, why did you bring a suit?"

"Just in case."

"In case what? You have a meeting at the bank?" Not once

have I seen Nick in anything other than his jeans and leather jacket, or that Elvis jumpsuit. And of course there was that one night when he was wearing nothing at all. But who's keeping track of his wardrobe anyway?

"You just never know," he says, and I think about Jeremiah and his family for a moment. People always say we never know when our time's up and it's so true. "What about you? You going on a date?"

On the off chance of a nice night out, I packed a relatively tasteful dress with me—navy blue, not black. "It's either this or jeans," I say, wheeling my two-ton suitcase over to the door with my garbage bag pillow tucked beneath my arm. "C'mon. Let's get this over with."

So here we are in our road trip best at a funeral for a guy we never knew existed until last night. Soft harp music sounds through the room—the kind that plays softly at Hallmark stores. Entering the funeral home is about as nerve-racking as waiting to go onstage. I haven't been to one of these since my dad's. Everyone's dressed in mourning attire, and they all have the same question on their faces—*How did he go so young?*

The only question on my mind: Do I *have* to be here?

My phone buzzes in my bag. It's Imani, probably calling me back from last night. I'll call her later—don't want to explain this very odd outing. A group of people pass us wearing American flag pins on their lapels and carrying handheld flags too. Hard to tell if Jeremiah was a veteran or if they're observing our Independence Day—whose flashy tradition is somewhat responsible for his death.

"Think there'll be a firecracker finale?" I ask.

"What kind of person dies from fireworks?" Finally, he says something honest about this whole thing.

I pat Nick's shoulder. "The kind that thinks you're hilarious."

"I'm gonna go find Jordan and figure out where I'm supposed to be." Nick buttons his suit jacket and rushes off.

"Wait," I call after him. "Don't leave me . . ." My words trail off as he makes his way through the crowd. "Shit," I mutter under my breath. The reality of this whole thing sets in. Somebody died (probably Nick's number one fan).

"Sweetie, you look lost." A woman approaches me. "Are you here for the Jeremiah Hill service?"

"Uh, yeah," I say, adjusting my glasses.

"Well, okay. Now, you must be from out of town."

"New York," I say.

The woman narrows her eyes in suspicion. "You don't sound like you're from New York."

"Well, I am."

"All the way from New York just to pay your respects to Jeremiah. Well now, y'all must've been good friends."

"Not exactly."

"Oh." The woman's eyes widen. "Oh, I think I know who you are now." She leans in, whispering, "Just steer clear of his wife, okay, honey?" The woman pats my arm in a condoling kind of way and walks on.

Steer clear of his wife?

Oh, no. Does she think?

"No, I'm not—" I call after her, but she's already gone. Great. If this place is like the small town I grew up in, word will get around that I'm Jeremiah's mistress before the eulogy's over.

I wander farther inside toward the glow of a mounted TV screen playing a slow montage of photos. A shirtless Jeremiah poses with a can of Miller Lite on the dock of a river. Unlike his brother, he's tanned with dark hair, slicked back. And it looks like he was no stranger at the gym. I tilt my head as I take in the photos. He can't be much older than me. Maybe even my age. Handsome too. A photo of him leaning against the tail of a black F-150. The license plate reads *PUMPIN*. I raise an eyebrow. What does that mean? The photo fades into the next, Jeremiah and a handful of bros pumpin' fists at a nightclub.

Ah, got it. Perhaps his other woman is from the Jersey Shore instead of the city.

Jeremiah's people seem to be filing into another room and taking their seats. I glance around for Nick, who's standing in a corner with his head lowered.

Is he crying?

I hurry over and tap him on the shoulder. "You okay?"

He startles. "Yeah, fine. It's just weird. He's like younger than me. One day here and one day . . ."

"I know. Boom!" I mime an explosion and he startles again.

"Excuse me. Are you Nick Leto?" A woman, whose perfume entered the room before she did, asks. Nearly as tall as Nick, she seems to have caught him with her crystal blue eyes.

"Yeah," Nick says.

"I'm Holly, Jeremiah's wife." She extends her hand as if she wants Nick to kiss it and whisper *enchanté*.

He takes it and gently lays his other over hers like a Southern pastor. "I'm so sorry for your loss."

"Yes, it was a shock. He and some of the other guys put on

the firework show from a barge out on the lake every year. They get a little drunk out there while they test a few before the big show, but he's always safe. I mean, a few burns here and there. And then there was that one time his sleeve caught fire but it was fine as soon as he jumped in the lake. That's why he started goin' shirtless out there." Holly's eyes glisten with tears. "I just never thought something like this could happen to my Jer-bear. I mean, how many people actually *die* from fireworks?"

"About seven people every year in the U.S."

Holly and Nick gape at me.

"I looked it . . ." Not the place to cite a Google search. "Never mind. I'm sorry for your loss."

"He was only thirty years old," she continues. "There's so many things he didn't get to do. We didn't even get a chance to start our family yet." She sniffles back tears. "Anyway, we better get in there. Thank you again, Nick, for showing up. It would have meant so much to him."

"Of course," Nick says. "Happy to do it."

Nick and I settle near the back on a cold, hard wooden pew. Aren't funerals uncomfortable enough without the sixteenth-century furniture?

"I can't believe we're doing this."

"Did you have a bad experience at a wake or something?" Nick asks.

"No," I say, though I'm not sure it's totally true. My phone rings again. Imani for the second time. This time I send her a text.

OLIVIA: I'll call you later.

After a quick introduction, the emcee (if that's what they're called at a funeral) starts the show. "Now we have a special guest. Nick Leto, Jeremiah's favorite comedian, is here and he'd like to tell a few jokes in his honor."

"Wish me laughs," he says out of the side of his mouth, and rises to his feet. The knot in my stomach tightens more and more the closer he gets to the stage. The room is silent. Yikes, a dead crowd is never a good start.

Nick takes the mic. "Good morning, Mississippi! You ready to liven up this funeral?" Oh, no. "I didn't know Jeremiah but from what I can tell he was a great guy. A guy who loved to laugh, is that right?" The crowd nods and throws yeses his way. "I'm told that if Jeremiah were here, he'd want to hear some jokes, so what do you say? Can we share some laughs for him?" Everyone agrees and Nick begins.

My phone vibrates in my hands again. No surprise, it's Imani. This time, I get a sinking feeling in my gut. Something might be wrong. I better take this. I quickly sneak out the back and walk outside into the sweltering Southern heat.

"Hey, Imani, everything okay?" I answer.

"Do you not have reception down there?"

"Yeah, sorry. I'm kind of at a funeral right now."

"A what?"

"It's a long story. I'll tell you later. What's going on?"

"I need to talk to you. It's really important," she says. Uh-oh.

"Okay, what is it?" I find a wooden column to lean against and brace myself.

"I got a promotion." A promotion? That should be good news. Why is she saying it with an *I have terminal cancer* tone?

On the off chance I'm reading this whole thing wrong, I respond strictly to her words. "Imani, that's amazing. Congratulations!" With all the overtime and effort she's put in, why isn't
she over the moon right now?

"It's in Frankfurt."

Excuse me? I blink my eyes quickly as if clearing away fog.
"Did you say Frankfurt? As in Germany?"

"Yep."

"Like an ocean away?"

"That's the one."

Oh, no. No, no, no, no, no. This isn't happening. "So you're
moving to Germany?" I clarify, trying to imagine Imani going
back to the home of Oktoberfest and punch buggies.

"Yeah. I leave next week to start, then I'll be back for the rest
of my things in a month."

"Next week? But that's so—"

"Soon, I know."

I take in a deep breath, trying to pace my racing heart. Let
me get this straight. My best friend and roommate is moving
halfway across the world almost immediately and I'll be left with
a lease that I can't possibly afford because I just got fired from
my only real paying job.

"Olivia, you there?" she asks.

"Yeah, sorry. Just trying to wrap my head around this."

"I know, me too. I thought this might happen but I didn't
want to say anything until I knew more." Is that why she's been
up my ass about finding a new job? Why hold out on me? Would
it have made a difference if she hadn't? Oh, God, I don't know
what to say. What to think. Or what to do. I can't handle this
right now.

"Listen, I really am at a funeral so I'm gonna have to call you back."

"Are you okay?" She already knows the answer to this.

"Yeah, I'm fine. I'm just . . . I'm really happy for you. Seriously. I'll call you later."

n a daze, I walk back into the service. Nick's still onstage, or whatever it's called, holding his gaze to the ceiling. "Well, Jeremiah, I wish I had the chance to meet you. I know that wherever you are you're driving one helluvan F-150 with a license plate that says *PUMPIN' Forever.*" The room swells with heartfelt laughter. And by the response, Nick actually killed at a funeral.

I want to join in with the others but I feel like I'm in mourning. In the same way Jeremiah's death changed the lives of his family and friends in an instant, Imani's news changes mine. The Olivia Vincent Plan was supposed to be simple. Easy even. Road tour hiccups made it hard. But now it's like my plan's dead in the water.

I guess sometimes you're the firework and sometimes you're the idiot it kills.

Nick takes his seat next to me. "Hey, where'd you go?"

"I had to take a phone call," I say, keeping my eyes focused on the large wooden crucifix hovering behind Jeremiah's casket. Dear Lord, *have mercy* on my soul!

"Everything okay?"

"Yeah." I force a smile. "Everything's fine." Except everything is *not* fine.

Jeremiah's brother, Jordan, takes the mic and begins his eulogy. His words bring me back to the day I took the mic at my dad's funeral. I'd been onstage many times at comedy clubs but nothing quite compared to speaking that day. I'm not the kind of person who cries or falls apart. And if I do, it's in private (like doors bolted shut, soundproof walls kinda private)—not in front of a room of people.

I still have it somewhere, my scribbly eulogy on a folded legal sheet. It was short. Just a single page, but I must've written it over and over again until every word was perfect. Exactly like a good joke. I hardly remember being up there. But I do remember telling myself—*Just read the next sentence. Don't think about it. Just read.* And that's what I did. Because if I thought for a second that my dad was really gone, I would've lost it there in a roomful of people. The way Jeremiah's brother is starting to lose it now.

This might be a stranger's funeral somewhere in Mississippi but it feels just like that dusty day in May. Only worse because now Imani's leaving me too. How am I going to do this on my own? And this time, I really am all alone. The shock and sadness of it all swirls in my chest, bubbling up my throat. I swallow it back but then my eyes begin to burn and flood.

Uh-oh, I can't stop it. I open my mouth thinking I'll take a quick breath but nothing goes in. It only comes out.

All of it.

At once.

"Waah!" I wail, throwing my head back, bawling more than everyone at the funeral combined. Sobs spill out as tears flow down my cheeks like a torrential downpour on an April afternoon in the city. The one day you don't bring an umbrella.

"Oh my god, what?" Nick whispers, grabbing ahold of my shoulders. "What are you doing?"

But I can't make words, it's just a jumbled mess—like my life.

"Get it together, Olivia. Everyone's staring at us," Nick mutters.

"Waah! Aah, aah, aah!"

"Okay, crybaby, let's go." Nick helps me up to my feet and ushers me out of the room, apologizing to everyone on our way out.

Outside, beneath the awning's shade, I struggle to breathe and swipe my hands across my wet cheeks. Nick stares at me, as clueless as a new dad with a dirty diaper. "What's the matter with you?"

"My life is a disaster!" I cry out.

"What are you talking about?"

"Imani just called. She's moving to Germany in a week. A week! And now I have no steady income to pay the rent for our apartment. If I don't get this audition, or even if I do, I'll have to go back to a job I hate. And—and I have no one left. Like no one. I'm alone. I'm gonna die alone," I manage to say through sobs of grief and frustration.

"You're not alone. What about your dad? Your family in Texas?" Nick's assuming things. I never actually told him I have people in Texas.

"He's de-e-ead." I blubber the truth. The pain.

"Wait, your dad died?"

"Ye-e-e-e-es! He died and left me alone. All I have left is student debt, which will follow me to my grave!"

You know when a child is having a total meltdown at the checkout in the grocery store because his mother refuses to buy him a candy bar and his nap time should've started twenty minutes ago? That's what I sound like. I might as well plop down on the ground kicking and screaming.

"Okay, okay." Nick makes his voice soft and soothing. "Calm down. It's gonna be okay."

"I don't know if it is. I never thought any of this stuff would happen to me but it did. And I feel helpless." I finally look up at him. "I just want to be a stand-up. I want to make people laugh. Why is that so hard?"

"Come here." Nick pulls me in, swaddling me in his arms, and his heart beats against mine. I take a deep breath of his scent, all mixed with leathery cologne and cigarette smoke. He rocks me back and forth and strokes my hair. "I understand. I know what it's like to feel like the world has left you for dead. But you're tough."

I whimper at his words, almost wanting to fight them.

He continues. "Don't give up. You're gonna make it. And I'm gonna help you land the *Late Night* audition." More tears spill out of me. And I don't know if they're because of his sweet generosity—the brief relief and glimmer of hope he's offering—or because of the fear that it won't matter because the other shoe always drops. Nick lets me go and swipes his thumbs over my wet cheeks. "I'm a survivor. And a true survivor can always recognize another. You're strong. You're a winner. I know you'll get through this. I believe in you."

I sniffle back tears, stunned by my breakdown behavior and by Nick's sweet support. "Thanks. That means a lot." I take another deep breath and clear my lungs. "Should we go back inside?"

"In a minute. This is the strangest funeral I've ever been to. I need a smoke." He lights up and takes in a long drag. "I'm sorry about your dad. When did it happen?"

"Two years ago. He was only forty-eight."

"Shit. How did he die?"

I glance at the cigarette in his mouth then draw my gaze up to his eyes. "Lung cancer. From smoking."

Nick exhales a plume of smoke, the realization shifting something in his expression. Like it all makes sense now. He takes a good look at the cancer stick gripped between his fingers, then kneels down and smashes it into the sidewalk like a nasty bug until the smoke is extinguished.

The door behind us swings open. Holly, Jeremiah's wife, stomps toward us, red-faced and trembling, eyes shooting daggers aimed at me. "How dare you come to my husband's funeral!"

Oh, shit.

She jabs her finger into my shoulder, shoving me back. "You think I don't know who you are, you big-city hussy bitch! How dare you show your face here, making a scene with your tears. I'm his wife!"

What is she talking about? Then I remember that woman I met—*Just steer clear of his wife, okay, honey?*

"No, you don't understand, I—"

"Oh, I understand perfectly. You think I'm just the idiot hill-billy wife but I did two years in community college too, you four-eyed floozy!" Holly's removing her star-spangled earrings one at a time.

I step back and Nick moves in. "What are you doing?"

"I'm gonna kick your ass, Yankee ho!" She lunges at me but Jordan grabs her at the last second, keeping her at bay.

"Run!" Nick yells, and we jet off for the Jeep.

"Hooo-lllyyy shhhhh-iiiiitt," I say, picking up speed. Holly's on our tail like the Hulk. I've never seen anyone in platform stilettos run like that. I jump in the Jeep and slam the door. Since there's a crowd of people behind us, Nick can't back out without knocking someone over like a bowling pin.

"What are we gonna do?" I say in a panic.

"Hold tight." The ignition kicks on. Mötley Crüe's "Kick-start My Heart" blasts through the speakers. The engine rumbles and Nick steps on the gas, plowing over the grassy curb. He swerves left to miss the cars parked across from it, then makes a sharp right onto the road. And we're off! I grip on to my headrest, staring out the vinyl back window, which is flapping in the breeze.

Rest in peace, Jeremiah. PUMPIN' Forever.

Thirty-One

Nick white-knuckles it all the way to the highway—both of us staring out ahead. Shell-shocked. Slowly we turn toward each other. Tension fills the Jeep from the front to the rear windshield. Until finally, it breaks.

Hahahahahahaha!

Huge belly laughs barrel out of us one after the other. Those good, deep, rich laughs that threaten your bladder control (you know what I'm talking about).

"We just dodged a catfight," Nick says between chuckles.

"No one's ever come at me like that—earrings off and everything." I can hardly breathe. "Okay, but seriously. No more funerals this tour."

"Agreed. Well, unless they're paid."

"I hope his real side piece is far away from Mississippi. That woman's out for blood." I hold my stomach, laughing so hard that my cheeks hurt. Then the tears start coming. "Oh, no!"

"Are you crying again?"

Through laughter and swiping at trickling tears, I say, "Yes. I swear I never get this emotional."

"Maybe you needed it." There are so many things I could cry over but I don't want to. How does it help anything? It doesn't—better to just suck it up and keep going. "So how come you never said anything about your dad? I wouldn't have been such a scumbag about smoking if you told me."

"Probably the same reason you didn't mention your divorce. I don't really know how to talk about it. I guess it was bound to come out sometime. This tour has strangely brought up a lot of stuff about him."

"Like what?"

"Like this Jeep, which is basically a newer version of my dad's. Your damn '80s rock playlists and . . ." I stop myself, not wanting to say it out loud. Not even wanting to think it.

"And what?" Nick asks.

I let out a long sigh. The man's already seen me cry. I might as well tell him this. "He wasn't keen on me doing comedy. I keep thinking about what he said." Nick glances at me, and even behind his Wayfarers I can see a curious look in his eyes. So I continue. "Back when I was in college, there were these open mic nights on campus. One night, I had a hard lemonade and went onstage. Even with liquid courage I was still so nervous. But the moment I heard my own voice over the sound system, it soothed me, which I know sounds so narcissistic."

"No, I get it. Holding the mic is powerful."

"Exactly. So I made some off-the-cuff cracks about the university, and I actually got a few decent laughs. And that was it. I was in love. I knew that night this is how I wanted to spend my time. Not stuck in an office somewhere, blinded by fluorescent lights and trying to prove my worth with every single legal brief.

"So I started performing, and performed some more, and eventually went to mics off campus. And since my dad was such a fan of stand-up, I decided to tell him about it, somehow thinking he'd be supportive. Maybe even tell me to quit school and just do that, which is what I secretly wanted to do anyway. So I came out as a comic."

"Uh, I know how that goes. What did he say?"

"He looked at me like I was turning tricks or something. And then he said to me . . ." I pause, not wanting to say it because it hurt so badly when he did. The sting of his words still hasn't completely faded. "He said, 'You're never gonna be able to take care of yourself if you're a stand-up comedian.' He said I should finish my law degree and get a job so I could afford to go see the best comedians live. That that would be a better use of my time and talent."

"Ouch. That's pretty brutal."

"It broke my heart but . . . he was my dad, and he hadn't steered me wrong before so I listened to him. Well, mostly. I still performed when I could but at that point it was just an outlet, the one place I felt like I was being myself, and accepted for who I really am."

Nick smirks. "I knew you were a bit of a rebel."

"I wish I had been all rebel because now he's gone. For all the time I've been an attorney, I believed he was wrong to discourage me. But now, without steady income and Imani moving across the world, I'm starting to wonder if he was right. I don't know if I'll be able to take care of myself if I'm just a stand-up comedian." I half expect to break down and cry. Again. But I don't. Actually, in a funny way, I feel better. Like saying what

I'm afraid of gives it less power over me. Even if the fear is legitimate.

"Everyone in this business has to pay their dues," Nick says. "And sometimes, yeah, that means getting a second job. Especially in a city like New York. I mean you were a fuckin' lawyer and you still needed a roommate to live comfortably. It's unreal. But here's what I know for sure. No matter how you pay your bills, getting up on that stage every night *is* how you take care of yourself."

It sounds strange but I get what he's saying. For people like us, stand-up is self-expression, self-realization, and self-care. Like fresh air, allowing me to breathe and survive in this wild world. He continues. "If I didn't have the stage, I'm sure I'd be dead by now too." I think back to the photo of my dad. A photo I'm not quite ready to share with Nick. But I wonder, if my dad hadn't given up on stand-up, would he still be alive today? "And, Olivia"—Nick brings me back to our conversation—"when you want something big, something worthwhile, there's always going to be a good reason not to do it."

"Do you have any good reasons?" I ask.

He looks over at me like he's reluctant to speak. "I guess since you told me all that stuff about your dad, I can let you in on my story."

"Let's hear it."

"I love stand-up too. Or at least I did until it came between me and the other things I always wanted."

"Like what?"

"A family," he says quietly. "I found a nice girl, we got married. She seemed supportive of my career, wanted to have a baby even though I was on the road half the year. But I did it so we could save up and not have to worry about taking care of our kids. We tried for a year to get pregnant." He takes a moment like he still feels the sting of whatever happened next.

"And then one day, I got back early from an out-of-town gig. I wanted to surprise my wife so I went to Palermo and picked up a couple cannolis, the kind she likes with the cherry on top. Before I unlocked the door, something felt off. Like the hairs on the back of my neck stood up. And when I walked in, half of our things were gone. I thought probably someone broke in but there was no mess, no broken locks or windows." He fidgets his thumb on the steering wheel, keeping his eyes on the road ahead. "I didn't want to believe it but I knew what happened. When I called her, she said that she'd moved out, that she met someone else. Then, later she told me that she'd been on birth control pills almost the entire time we tried to get pregnant."

"Oh my god."

"Yeah, she said that she couldn't possibly bring a baby into the world with an absent father and husband."

"Damn, that's cold," I say.

"Yep. That was it. I blamed comedy. Comedy got in the way of my marriage."

"You know that's not your fault, right? Or comedy's. She just wasn't the right person. You know that?" I offer.

"Yeah," he says, the word getting caught in his throat.

"Shit, man, you're just as much a mess as me. How are you gonna help me land this audition?" I ask in jest.

"Because I've done it before, remember?"

Thirty-Two

It's Independence Day. A day that we celebrate freedom (from our buddies, the British). With no job, no Imani, it's a different kind of Independence Day for me. I'm no longer under anyone else's control, no longer dependent on anyone for my livelihood, no responsibility to anyone else but myself, and free to make my own way. I had no idea liberation would feel so uncertain.

I need an anchor. A good show with lots of laughs would help.

New Orleans has an electric vibe—one I've never quite experienced before. It's as charming in person as it is on television—colorful town houses, bushy palm trees, and zydeco street musicians. We're performing in a club in the heart of NOLA—The Wild Moon. I know, sounds more like a pagan store than a comedy club. It's really neither, hosting both comics and bands—I dunno, maybe witch shows too.

With my stage time just minutes away, I set my legal pad aside and let out a nervous breath.

"How you feeling, Olivia?" Nick asks from a lounge chair in the corner.

"Honestly? Pretty raw."

"Good. Raw is good."

"Yeah, well, it doesn't feel good and I could really use a win tonight."

Nick leans forward and I feel a pep talk coming on. "Can I give you some advice?"

"Please." I sit up straight.

"Go out there and just have fun. Pretend you have a hard lemonade in your system and you're going up for shits and giggles."

"Shits and giggles? It's been so long since I've done that. I don't think I remember how."

He doesn't respond, just stares at me, tapping his chin. "Let's jog your memory then. Tell me a joke. Not one of your jokes. Just a fun joke. The sillier, the better."

A silly joke, huh? I snap my fingers, trying to conjure something. Then, I remember the joke my dad loved to tell. It always got a laugh. "Okay, I got one. Stop me if you've heard it."

"Doesn't matter. Go," he says.

Here goes nothin'.

"There's a pirate ship sailing along the sea—a captain, a first mate, and a full crew on board. One day the first mate comes running up and says, 'Captain, Captain! There's a ship on the horizon!' The captain says, 'First mate, bring me my red shirt. We'll go to battle.' First mate brings him his red shirt, they defeat the ship, and sail on." I've got Nick's attention now.

"Next day, the first mate comes running up again and says, 'Captain, Captain! There are three ships on the horizon!' Captain says, 'First mate, bring me my red shirt.' So the first mate looks at him and says, 'Captain, how come every time we go into battle you ask me to bring you your red shirt?' The captain says, 'Good question. You see, this way if I'm shot during battle, the blood will blend in with my shirt and the crew won't get scared and run away.'" I nod as if I'm the first mate. "The first mate says, 'Very smart, Captain.' And he brings him his red shirt and they defeat the fleet. Next day, the first mate runs up to the captain and says, 'Captain, Captain, there are sixteen ships on the horizon.' Captain says, 'First mate, bring me my brown pants.'"

Nick applauds with a chuckle. "That joke is the definition of shits and giggles."

"No kidding," I say, feeling better. More playful.

"Now go out there and have fun."

"I will. Thanks." I turn for the door but then look back. "Hey, wish me laughs."

Nick's smile grows wider as his gaze meets mine. And all I can think is I want more than laughs with him. So much more. Is that even possible with my dad's death and his divorce hanging over us? Can two stand-ups really make a couple?

A couple, Olivia? You cry in front of the guy once (or twice) and now he's your soul mate? This is exactly why I don't get emotional. Once you open that door, who knows what will come out. Or who you'll let in. Nick sees me off with a salute, reminding me I have a show to do.

Hovering in the doorway at the back of the room, I notice the crowd is less dense than I expected, given the masses of people outside. Perhaps locals aren't as interested in stand-up as they are the outdoor festivities like hosting backyard barbecues, drinking cold beers out of coolers with melting ice, and setting off illegal fireworks (RIP, Jeremiah). If I can have a little fun, maybe I have a chance of being explosively spectacular onstage.

I stretch out my hands and my mouth and adjust my glasses as the emcee calls out, "Please give a howlin' welcome to Olivia Vincent!" The audience cheers and howls like a pack of wolves. I never got a welcome like that before but it's a lot of fun. I grab the mic and feel my wild emotions from the day begin to steady. As I go through my set, something about performing feels different. Lighter. More open. For the first time since I left New York, I feel exuberant, *full of beans*, as my grandma would say.

The crowd is loving it. Loving me. Laugh after laugh after laugh. All the laughs. Finally, I'm connecting with the audience in a way I haven't in a long time, maybe ever. How refreshing to forget the fear of all the things that could go wrong. My last punchline lands with a bang and the crowd explodes with applause.

Yes! Oh, yes! That feels good.

"That's my time, everyone! I'm Olivia Vincent and I'm back!" I wave and capture the crowd in my mind before returning the mic.

Offstage, Nick waits with a proud smile, rivaling mine. "I knew you could do it."

Without a second thought, I reach for him and wrap my arms around his neck. His leather jacket squeaks in the crooks of his elbows when he squeezes me back. "Thank you, Nick. Thank you for not letting me give up."

He kisses the top of my head the way only someone who loves you can. Gentle and genuine. "Bernie was right about you," he says, holding me steady. "You got somethin', kid."

That old familiar pitter-patter in my chest kicks into high gear. It's so loud that it feels like his chest is vibrating too. Is he feeling what I'm feeling? And is it a road we should go down?

"Welcome to the stage, Nick Leto!" the emcee calls, and Nick and I let each other go.

"Wish me laughs," he says, and hikes away.

After the show, I join Nick at his merch table, where we chat with our newfound fans until they rush out to find a good spot to watch the firework show.

"Sold a lot of shirts tonight," Nick says, holding up a single tee. "Just one left."

"You know what?" I say. "I want to buy it."

"Really?"

"Yeah, so what if I have no room in my suitcase." I pull out my wallet and hand him my credit card.

He refuses. "Nah, your money's no good here."

"What? I can buy the shirt," I say, actually wanting to spend what little money I have left on it.

"I know you can but I want to give it to you." He hands over the black cotton shirt and I fold it over my arm, gently smoothing it out.

"Thank you. Can I at least buy you a Fourth of July drink?"

Nick checks his watch. "Sure, but let's get it to go. Fireworks start in half an hour."

We grab a couple of beers from the bar in plastic go-cups (the only legal way to drink in public in these parts). The chilled barley-flavored beer is deliciously crisp—the perfect companion to a hot summer night in Louisiana.

Outside, the sky grows duskier by the second as we head toward the river. The sticky air clings to my skin like these pleather pants. Walking along the Mississippi in eighty-six-degree weather, I know I'm not the only one sweating.

"Hold on. Have you ever had a beignet?" Nick stops and wiggles his brows suggestively.

"Is that a French sex thing?" I say, because that's how he makes it sound.

He snickers. "It's a French donut but some do describe the experience as orgasmic."

My cheeks redden at the word. Am I embarrassed because he knows I haven't had one in a long time or because there's still a part of me that wants to have one with him?

"There's a place famous for 'em not far. You up for it?" he asks.

"As long as I don't have to fake it," I joke. Nick takes it in stride and steers us in another direction.

After getting through the line at the famous café, Nick and I find a space against the building on the sidewalk. Horns from a nearby brass band blow with fervor while a slew of people saunter up and down the street. It's like being back in New York on a warm summer night but with a more soulful soundtrack. I gaze up at the night sky, feeling the anticipation in the air. Everyone here is waiting for the show to begin.

"You ready for this?" Nick opens the paper bag and I reach inside, pulling out a palm-sized square of fried dough, a mound of powdered sugar cascading off it.

"So it's like a funnel cake?" I ask.

"Funnel cake ain't got shit on this beignet." Nick takes a bite, his lips covered in white sugar.

"You look like Tyrone Biggums." I laugh, sinking my teeth into the warm pastry.

"And now so do you."

The airy dough melts on my tongue like a heavenly cloud sprinkled in rainbow and fairy dust. I moan an insatiable, "Mmm, mmm, mmm! That . . . is . . . amazing."

"Told you." His gaze falls, landing softly on my mouth as I sweep the sugar off my face. "You still have a little . . ." Cupping my cheek with his hand, he gently glides his thumb over my lip. He may just be wiping powdered sugar away but he takes my breath with it. I'm transfixed by the hungry look in his warm brown eyes and I'm dying to indulge. I think he is too.

I tilt my chin and part my lips, eager for him to dive in. Fireworks ignite overhead and I brace myself for one of those magical, movie-like moments. The kind that make the world stand still.

"Hey! Didn't we just see you at The Wild Moon?" a man asks, the smell of liquor on his breath. Yanked from our moment, Nick and I turn his way and take in the group of friends surrounding him.

"Yeah, how's it goin'?" Nick offers with a nod.

"That was a funny-ass show, man." The intruder points to Nick, then looks at me. "You guys are cool."

"Thanks a lot. Happy Fourth," Nick says with a steady-hand wave. The man and his friends shout their drunken farewells and move along. I wait for Nick to say something, pick up where we left off. But he doesn't. Now it's up to me to grab him and tell him to stop being an idiot and kiss me. But I don't. Our firework moment's faded to black. And our Jerry-and-Elaine dynamic prevails. So I reach for another beignet and take a sugary bite.

So much for orgasmic experiences.

Thirty-Three

WELCOME TO TEXAS.

The Lone Star State flag greets us from a highway sign as we cross the border. Yee-freaking-haw.

"Home sweet home, huh?" Nick says as Bruce Springsteen sings "I'm on Fire" on the stereo.

"Something like that," I say, staring out at the long stretch of two-lane highway in front of us. No matter how this place makes me feel, Texas is my home. Sure, I had my reasons for staying away so long. But driving in this Jeep on I-20, I'm not sure if they were good ones anymore.

I take a deep breath as we ease into the state. That's when I spot the real welcome sign. "Oh my god, did you see that?" I practically jump out of my seat.

"See what?"

"The sign for Whataburger."

"Whata-what?" Nick spits out.

"What-A-Bur-Ger." Maybe he'll understand that. "I told you

about it. Best burger in the world. Can we go? Pleeeeaaassse!" I bounce in my seat like a little kid who's just seen the sign for Disney World.

Nick chuckles, watching me wiggle with excitement. "Okay, water burger it is."

"You make fun of the name now but soon you'll be singing a different tune, my friend."

"You are the burger queen."

"That I am."

Seeing the orange-and-white w sign when we pull into the parking lot almost brings tears to my eyes. Almost. It's been too long.

"So this is it, huh?" Nick asks, underwhelmed.

"C'mon, lunch is on me." Nick's been uber generous this trip. Now it's my turn to treat him to a real Texas burger. The smell of those delicious grilled patties brings me back as I saunter up to the counter.

"Welcome to Whataburger, what can I get you?" the cashier in a bright orange polo asks.

"Yeah, can I get a double meat, a bacon and cheese, fries, an order of onion rings, and two chocolate milkshakes?"

"Yes, ma'am! Will that be all?"

"Throw in a sweet tea." We're in Texas, after all. The cashier tallies up the order and I hand over the cash.

"You're ordering for me?" Nick asks.

"Trust me, this is my burgerhood, okay? I know best." We take our table number and find a booth along the window.

I look out over the trees across the parking lot to that open blue sky. It's funny, even though we're in a tiny town outside of Longview, somehow I feel like I'm around the corner from my dad's neighborhood. Like he's just a few blocks away and I can see him anytime. Ask him anything I want.

Too bad that isn't true. And it'll never be true again.

"So what part of Texas *are* you from?" he asks.

"Someplace you've never heard of." Why start with all the geography questions when it doesn't actually matter.

"Is it near here?"

I shake my head. "No, but we'll pass it on the way to El Paso."

"Well, maybe we'll drop in and have a little burger visit there if you want."

"Yeah, maybe." Part of me desperately wants to be there in Midland and the other part of me wonders if I'll be able to breathe when we pass through.

"Here you go!" A staff member slides a full tray between us. My mind completely shifts focus to the feast in front of me. Wide-eyed and salivating, I'm dying to dive in, but I gesture for Nick to unwrap his burger first. He takes a big bite, and I watch him the way he watched me last night with the beignet.

"Eh?" I ask, encouragingly.

With a full mouth, he manages a smile. "Oh, yeah. That's good. Really good."

"Yeah, take that, Shake Shack."

"Whoa, let's not go that far, Texas."

Now it's my turn. I've waited long enough. Feeling the weight of all those gorgeous ingredients in my bacon cheeseburger, I ease it into my mouth. Not too fast, not too slow, wetting my lips before I take the first bite. First bite in forever.

"Oh, God, I missed this," I say.

Nick wipes a little mustard from the corner of his mouth and sets his burger down. "So if you could have a burger with any comedian, dead or alive, who would it be?"

I want to say my dad. Even if he took the mic for only one night, I'd count him as a fellow stand-up. But that's not what Nick's asking, so I say the closest thing to it. "Eddie Murphy."

"Good choice. I bet he'd be a blast to have a burger with."

I let out a small laugh thinking about the McDowell's scene in *Coming to America*. "Yeah."

"Why Eddie?" Nick asks.

"He was my dad's favorite," I say, keeping my eyes on the bacon. "What about you?"

"I'll go with Bill Hicks. He grew up in Texas so he'd probably enjoy a Whata . . . whatever kinda burger this is."

I raise my milkshake, thinking of the late, great comedian. "To Bill Hicks."

Touching his paper cup to mine, he adds, "To your dad." Tears threaten again but I swallow them back with another burger bite, stuffing in an onion ring for good measure.

Nick sets his meal down and dusts his hands. "Okay, let's talk shop. Last night's performance was a good start. Now, I want you to take that playful energy into tonight, but I also want you to think about a few other things."

"Like what?" I manage with a mouth filled to the brim.

"For instance, I've noticed you don't allow a lot of silence during your sets." That makes sense. I'm not big on silence. Too high a risk of my mind running away. Nick continues. "But it's good to have some. Start by sitting in it a second longer than you want to. It helps build the anticipation. It works great on late-night TV."

"You're the expert. I'll give it a try. Anything else?" I ask.

"Yeah, remember when you told me about watching Margaret Cho for the first time?"

"Uh-huh."

"Between now and showtime, I want you to find a way to reconnect with when you fell in love with comedy in the first place."

"Okay . . ." I can't say there was one moment when I fell in love with stand-up, it was many little moments—listening to comedy records with my dad, watching stand-up on cable, seeing live comedy for the first time. "What about you? When did you fall for stand-up?"

Nick leans back in the booth, his eyes on the ceiling as he rubs his stubbled chin. "Man, I haven't thought about that in a long time," he says with a chuckle, and allows an extra second of silence. I lean forward, stuffing a fry in my mouth. "For me it was when I was sixteen, I think. My uncle was in his twenties, living in the city, and somehow snagged us tickets to see Jerry Seinfeld live."

"Wow! What was that like?"

"I don't know if I've ever laughed that hard in my life. He was just so effortlessly funny. And seeing him live was so much better than any televised special I watched. That was a tough time in my life but for the hour that Jerry was onstage, I forgot about all my bullshit and just enjoyed life for a bit. Sometimes I forget that's what this is really about."

Funny, eating burgers with Nick does for me what Jerry did for him that day. For just a bit, I forget about my precarious career situation, Imani's across-the-world move, the *Late Night Show* audition, and all the other details that have been nagging me on this tour. It's nice to be in the moment. Maybe that's why

I fell in love with comedy too. Because when something's really funny, and you're laughing so hard your stomach hurts, there's no better place to be.

Back on the road with the sun bright overhead, gentler rock music on the radio, and the steady rhythm of the road, I pass out. Next thing I know, the Jeep comes to a stop and a hot, smoky breeze wafts over my face. And where there's smoke, there's Nick burning up his lungs. I drag in a deep, polluted breath and take in the city stoplight ahead.

"Are we in Dallas?" I ask, sliding my fingers behind my lenses, rubbing sleep from my eyes.

Nick extinguishes his cigarette and exhales what's left out the window. "Yep, just a few blocks from the club. We have to stop by and get the condo keys from Bob."

"Damn, I was really out," I say, recognizing the soft melody on the radio—"The Flame" by Cheap Trick. "Was I snoring?"

Nick smirks. "What do you think?"

"I bet you'll be glad to have your Jeep all to yourself again next week."

"Eh, I kinda like having you around." He takes his eyes off the road and smiles at me. My heart flutters and I can't help but respond with my own dopey smile. It'll be weird not to see him so much. Will our friendly Jerry-and-Elaine relationship continue in New York? Will we be more? Then again, he's a road warrior and surely within a few weeks he'll be traveling with a new feature. But, he did just say he likes when I'm around. So I ask, "Does that mean you want me on your next tour?"

His gaze returns to the highway. "Actually, I decided to take some time off the road for a while."

"Really?" Not at all the answer I was expecting. I want to ask if that means he's planning to hang out with me in the city. Does he like the idea of going to farmers' markets together on Saturday mornings and playing Funnies on Saturday nights as much as I do? I might be brave enough to make a fool of myself onstage in front of strangers every night but I'm not quite brave enough to ask Nick if he feels the same about me.

"Oh, hey, it's right up here." Nick points ahead, turning the corner toward Classics Comedy Nightclub. "You're gonna love this place. Bob is a class act. Super nice guy. He opened this place back in 1985, I think."

"Wow, this place is older than I am. How many times have you performed here?"

"I think this is number six."

"Damn, you drove all the way from New York to Dallas six times?" No wonder he wants some time off.

"Not exactly. I'll usually fly out. Do some shows here, Houston, a couple in El Paso . . . Wait. What the hell!" Nick and I gawk at the scene from the Classics Comedy Nightclub parking lot.

I gasp. "Oh my god."

Red-and-yellow flashing lights flicker atop fire trucks and other service vehicles. What I imagine was once a lone brick building is now charred around the edges. The melted marquee is hardly recognizable with the roof partially caved in. Wispy clouds of black smoke smolder out the openings like a poor man's chimney. Our gig gone up in flames.

A total disaster.

So much for my reprieve.

Thirty-Four

The Jeep stalls at the edge of the parking lot and Nick rushes out toward the crispy building. I'm hot on his heels.

A red suspender–wearing fireman keeps him at bay with a strong hand. "Sir, you're going to have to exit the parking lot."

Nick rips off his shades, a horrified look in his eyes. "Was anyone hurt? Where's Bob?"

"No. No one was in the building when it caught fire. But again, I'm gonna need you to leave the scene while we get this under control."

Good Lord. Can we have *one* day on this tour where everything goes according to plan? "We're supposed to perform tonight," I say.

He raises an eyebrow. "*You're* a comedian?"

I step up. "Yes, I am."

"Well, no one's performing here anytime soon."

Nick paces, clawing his fingers through his hair. "What the hell happened?"

The fireman looks back at the destroyed club. "We're still looking into the origin of the fire, but it looks like someone left a lit cigarette in the office." Nick and I trade glances. "But you didn't hear that from me. Now, please. You two need to go. I'm not kidding."

Not to rub it in but . . . "Told you smoking kills," I say.

Nick gives me a sideways glare. It's like he's really beginning to resent this truth but not enough to quit himself. "I'm calling Bob." We head back to the Jeep and after a minute, he hangs up without a word.

"No Bob?" I ask.

"No Bob. No job. And no place to stay." Nick starts the engine, looking over the scene again. "Ah, man. I love that club!" he says, pouting.

"What are we gonna do now?"

"I've been driving for eight hours already. Let's just get a motel and forget this whole thing ever happened."

A whole night free and Nick wants to spend it moping in a motel in Dallas. And we can. It would be easy (and somewhat necessary) to catch up on my sleep. But I'm here. In Texas. So close to home. What if the comedy club fire isn't a disaster? What if it's an open door? An invitation to go back to Midland and maybe get some answers.

"Pull over," I say, gripping on to the dashboard.

"What? Why?"

"I want to show you something."

We find ourselves at the back of a busy Walmart parking lot. I get out of the Jeep, open up the back, and dig into the front pocket of my suitcase. Eddie Murphy smiles back at me from the old album cover. My hands begin to tremble like I'm about to reveal the biggest secret of my life. Back in the cab, Nick waits, fidgeting to all hell, but he stops when I hand him the record. "Remember when I told you my dad loved comedy?"

"Yeah."

"This was his. He listened to it in his last days. Laughed every time like it was the first time he heard it," I say, and Nick flips it over, tracing his hand over the set list on the back cover.

"I know this one. It's funny," he says.

"It is. Sometimes when we'd listen to it, I'd feel guilty for laughing. It didn't seem fair, you know? That I could have all this time to laugh and listen to great comedy and great music and he couldn't. His time was up." Nick listens quietly and I clear my throat. "Anyway, he said I could do whatever I wanted with all of his things, but that he wanted me to keep *this* album."

"It must've meant a lot to him." He looks at me, setting the record against the steering wheel. "Why are you showing this to me now?"

"Because after his funeral, we all went back to his house. It was weird because it felt like he was there even though of course he wasn't. I had basically moved back in to take care of him. And that night was the first night I was totally free to go back to my own place. But even after everyone had gone home, I couldn't bring myself to leave. So I sat on the living room floor and put this record on again. When I pulled it out of the sleeve, this came with it." I slip out the photo of my dad and hand it to him.

"Is this him?" Nick sounds as surprised as I was the night I found it.

"Yeah."

"Whoa, whoa. He was a stand-up too?"

"Crazy, right?"

"You look like him," Nick says, smiling. "Same nose. Same smile."

"Yeah, I guess the apple doesn't fall far from the tree," I say.

"Where's The Hoot?"

I shake my head, taking my dad's keepsakes back. "I don't know. He never told me about any of this stuff. But I think he must've left it for me to find. Anyway, I was thinking instead of staying in Dallas, maybe we can drive to my hometown. Maybe I can get some answers there."

"Where's your hometown?" Nick reaches for his cigarettes again but then drops them like they're on fire.

"Midland. It's on the way to El Paso. About four hours away."

"Four hours?" Nick vetoes the idea with his tone. "I don't know, Olivia. I think it's really cool that you shared that with me and I'd love to help you out, but I can't drive another mile. I'm sorry."

"Well, then, let me drive. It's a straight shot on the highway. You can sleep and I'll get us a place to stay." If he doesn't hand over the keys to this Jeep, I might just have to hijack it. "Please, Nick. I swear I'll be a perfect angel with your Jeep. You said you would help me land *The Late Night Show* and I think this will help. I know it will. Please," I beg.

He shakes his head and I'm sure he's going to say, *No, capeesh?* But he clenches his jaw and says, "All right."

"Really? I can?" I cheer and he nods. "Does that mean I command the radio too?"

"Don't push it."

It's a miracle I don't get a ticket. After four hours, passing a slew of stinky cow farms along the way, we arrive in Midland about forty-five minutes ahead of schedule. Nick's passed out cold with his sunglasses barely hanging on his face, looking like Bernie. From *Weekend at Bernie's*. Not our agent. I pull off the highway, braking at a red light.

Nick startles himself awake. "Oh my god, I had a nightmare I let you drive the Jeep."

I glance over at him and give a flat, "Hardy-har-har."

"Bring me my brown pants," he jokes, then takes a swig from his water bottle and sits upright. "So this is your hometown, huh?"

"Yep." Driving around the loop feels familiar and foreign all at the same time. Finally, after two years and four hours, I pull up to my destination. My mouth's bone-dry, heart pounding in my chest. I've had the entire trip to mentally prepare for this moment but I don't know if I'm really ready. Will I ever be ready?

Nick peeks out the windshield and reads the garage sign. "Midland Auto."

"It's my dad's auto repair shop. Well, it wasn't technically his but he was such a longtime, dedicated worker, it might as well have been."

Nick sets a gentle hand on mine, nearly distracting me from my mission. "Want me to come with you?"

As much as I'm loving his support, I can't bring him inside. I'll get grilled for sure. "It's probably best you wait here. I won't be long." I inhale that hot, dusty Midland air, then step out of the Jeep. Nick does the same.

"Hey, Olivia," he calls. "Good luck."

I smile and raise a pair of crossed fingers. Inside, the garage looks exactly the same—like being in a time warp. All of the techs either have their heads under hoods or bodies beneath engines.

Oh, there he is. The one I came to see.

The man lifts his head out from under a hood and wipes his wrench with a greasy, dull red shop towel. His black hair is sprinkled with more salt and pepper and his face has filled in some since the last time we met. But he's still my Uncle Artie.

"Hey, Tío!" I call.

His eyes are awestruck, like he's seen a ghost. "*Mija?* Is that you?"

No one's called me that in ages. I guess I really am home. And it's okay. "Yeah, it's me."

"Oh my gosh, Livy, get over here." He waves me forward, walking my way, and embraces me in a *long time, no see* hug. The smell of sweat and grease brings back memories of my dad coming home after a long day's work. Artie isn't my uncle by blood but you'd never know the difference. He was like my dad's penguin. Of course, bros would never say some sentimental shit like that. "What are you doing here?"

"I'm just passing through on a comedy tour. I thought I'd surprise you." When really, I surprised myself.

"Mission accomplished. And perfect timing. I'm heading home for dinner now. You'll come with me?"

"Yeah, sure." I tug on my ponytail. "But I've got a friend with me."

He cleans off his wrench. "Okay. Bring her too."

"It's a guy. Nick. He's headlining the tour."

Artie raises a brow and peeks over my shoulder. "Uh-huh. And where is this Nick guy?"

"He's outside. I asked him to wait there."

"Well, don't be rude. Introduce me to your *friend*." Artie makes a beeline for the exit, ditching the friendly smile he sported for me. Uh-oh.

I chase after him, pulse racing. I should've prepared Nick for this. "He's my colleague so be nice to him."

He makes a clicking noise with his tongue. "Why wouldn't I be nice?"

Growing up, Artie took the protective role when it came to boys I was hanging out with. Probably because my dad was always chill about them as long as they didn't interfere with my studies and brought me home on time. Artie always had resting gangster face, giving my boyfriends a hard time, almost verbally hazing them. "Are you trying to scare my boyfriend away?" I'd complain, and he'd say, "*Mija*, if he can't take a joke then he has no business being with you. You should be thanking me."

Outside the garage, Nick leans against his Jeep, taking a long drag from his cigarette. When he spots us, his eyes bug out and he ditches his smoke. I run ahead, beating Artie to the punch. "Artie, this is Nick. Nick, meet my Uncle Artie."

My road buddy offers his hand. "Good to meet you, sir."

Artie takes it without a sliver of a smile. "Uh-huh."

I smack Artie's arm. "Be cool, Tío."

"We're just talking," Artie remarks gently, then turns back to Nick. "So you and Livy will come to my house for dinner tonight." It sounds less like an invite and more like an order.

"Yes, sir."

Thirty-Five

Nick and I sit across the dining table from Artie and his wife, Carla. We pass serving dishes politely to one another—tender, leftover brisket, feathery cilantro, bits of onion, and warm corn tortillas. When Nick agreed to come here, he couldn't have anticipated walking into an interrogation. He bravely endures Artie's *friendly* third degree while Carla and I continually scold him between bites. My road buddy takes it on the chin like a champ.

"So, Livy," Carla says, commanding my attention, keeping the heat off Nick for a moment. "How's law firm life in New York?"

It's a good thing I took this big ole bite—buy myself a second. "It was very busy. Stressful. Such a grind."

"Was? Did you say *was*?" Artie narrows his eyes at me.

"Yes." I flash them my sweet niece smile. "I'm no longer working there."

"Then what are you doing?" he asks.

I send him a *you're being silly* sort of wave and chuckle. "Touring the country, of course. Livin' the dream." My surrogate aunt and uncle look somewhat horrified at the news. But I remember what Nick said back in Atlanta about not needing others to validate my choices. It's easier said than done when I see my dad's and Imani's concern mirrored in their eyes.

Nick clears his throat and places his hand around my shoulder. "Actually, Olivia has an audition next week for *The Late Night Show with Anderson Vanderson*."

"That's right!" I say, thanking Nick with a look.

Carla drops her taco. "Anderson Vanderson! I love him!"

"Why are you touching her like that?" Artie points a hostile finger at the outsider.

"Huh?" Nick flinches away with his hands up. "I'm not touching anything."

"That's right, young man."

I roll my eyes. Oh, Lord.

"So you're like a *real* comedian now?" Carla asks.

"Can you believe it?" I say, trying to sell the idea. But I'm not here to talk about my comedy career. I'm here to ask about my dad's.

"Are you staying nearby?"

Nick and I trade *uh-oh* glances. "Yeah, we'll get a place nearby."

"Two rooms, right?" Artie adds. He doesn't know the half of it.

"Yes," I say.

Carla slaps another heap of rice on my plate, then piles the rest on Nick's. "Why don't you both just stay here. We have the extra room."

I'm familiar with the extra room. Not because I spent a lot of time there but because Artie's holding some of my dad's things there for me.

"But you take the couch," Artie orders Nick. "I don't know what kind of funny business you've been up to but you won't be fooling around under my roof."

My cheeks go hot like burnt biscuits, then Carla comes to my aid. "Artie! Livy's a grown woman. She's not that little toothless pipsqueak hanging around the shop anymore."

"If Vince were here—" he starts.

"If Vince were here, he'd offer Nick a beer!"

Nick turns to me, a swirl of wrinkles on his forehead. "Your dad's name was Vince Vincent?"

"No, Vincent's my stage name." I shake my head and watch Nick add up the details.

It was the name I chose back when I started doing stand-up in college. Before my dad knew. I never told him about using his name. A homage to the man who passed down his love of the art to me. When I moved to New York, I wanted to change it. Let everything from my past go. Everything but that Eddie Murphy comedy album. I had another stage name picked out and everything. But when it came time for me to sign up for the open mic, I wrote *Olivia Vincent*. And that was that.

"Speaking of," Artie says. "Where's your next show? Are you performing at the LOL Lounge in Odessa?"

"El Paso," I say.

"That's a long drive," he says, though not compared to what we've driven so far. "I insist you stay here. Rest up for tomorrow."

I swallow a bite of rice. "I'll stay but I'm sure Nick will be more comfortable in a hotel."

"Why? Is something wrong with our couch?" Artie asks.

"Tío—" I start.

Nick places his hand on mine beneath the table. I know it's meant to be an innocent sign to stand down but it feels so forbidden in all the right ways. "Thank you, Artie. I'd be happy to stay the night."

Thirty minutes later, the sun's gone down and I'm helping Nick dress the sofa with a sheet. "You really don't have to stay over."

"Yeah, right. I'm not saying no to that guy. He's scarier than the mob," Nick mutters quietly even though Artie's way out of earshot.

"Eh, he's all bark."

Nick plops down on the couch and yanks off his shoes. "So what's the plan?"

"What do you mean?" I ask.

"I mean, I let you drive my Jeep and now I have to sleep with one eye open in case your uncle tries to murder me in the middle of the night. You said you needed to get some answers. So are you gonna talk to him?"

Now that I'm here at Artie's house, the moment has finally presented itself and even Nick can see I'm stalling. "It's getting late," I say.

Nick gives me that *you're being ridiculous* look. "Don't be a wimp. He's still up."

"All right, I'm going."

"Good," he says, leaning on the pillow. "Leave your door cracked so you can hear me scream for help."

"Good night, Nick." I turn out the light.

"Night."

I wander back to the spare room and find the photo in question. Sneaking out the back door, I step through the dark dirt yard to the detached garage. Artie's fiddling with something while ESPN plays in the background.

"Isn't it past your bedtime?" I ask.

"Nah, I hardly sleep." He pulls up a stool. "Come sit down and visit with me, Livy." I take a seat and push my glasses up the bridge of my nose. He snickers. "You're so much like Vince." Yeah, and I'm about to find out just how much. "You push up your glasses just like he did."

Now there's a shared habit I never realized. Funny how we subconsciously mirror little things our parents do. "Hey," I say, my voice a little shaky. "I need to ask you about something."

"Anything, *mija*. What is it?" he asks, and I hand over the old photograph. Artie squints in the light, then his expression unravels. "Oh, wow, I remember this."

"You do?" My heart nearly leaps out of my chest. I knew he would have some answers for me. This simple affirmation is worth all the trouble (not sure Nick would agree).

"Yeah." He laughs. "That was at The Hoot."

"So you knew my dad did stand-up?"

"Yes, ma'am." Artie can't take his eyes off the photo, in the same way I couldn't when I first discovered it. "He was a funny guy."

"Because I had no idea. Not until I found this."

"Well, Livy, it was a long time ago. Must've been '83, '84. We were still in El Paso." So it was before I was born. Makes sense. "Look at those pants." Artie covers his mouth, and his cocoa-brown eyes grow misty. I may have lost my dad but he lost his best friend. If Imani died, I think I'd be misty-eyed too. "We were so young back then." Then my super tough, auto mechanic uncle wipes a tear from the corner of his eye.

See, all bark.

I let him have a moment to take it in. At the same time, I'm ravenous for the details. "So what's the story?"

"Well, he loved stand-up. Just like you. When we were kids, we worked at the nightclub sometimes. This place, The Hoot. Setting up band equipment. A lot of low-key music—jazz, R and B, that kinda thing."

"So then what?"

"Then they started booking stand-ups and one day he decided to go onstage. He didn't really know what he was doing so he'd mimic other comics with his own material. Sometimes he was like Cheech Marin and sometimes he was like Steve Martin and sometimes he was like Eddie Murphy. He never really found his own style."

I laugh, easily able to imagine him putting on a show in a Marin, Martin, or Murphy flavor. "Is that why he stopped?"

Artie hands the photo back to me. "I don't know. I think once your mom got pregnant with you, it got harder and harder for him to do things like that."

Knowing her, I'm sure she ditched us both any chance she got. I let this sink in. "So he gave up his dream because of me? Do you think that's why he never told me about it?"

"Who knows, *mija*? Only he could really say. But knowing him, I think he was okay with growing up to take care of you and just being a fan of good comedy."

That sounds familiar but it still doesn't add up.

"I just don't get it. How could he discourage me from stand-up when he himself did it? I mean, what a hypocrite. Then he leaves the evidence for me to find like he's playing some mystery game that I can never solve. It's not fair!" I have half a mind to tear up the photo, forget I ever saw it, forget everything he said about stand-up, and move on.

Artie exhales a heavy sigh. "You're right. It's not fair. And you have every right to be angry. But your dad, well, he didn't know anything about raising a daughter by himself. He just had to figure it out. At the shop, he'd always say to me, 'If I can just get her through this next year, it'll be okay.' He never knew if he was doing the right thing but he did his best. And when you went away to UT, he was so proud of you. Like he knew you were gonna be okay. But when he found out you were doing comedy, it scared the living shit out of him."

"Really? He said that?" I ask.

"In so many words, yeah. I dunno, maybe on some level he knew he wouldn't always be there to take care of you if you needed it and he wanted to make sure you could take care of yourself."

Something about his words rings true, but the truth is, we'll never really know how he felt. Or what he wanted me to take from finding the photo. I lower my head, wishing that somehow I could have a little more time with my dad to ask these questions and so many others. "If only I could talk to him, you know. There's so much I want to know."

"Then talk to him," he says, making the idea sound so easy. But it's not, even if all I have to do is say things out loud. "There is *one* thing I do know for sure."

"What?" I ask.

"He loved you no matter what. And speaking as a father myself, the rest doesn't really matter as long as you're happy."

Who knows if my dad would share his sentiments exactly but it's nice to think he might. After all, I don't think I'd choose anyone over stand-up but he chose me. How can I be angry about that?

"Thanks, Tío," I say, relieved to have some questions answered. "You still have his records, don't you?"

"Right where you left 'em."

Artie and I retire to our respective rooms, careful not to wake Nick—assuming he's even asleep with both eyes closed. The poor guy must be exhausted. I creep over to the guest room closet and crack open the door, quiet as a country mouse. There it is. The box of my dad's vinyls. Then, I hear someone slinking down the hallway. It's Nick coming out of the bathroom. "Psst," I hiss, waving him into my room.

"What's up?" he whispers.

"C'mere, I want to show you something." I shut the door and lift the top of the storage box, inviting him to sit on the floor next to me.

"What's this?"

"These are all my dad's records." I begin pulling them out one by one. "George Carlin. Richard Pryor. Rodney Dangerfield. Redd Foxx."

Nick holds each of them like priceless artifacts of the past. "These belonged to your old man?"

"Yeah."

"The guy had a good sense of humor," he says.

"It's not just comedy. Check these out." I walk my fingertips to the other side of the box and begin pulling out his favorite music. "Journey. The Eagles. Tom Petty. Boston."

"Wow. Let me see those." The two of us fish through the row of records like we're in an indie music store in the Village, pulling out gems in awe. "Do you think he has other photos hidden in any of these?" Nick asks.

The idea hadn't occurred to me. The Eddie Murphy album was the only one he asked me to keep. Clearly my dad could keep secrets. "It's possible but I doubt it."

"Let's scope it out." Nick flicks his eyebrows, intrigued by the excursion. It's cute that he's curious about my past. A quality that's making me want a future with him.

We split the record collection in two and slide out every vinyl from its cardboard sleeve—through The Who, Bob Marley, Def Leppard, and even Mungo Jerry, there isn't a single hidden item.

"Bingo!" he says, holding a copy of Guns N' Roses' *Appetite for Destruction*.

My heart stops when I catch a glimpse of the faded photo. A tiny me sits on the hood of my dad's Jeep. The sunlight highlights my little ringlets a honey brown. My dad stands close, squinting in the glare. His hands hover nearby like a fail-safe in case I fall.

"Is this you?" Nick asks.

"Yeah. I don't know if I've seen this before." I turn it around and read *Livy and Vince Sept. '89*.

"So that's the famous Jeep, huh?"

"Yeah," I say, unable to take my eyes off the photo.

"Any idea why he hid it in here?" Nick holds up the '80s metal album. At first glance it seems like an odd place to stick a photo of yourself and your toddler. But knowing him, it was the perfect place.

"'Sweet Child O' Mine,'" I say. "This was taken around the

time my mom left. He packed up all our belongings and we came here to Midland where Artie had moved and had a job waiting for him at the shop. It was just the two of us—like him and me against the world or something. He used to sing that song to me every night before bed, like it was the only lullaby he knew."

Nick smiles. "I thought you hated that song. You always veto it."

"No, I could never hate it. I just haven't been able to let myself enjoy it since he died." I stare at the photo, thinking back to all of those little father-daughter moments, knowing that all along he was just trying to keep me safe. Maybe Artie's right. If I want to talk to him, I should talk to him. "Hey, you wanna take a drive?"

Thirty-Six

For the second time today, I'm behind the wheel of Nick's Jeep (a miracle, I know). It's nearly midnight when I pull up to the iron gate of the storage facility and punch in the code.

"What are we doing here?" Nick asks.

"You'll see." I park Nick's Jeep and we hike up the aisle of garages to number 382. As I lift the door open, a wave of heat streams out of my unit. It's as dark as a cave inside.

"Would you mind turning on your flashlight?" I ask.

Nick and I aim our phone torches inside, shedding a light on a 1981 black Jeep Laredo, specks of dust swirling in the glare.

"Holy shit! You still have this?" Nick walks over and places his hand on the round headlight.

"Of course," I say, smiling at the old hunk like it's my Uncle Jeep. "Can you help me push it out of the garage?"

I climb in, release the brake, and shift it to neutral. With Nick at the back and me wedged in the driver's side door, we throw our weight forward. The Jeep inches on and I steer it in place, the same way my dad would when we'd get stuck on the road. "Okay, that's good," I say when it's nearly all the way out of the garage. I step back and take in the relic beneath the glow of security lights and the moon. It hasn't aged a day.

"This is so badass," Nick says, running his hand along the hood. I snort a laugh. My dad would've liked him.

"Hop in," I say, taking the driver's seat, and I reach for my dad's handcrafted wooden urn tucked away in the back. The vase-shaped surface is smooth, save for some dust, and it's heavier than I remember. "I think you put on some weight, Pop," I say, heaving it onto the center console.

"What'd you say?" Nick asks.

"Not you. This. This is my old man."

"You keep your dad's ashes in a storage facility?"

"When you say it like that it sounds bad but yeah, he wanted to be buried with his Jeep."

"Should I have brought my big shovel?"

I giggle. "Now there's the start of a funny joke. Two comedians diggin' a grave for a Jeep. One says to the other—"

"Let's bury you instead?" Nick adds, and I shoot him a look. "Too dark?"

"Are you kidding? Look where we are." No way Nick could've conceived of this scenario when he warned me to be prepared for anything. I know I couldn't.

"So, you gonna take him on a drive?" he asks.

If only that were possible. When you're raised by a man, you learn to communicate like a man. Not face-to-face but shoulder to shoulder. If we ever needed to talk about something important or hard, he'd take me for a drive. And it worked. Somehow it was always easier to say what I was feeling when I could stare out at the road ahead. "Nah, I doubt the Jeep would run after being benched for all this time."

"Okay, well, why don't I leave you two to catch up? I'll wait in the parking lot."

"Thanks. I won't be long."

"Take your time." He begins walking away but stops short and turns back. "Wait, do you mind if I talk to him for a second?"

"Um, okay . . ."

Nick wedges himself in the open door and leans on the frame. "Hey, Mr. Vincent—"

"You can call him Vince," I say, watching a guy I could see myself bringing home to meet my dad have some kind of moment with his remains. It's a thoughtful gesture, given the circumstances.

Nick clears his throat. If I didn't know any better, I'd say he's a little nervous. How sweet. "Right, Vince. I'm Nick Leto. I'm on tour with your daughter. But you probably already know that because you're um . . . you know." I press my lips together, keeping a chuckle at bay while Nick navigates this conversation. "Anyway, I haven't known Olivia long but I feel like I've gotten to know her pretty well over the last week and a half. And I know when you were alive, you weren't too thrilled about her performing stand-up. If I had a daughter, I might feel the same way. It's tough but she's really good. She makes people laugh. From what I know about you, that's something you'd appreciate.

"So I wanted to say I think you'd be proud of her. I know you're worried about her taking care of herself but you don't have to because she's pretty badass. I don't know many women who can teach a man how to change a tire on the side of the Jersey turnpike."

With his heartfelt words, the mood shifts from awkward to sincerely tender. Quiet tears cascade down my cheeks. And I let them. Because as I grew up, I just wanted my dad to be proud of me. I never really knew for sure if he was because he wouldn't come out and say it. Instead, he'd say, *You did good, Livy. You did good.*

Nick continues, "So that's all I wanted to say. That and you have a really sweet ride." He pats the top of my dad's urn and looks up at me. "You okay?"

"Yeah," I say, sniffing back a sob. "Thank you for saying all that." Nick acknowledges my gratitude with a nod then leaves me to express myself alone.

I run my hand along the black-painted wooden console he made when I was a kid. The semigloss finish feels missed on my palm, and I loop my finger around the oversized cup holders— specially made for his beloved Big Gulps. I trace the fabric of the dusty vinyl seats, scratching against the grain with that funny *zip-zip* sound. Gazing over the circular gauges on the dash, the knobs, and the cassette player brings me back. I find the keys in the metal glove compartment, right where I left them. The Jeep won't run, I know that, but if I can't take a drive with my dad, I can at least fake it.

I turn the ignition. There's no life left except for the faint radio static coming through the speakers. "Whoa," I breathe out. The engine may have kicked the bucket but somehow the battery's still kickin'. I grip the skinny, leather-wrapped steering wheel and look out across the way at a row of closed garages, picturing a stretch of open road on a sunny afternoon. No different from the one I drove earlier. Now that I'm here, I don't know what to say first. Why is it easy talking to a crowd of strangers and impossible talking to my invisible dad? Makes no sense.

So I just open my mouth and say the first thing I can think of. "Hey, Dad . . . I thought I'd know what to say when I got here but this is harder than I thought. I hate that you're gone . . . and I hate that I've stayed away so long." I wipe a tear from the corner of my eye. "Why did you leave me that picture? And why didn't you tell me about The Hoot? I have so many questions that I'll never get the answers to. Maybe you were too proud or maybe you lacked the courage." I hold my breath, wondering which is true. Or if neither is.

"You and I are so much alike in so many ways, but I'm not too proud to say that I am afraid of what you said. I'm afraid that I might not be able to take care of myself with stand-up. I am afraid." My voice cracks and I take a breath. "But I also really want to try. I didn't have the courage to tell you that before but I do now. And since you're in an urn, you really can't argue with me—so that's new.

"When it was just the two of us, you found the strength to take care of me. You figured it out. It must've been hard. Maybe the hardest thing you ever had to do. This might be the hardest thing I ever do too but I'll figure it out. Because I have to. I think you can understand that. Please understand I'm not trying to be ornery. I just want to be true to me."

I shut my eyes, soft tears trickling down my face and fogging my glasses. For the first time since the funeral, I let myself feel all the things I couldn't before—the grief, the loneliness, the ache for more time, but also a deep sense of appreciation for this moment. Alone in the Jeep. With my dad.

The static on the radio begins to clear away like clouds after rain. A faint, electrifying guitar riff sings to me and my heart stops. Is it? I turn the knob to help it along until it's sharp. *"Whooooa, sweet child o' mine."* I look at the passenger seat, half expecting my dad to be sitting there grinning. And even though I can't see him, he's around—in a song, in a joke, or in the Jeep. Artie's right. Dad loves me no matter what.

Thirty Seven

G ood God, Livy, whatchu got in here?" Artie asks, dragging my suitcase out to Nick's Jeep.

"Just a few things," I say.

"Women," he says, handing it off to Nick, and the two share
a very agreeable bro moment.

Aw, they made friends.

"Don't forget your garbage bag pillow. Next time, don't run
off so fast, okay?" My uncle brings me in for one last hug before
we drive west.

"Okay," I say, wishing I could stay a little longer (if you can
believe that).

"Listen, *mija*, if you ever need anything, anything at all, Carla
and I are here. You're family." This is a fact I never should've
forgotten. And I make a silent promise to remember and come
back soon.

"Thanks, Tío," I say. "That means more than you know."

Nick finishes loading the luggage in the back and offers Artie a hand. "Thank you so much for your hospitality."

"You're welcome. Now, you kids be good."

Nick salutes the sergeant. "Yes, sir."

Carla wraps me in one last mama hug and hands me a warm paper bag. "It's just a little snack for the road." I thank her and hop in the Jeep. "Good luck with your *Late Night Show* audition!"

"Don't wish me luck. Just wish me laughs," I say, buckling my seatbelt, and we're off to the next show.

"Take the Money and Run" by the Steve Miller Band plays on the radio. "How you doin' over there?" Nick asks, approaching the neighborhood stop sign.

I smile, satisfied with . . . well, everything. "Doin' good. What about you?"

"I'm not sure. I made an important decision," he says, his tone turning serious.

"What?"

Nick slides his sleeve up his biceps, a square flesh-colored patch adhered to his skin.

"Nick Leto, are you telling me you're a quitter?"

"Yeah, I got a lot of life to live. I don't want my time to be cut short."

"I have to say, that patch is kinda hot," I tease, playfully biting my lip and winking at him, unabashed. A smoke-free Nick is really sexy though.

He flexes his biceps. "How 'bout now?"

"Ooh! So healthy." The two of us share a laugh and head off down the hot, dusty road singing, *"Headed down tooo old El Paso!"* Somehow over the course of twelve states, Nick's become more than a headliner, more than my road buddy, more than a crush. He's become a real friend—the Jerry to my Elaine.

Later that evening, we pull into the El Paso Funnies comedy club parking lot, decorated with desert palm trees and an unobstructed view of the gorgeous Franklin Mountains. It might not be New York City but it's still a piece of my favorite club. I step out of the Jeep and take a deep breath, exhaling with, "Ah, it's good to be back."

"Yes, it is," Nick says.

The outside doesn't look like much, kind of like the New York location, but the inside is huge—like two clubs in one. I walk the perimeter of the main room, passing the crammed rows of empty tables and gazing at the signed headshots framed on the walls. Wow, for a club on the edge of Texas, it's hosted nearly as many legendary stand-ups as the one in Manhattan.

"C'mon, the greenroom back here." Nick points ahead.

Inside, there are even more framed photos on the dark blue walls but instead of headshots, they're snapshots of performances going all the way back to the '80s. I had no idea this place was a comedy landmark. I guess El Pasoans, my dad included, love to laugh. Nick and I stare at each picture, enthralled like we're in some kind of comedy museum.

"Holy shit, Brett Butler's been here! Now there's a funny Southern woman," I say, wishing I could've seen her live. "And Pablo Francisco, Steve Harvey."

"Here's Bill Hicks," Nick says, pointing to a small photo in the center.

I briefly look over all the others. "Are you up here at all?"

"Nah, I don't think I'll make the cut."

"Well, not with that attitude." I give him a playful shove. "I want to be up here one day." And I really do. Looking at all the legends who make stand-up seem so easy and who probably started out like me. It's something I tell myself all the time in New York but I really have lost sight of it since we left.

"Speaking of," Nick says. "Do you remember what we talked about yesterday at Whataburger?" It takes too long to answer because he's snapping his fingers in my face. "'Livia, you listening?"

"Sorry, I was thinking about burgers."

"Of course you were."

Regaining my mind, I say, "I remember. Be okay with silence and reconnect with when I fell for stand-up."

"That's right. And what did I teach you the night before?" He paces, hands held behind his back like a martial arts sensei.

"Just have fun," I say, thinking I get an A-plus.

"Good. Now this time, I'm going to leave *you* to prepare." And he does. It's just me, my yellow pad, and my past recorded sets. New Orleans was strong but I really want to nail it here in my dad's hometown. I have to earn my spot on the Funnies wall.

Later, after Nick wishes me laughs and the emcee calls me to the stage, I take the mic, but this time I feel better than steady. I feel electrified (and not because it's so dry here that I get a shock anytime I touch something).

"What's up, El Paso!" I begin, moving the mic stand off to my side. "Glad to be in the company of my fellow Texans." I get a few cheers. "That's right, I was raised in Midland, which is a very . . . astute name for a city that's not even in the middle of the state. But okay." I get my first laugh. This crowd doesn't need a geography lesson. "Yeah, I was raised by a single dad"—I hold a pause for an extra beat then continue—"which explains why I'm now a stand-up comedian." Another laugh.

I imagine I'm back in New York, and at the same time, remain present with this audience. This crowd of comedy lovers. I say a line and sit in the silence just long enough for me to panic that I've lost them only to see that they're listening even closer. Even more engaged. That's a neat little party trick. I think about the Eddie Murphy album, the Margaret Cho special, the first time I made my dad laugh. I let all of the shitty sets of my past, particularly on this tour, go. I'm still standing. Still crackin' jokes. But something feels different. More honest—even if my jokes aren't exactly *true* stories. I feel like I'm connecting with this audience in a different way than ever before.

I always thought I was being myself onstage. But how could I be myself, my whole self, when I was hiding from part of my life? Parts of my story. By the time my set's over, everyone's grinning. I capture the crowd in my mind, filing it away with the other great nights. "That's my time, everyone. I'm Olivia Vincent. You've been great. Seriously, you're awesome!"

Nick waits for me offstage, leaning against the wall, smiling my way. His eyes pull me in and I'm tempted to grab his gorgeous face and lay one on him for being, well, for being him. "You did good, Olivia," he says. "Really good."

After nearly three thousand miles, I'm finally getting somewhere.

Thirty-Eight

got an idea," Nick says, locking the door to the El Paso comedy condo. "Why don't we go topless?"

I cup my hands over my chest. "Like Vegas showgirls?" Because that's where we're headed. Las Vegas.

He chuckles. "I'm talking about the Jeep. But I wouldn't mind seeing that."

"Totally. You in a diamond thong. Where do I sign up?" I say, giving my tush a little tap.

"Play your cards right . . ." Nick leaves me with a wink and begins dismantling the soft top.

We ride off into the desert on I-10 toward New Mexico. With the sun on our faces and the wind whipping through the Jeep, we cruise on singing Queen's "Don't Stop Me Now" at the top of our lungs.

"I'm having such a good time!" I shout over wind, road, and Freddie Mercury.

"What?" Nick yells back, lowering the volume.

"I said I'm having so much fun. I don't want this tour to be over."

He grins, hair dancing in the breeze. "It's one for the books."

"Maybe I should ride back with you in the Jeep," I say, thinking that only six days ago the idea of going one more mile with this man was enough to make me want to take the wheel and careen us into a smoke shop.

"Don't you need to get home?" he asks with his wrist resting at the top of the wheel.

"Yeah, you're right." I gaze out the window through my prescription sunglasses at the purple and red hues of the mountains up ahead—taller than the tallest skyscrapers in New York. Now that I'm beginning to confront my issues, I've got another challenge looming. "I need to find a new roommate and I don't even know where to begin."

"Just put an add on Craigslist that says *smart, sexy, funny female looking to fill some space.* You'll break the server."

"You forgot to mention *dick pics welcome.*"

He snaps his fingers. "Now you're thinking."

I'm not sure if what I'm about to ask is a good idea but it feels like it has potential. Like it could work. "Would you be interested? I've got a two-bedroom on the Upper East Side." I sing the location, hoping it'll entice him.

"Trust me. You don't want to live with me."

"I've practically been living with you for the past week and a half. I could do a lot worse than you."

"You could do a lot better too," he says, turning up the music and thus ending the conversation.

Okay, maybe asking a guy you've known for only a couple of weeks to move in comes off as borderline psycho but in my defense, Nick has something that a stranger from some roommate website doesn't have—my trust. Unless Tom Hanks is on there looking for a room to rent (how can you not trust that guy?). Still, I try not to take his cavalier rejection too personally. Maybe I'm getting a little carried away. Caught up in a moment that isn't meant to be carried back to New York.

The drive through Arizona and into Las Vegas is so breathtaking I hardly manage to get any work done. I totally recommend it. We arrive at our hotel near the top of the strip—the Isle of Riches Hotel and Casino. Surrounded by some of the most recognizable casinos, its dancing lights give it an amusement park vibe. And let's be real, Las Vegas is nothing but an adult amusement park.

"Home sweet home," Nick says while we wait in line. Warm chandeliers illuminate the square-patterned wall molding and golden hues of the carpet. Now this is a lobby. "You ready to hit the casino?"

"I think I've got about twenty dollars to spare," I say.

He throws me a *yikes* expression. "Then we better play the penny slots." Gambling with pennies sounds like my kinda game at the moment.

I rock on my heels, watching Vegas-goers as I wait to reach the reception desk. A couple not much older than Nick's D.C. waitress friend practically float by smiling from ear to ear. The bride in a flapper-style white fringe dress and simple veil. The groom in a leather jacket not much different from Nick's. I like the idea of a rebellious Vegas elopement. Especially with a guy like Nick. That's when I look at him—smoldering dark eyes, cavalier hair, and dimples that make me blush. Even a fleeting thought of marrying him can mean only one thing.

I've got it bad. Real bad.

"What?" he asks, catching me staring.

"Nothing," I say, faking it.

After walking the distance from the front desk to the elevator and down the corn maze of a hallway, dragging my deadweight suitcase behind me, I'm ready for a shower, my comfies, and something funny on TV. Preferably with Nick in my bed.

"Meet me in ten minutes?" Nick asks, holding the key card up to his door across the hall from mine.

"Sure." If we can't have a quiet night in, I'll take a fun night out. Besides, it's Vegas.

I'm dressed for the evening and swiping my lashes with mascara when there's a knock at my door. Nick must be itching to go blow some dough.

"Almost ready," I say, swinging the door open, but he's not and he doesn't look so good. "What's the matter? Did our show get canceled?"

"No."

"Then what is it?"

He drops his head, leaning on the doorframe. "I hate to say it but I think I'm getting . . . old."

"Yeah, what else is new?" I joke, inviting him in.

"You just wait, Olivia. Your thirties will getcha," he says, and I pop in a pair of earrings. "Would it be cool if we save the gambling for tomorrow? Maybe order some burgers and watch a comedy instead?"

I narrow my eyes at him, suspicious. "Nick, can you read my mind now? Because absolutely we can do that." Without wasting time, I kick off my Converse and grab a pair of cotton shorts from my open suitcase (which basically looks like T.J. Maxx threw up in it).

Nick and I settle in on my king-sized bed with a couple of burgers from In-N-Out, a top-choice burger place I haven't frequented since college. I take a huge bite and stuff a couple of fresh-cut fries in my mouth, leaving little room to breathe. Most nights after our shows, Nick and I settle in for a little late-night comedy for ourselves. It's becoming a highlight of my day. We take turns picking the content—sometimes it's a few episodes of a sitcom like *Seinfeld* or *The Office* and other times it's a stand-up special like Sarah Silverman's *We Are Miracles* or Jo Koy's *Lights Out*. Tonight it's my turn to pick and I found something really special to watch.

"So what's on tap tonight? Ali Wong? You won't shut up about her."

"Nope, check this out." I aim the remote and pull up Nick's half-hour stand-up special, *Born to Run*, from three years ago.

"Are you serious right now?" Nick says.

"Yes, I want to watch it so I can figure out why you titled it after that Springsteen song."

"How about I tell you and we watch something else." He grabs the remote, cheeks flushed like he's got a sunburn from the drive. Unless it really is a sunburn.

"As tempting as that sounds . . . no." I steal the remote back again, this time pressing play.

Nick shields his face with his hand. "This is embarrassing."

"What are you talking about? Do you know how many comedians would give their right ass cheek to have one of these? Myself included. They don't just give these to anyone."

"Your right ass cheek, huh?" he asks, and I shoot him a look. "Okay, we'll watch it once and never again, *capeesh?*"

"Yeah, yeah, *capeesh.*"

We spend the next thirty minutes snagging fries from each other's fry baskets while I snort laughter nearly the entire time. He uses very little of the same material I hear every night on tour. And he's beyond funny. Almost funnier than he is now, but I keep this observation to myself. He ends the special with the same slogan on his shirt—*buh-bye.* Now I get it. Now I really understand why people love him. Why fans like Jeremiah special-request him. He's a great stand-up.

"That was so good, Nick!" I say, giving his arm a friendly smack.

"Thank yoooou, thank ya very much." And now Elvis-Nick is back.

"Don't laugh at me but it's been really fun watching comedy with you. It's nice to share a laugh with someone sometimes, you know?" I say, wanting to meet his gaze but feeling shy.

"Yeah, I do. I was just thinking that the best part of my special was watching it with you. Listening to you laugh."

I look at him. Even if his words have me trembling inside. Now I see that he has swoony feelings for me too. He leans close, so close I can almost taste him—the smoke-free version of him. And I want to. So bad. And so what if we break the rules again? So what if we're more than Jerry and Elaine? We're Nick and Olivia.

Nick tilts his head and I breathe him in, gently closing my eyes.

Ding-a-ling-a-ling!

Ding-a-ling-a-ling!

The annoying ringtone from my phone is enough to take us out of the moment. Dammit! I glance down at the screen. It's Imani. "Hey, I should get this," I say.

"Yeah, I should get to bed anyway." He climbs off my mattress, snatching his shoes from the floor. "Good night, Olivia."

"Night."

I watch him leave my room and answer the phone. "Hey, I'm so glad you called."

"Are you okay? I haven't heard from you since I told you about Germany."

"I know. I'm sorry." I smack my forehead. "When you told me, I actually had a bit of a meltdown. I haven't been handling all of this very well, have I?"

"No, you haven't. But I'm glad you're finally seeing it."

I walk over to the window and look out at the shimmering lights of the Vegas Strip. "Imani, I'm seeing so much more clearly these days."

"What do you mean?"

"I mean, you're not wrong to be worried about me. I haven't exactly been facing reality. It's just that . . . reality isn't always fun. So I figure if I lift my chin and act as if everything is the way I want it, then everything will fall into place—work itself out without me having to do the work."

"I know, I'm a little jealous of that."

"It's a blessing and a curse, I guess. But I'm sorry for being difficult and I'm really sorry if I seem unsupportive of your move. I mean, I'm not crazy about losing you to Europe but I'm so happy for you. I love that things are falling into place for at least one of us."

"Thanks. I really needed to hear that," she says. "And things are falling into place for both of us, as long as one of us doesn't go bankrupt."

"God, if bankruptcy could get me out of these student loans, I'd blow all my money at the casino," I say, and she giggles. Hearing even the smallest laugh from Imani makes me realize how much I'm going to miss her when she leaves.

"Your audition's in a couple days. How are you feeling about it?"

"I feel good. Really good. I'm learning a lot on this tour. Like you wouldn't even believe," I say.

"I'm all ears."

I settle in, ready to share it all with my penguin. "Oh, girl, I have to tell you what happened. I went to Midland . . ."

Thirty-Nine

n the morning, Nick and I meet at one of the restaurants in the hotel for breakfast. The button on my jeans is starting to feel like it's gripping the denim for dear life and screaming—*Suck it in, honey!*—so I opt for an egg white omelet to offset all those burger calories.

"Tonight's your last show before your audition," Nick says, then snaps off a bite of his sausage link.

"I know." I sip from my second cup of coffee. I could hardly sleep last night thinking about it. Telling Imani the whole story didn't change her mind. And she was sure to remind me of the promise I made her before I left—if I don't land the audition, I'll call the headhunter as soon as I get home. Not that I could forget it. With her now leaving New York there's a chance I'll have to do that anyway. But as we say in the country—*Don't count your chickens before they hatch.*

Come to think of it, that saying supports Imani's stance more than mine.

Never mind. The point is I don't want to assume I need to make any big decisions at least until after the audition.

"We've got a big Vegas crowd later," Nick continues.

"I know. I'm ready," I say as if I've been training for this day my whole life.

"I think you can be readier. More ready. Which is it?" Nick and I must be losing mental steam. But we can't rest on our laurels now.

"Readier. You got more sage wisdom for me?"

"Yes, and this is it. No more lessons from me. The rest you'll have to figure out because I've got nothing left to share."

"Okay, hit me." I slap my hand on the table, practicing my gambling moves for later.

"Two things. First, you have a lot of funny material but it's not really about you. Infuse your story into your act. Think of that Charlie Chaplin quote. Trust me, you've got a lot to work with."

"I'll take that as a compliment?" I ask, unsure.

"Sure. Why not."

I've been avoiding it for a long time but I think he's right. I need to try telling parts of my story. My real story—not just all the modern dating stories I steal from Imani's adventures on Tinder. "Okay, I'll do my best."

"Now, there's one last piece of advice I have for you. But it might be the most important."

"Okay, what's that?"

"Trust your comedy."

I guess that's good advice, however— "Thanks, but I do trust my comedy."

"I say this as a friend, but half this tour you didn't and it showed. I know you have all this apparent confidence but I could hear the doubt in your voice in D.C., Mississippi, and Atlanta.

You can't doubt because when you do, you bomb. Not just you, all of us. Every. Single. Time. So"—Nick stands up and tosses some cash on the table—"I'm gonna leave you to prepare."

"The whole day?" I ask.

"Yeah. Use it wisely. I'll see you at the show."

Then, it's just me, my coffee, my legal pad, and my stories. Here we go.

When it's nearly showtime, Nick's nowhere to be seen so I hang out in the wings as the opening acts warm up the crowd with the help of the drinks being served.

"Hey." Nick taps my shoulder and I whip around.

"Where've you been? The poker tables?" I ask.

"Maybe. So how's it looking tonight?"

I flash him a folded legal sheet, the one I've been scribbling on all day. "Good. I thought a lot about what you said and worked out some new material I'm going to try tonight."

"Really?" His brows shoot up like he's about to tell me it's not a good idea. How can I trust my comedy if I can't also trust myself? So I hold firm.

"Yes. It's not like we have time for me to do an open mic. This is my chance."

"I feel the same way." Nick pulls something from his pocket, holding it between his shaky fingers. It's his wedding ring. Not a speck of drain gunk on it.

"Why do you have that?" I ask.

"I'm going to try some new material too. About my divorce. I think it's time. And I think it'll help."

I place my hand on his leather-clad shoulder. "I'm proud of you, buddy. Are you using the ring as a prop?"

"No, I thought maybe I could pawn it after the show," he says, stuffing it back in his pocket like it's nothing but a nickel.

"I don't know if the shops stay open that late." Who knows what kind of funny stuff people in Vegas pawn in the middle of the night?

"Then we'll take a drive and I'll chuck it in the desert or something," Nick says, and I watch his expression to see how serious he is. "I don't want this thing that happened to hold me back anymore, you know?"

I nod. "Take your pain and play with it."

"Exactly."

The emcee begins my introduction and I stuff my notes in my back pocket. "I have to go," I say, and lean up on my toes, laying a little kiss on Nick's cheek—right where his dimple is. "Wish me laughs."

His eyes lock with mine for a moment before I turn for the stage. I stretch out my hands, my mouth, and adjust my glasses as the emcee calls my name. "Let's give it up for Olivia Vincent!"

Now I have to trust my comedy.

"Hello, Las Vegas! How y'all doing tonight?" They all cheer. "You know, Vegas is a great city. I absolutely love it! Don't you?" The crowd gives a little cheer, like the city hasn't taken their money yet. "Yeah, it's amazing—the lights, the shows, the creepy men on the street peddling escort flyers. It's the best!" This gets a laugh so I take a beat. Make that two.

"Vegas isn't for everyone. In fact, for single women approaching thirty"—I point to myself with a cringing expression—"Vegas is the worst place you can be. Everywhere you go, some chick in her twenties is tying the knot. You know there are drive-thru chapels? That is the most American invention I've ever heard of.

What's next? Drive up for the vows, then drive around to pick up your divorce papers at the second window?"

Hahahahahaha! Hear that?

"I'm not gonna lie, I'm straight up jealous of young brides. They're always flaunting around in their bedazzled bride tops with their posse of girlfriends, who wish her well to her face but secretly think she's making a mistake by marrying *Gary.* I know, it's not a great husband name. Sorry, Garys—you'll have to die alone this round."

I don't know any men named Gary but I do hope he has a good sense of humor because the audience gets it. "But seriously, I'm just jealous because my bedazzled shirt says, *Always a bridesmaid, never a bride.* Except the *always* is crossed out and it says *never a bridesmaid.*" I gesture to my white T-shirt, getting into a little of my own story.

"It's true. I have married friends but never make the wedding party cut. You see, brides are very particular about the aesthetics. It's like they get engaged and then become judges of *America's Next Top Bridesmaid.*

"I'm not kidding. Did you hear about that bridezilla that kicked her friend out of her wedding party because the friend got cancer and lost her hair?" I make an aghast face. "I know, it's terrible. But don't worry. Karma will bite her in the ass. Because you know who she's marrying? Gary." Now I'm just being playful, having fun. "Ah, bless your heart, Gary."

"I know why I never get picked though." I let out a sigh. "Because I slept with the groom." This gets a nice laugh but I keep going. "I misjudged Gary. He is good in bed!"

I wait for the break, the silence after the laughter dies. "I'm kidding—I'm not a terrible human being. But I do wear glasses and brides don't make passes at friends that wear glasses. Seriously, have you ever seen a four-eyed bridesmaid? No, exactly, because if you did, the flash from the group photo would reflect off her lenses making it look like she's shooting lasers out of her eyes. And the only person allowed to shoot lasers out of her eyes is that bitch, bridezilla."

Considering it's the first time I've told this joke, the laugh is pretty respectable. I continue, "So yeah, I've never been a brides- maid but I *have* been asked to be a reference on a girlfriend's résumé, which is probably because . . . I wear glasses." The crowd laughs and I spot several four-eyed women in the audience who totally get it. They're my people. I transition into my usual set with some new material sprinkled in. By the end of it, the crowd roars with satisfying laughter.

"That's my time, everyone. I'm Olivia Vincent. You've been great!" I hand the mic off to the emcee and walk over to Nick, who's waiting for me.

"I got 'em all warmed up for you," I say, just like the first night we met.

"Now that's the kind of foreplay I like." It takes every ounce of strength I have not to grab Nick by the collar and pull him in for a kiss. Maybe more. But instead I wish him laughs and watch him walk onstage.

After the show, Nick completely sells out his box of merchandise. "I think that's everything I have," he says. "There's nothing left for L.A."

"What are you talking about, there's like five more boxes in the Jeep."

He takes a beat then it clicks. "Oh, yeah. Right. I forgot."

"You okay?" I ask. "Those nicotine patches going to your brain?"

He rubs the back of his neck. "Maybe. C'mon, let's play some poker."

"Wish me money!" I say, and we exit the auditorium.

Nick and I make our way over to the poker tables in the non-smoking section. "How 'bout some Texas Hold 'Em?" he asks in his best West Texas accent. But it's the worst.

"How 'bout you leave the accent up to me, cowboy?"

Just as we find an open table and place our bets, the guy sitting to Nick's right stares at us. He's wearing Nick's Buh-Bye shirt—fresh out of the box with folded creases and a blue collar poking out beneath it. "Hey, we just met you guys." He points to each of us and we greet them (again).

"I'm Chuck and this is my fiancée, Amy."

Amy stands over his shoulder with a pink cocktail in her hands. "Your bridesmaid bit was so funny. Is that true, you've never been a bridesmaid?"

"Sad, I know."

Amy pouts her lip. "Oh, bless your heart. Ohmigod!" The woman squeals so loud my ear's ringing. "I have a great idea. We have an appointment at the chapel tonight, and we don't have any witnesses." She looks to me. "How would you like to finally be a bridesmaid?"

"Are you serious?" I say, then look to Nick.

"Yes! You can be my maid of honor and Nick can be the best man. What do you say?"

We said no more funerals but we didn't say anything about weddings.

Forty

ick manages to move the other merch boxes around his
Jeep enough to reset the back seats so there's room for
the four of us.

"Where to?" he asks, after we load in.

"The Elvis Chapel," Chuck says, his arm cradling a blissful
Amy. Nick and I do our best to hold back the laughs growing
inside us but we can't.

"What's so funny?" Amy asks.

"Nothing," I say. "We just love Elvis."

After a short ride on the highway, Nick parks in front of an
Elvis wedding chapel. I don't know exactly what we're in for with
this wedding but I have a feeling it'll make great material. Inside,
we're greeted by a Chest Hair Elvis (trust me, you don't want me
to elaborate).

"You see the rug on that guy?" Nick says out of the side of his
mouth as we make our way toward the wedding hall.

"Jealous?" I ask.

Inside the hall, rows of linen-covered chairs lead up to a faux marble platform rimmed with twinkle lights that fade from purple to red to blue and white. Tall pillar-style columns flank the stage, complete with a set of silk flower arrangements. It's not exactly the fairy-tale dream but it's better than a drive-thru. The staff promptly serves us glasses of champagne.

"Shouldn't we wait until after the ceremony to drink?" I ask.

"No way, this is Vegas!" Chuck says.

"To Chuck and Amy!" Nick says, toasting us, and we all raise our glasses in celebration before shooting the bubbly back.

"You two are so cute," Amy says. "Are you together?"

I nearly choke on my champagne and Nick lays his arm around my shoulders. "We are. I asked her to marry me but she said no." If only that were true.

Amy doesn't seem to know how to respond so I take over. "He's kidding. We're just buddies. Like Jerry Seinfeld and Elaine."

"That was a great show," she says. "But I'll never understand why Jerry and Elaine didn't end up together. Instead they end up in jail!"

Nick looks at me. "We haven't been to jail on this tour."

"Something to look forward to," I say with a wink, when really I'm thinking Nick and Olivia should have the happy ending Jerry and Elaine never got.

"Now who's ready to get hitched?" JP Elvis enters the building, commanding our attention with his red-and-gold bell-bottom jumpsuit. Whoa. Now that's commitment. He instructs the guys to take their places while they get the music ready, and Amy and I step outside so she can collect her bouquet and make her grand entrance.

"I'm so nervous." Amy's flowers quiver in her hands. "Do you get nervous before you go onstage?"

"Every night. But once I pick up the mic, I'm good."

"Wow." She fans herself. "I can't believe I'm getting married."

"I can't believe I get to be a bridesmaid. Now I have to rewrite my joke."

She lets out a high-pitched laugh, clutching her bouquet. "How do I look?"

I take her in, her white minidress and pink peep-toe pumps. "You're glowing." Almost a little too much. "Wait, is this a shotgun wedding?"

"Honey, I hope not because I've been drinking cocktails all night."

Then, JP Elvis strums an acoustic guitar and begins to sing "All Shook Up." One of the staff members instructs us to proceed down the aisle. "I'm getting married!" Amy says.

"Yes, you are." I adjust my glasses, grab the mini bouquet, and begin the wedding march—well, more like a wedding walk. Nick catches my eye and the sensations of little butterflies flutter in my belly. With those eyes, that smile, it's impossible to look away. I feel myself blushing like . . . like a bride!

I send Chuck a congratulatory smile—and notice he's no longer wearing Nick's Buh-Bye shirt but his pressed blue button-down. I take my place across from Nick in front of the matrimony platform, thinking of that day-one lesson again—*Be prepared for anything*. I know I asked the guy to move in but I'm not remotely prepared for just how good Nick looks at the head of an altar. No wonder his ex-wife snagged him up.

Amy makes her entrance, gracefully, considering how many pink drinks she must've had. I look over at JP Elvis and it's hard to hold a straight face, but once the vows begin, I forget that we're in a little chapel in Las Vegas and instead I'm just watching two crazy lovebirds promise to love each other no matter what.

"Now for the rings," JP Elvis says, looking to the groom, then the bride.

Amy gasps as Chuck reaches in his pocket. "Oh, no, babe! I forgot your ring back at the hotel. Oh, crap, I'm so sorry."

Are rings even necessary for a Vegas wedding?

Just before JP Elvis declares this wedding a disaster, Nick speaks out. "I got it." He digs his heartbreak out of his pocket and hands it to Amy as if it's brand-new again.

"How do you have it? Are you one of those magician comics?" Amy asks.

"No, it was mine. Maybe you two will have better luck with it."

It's official. Nick's divorced and he's ready to move on.

The couple trade the rings and repeat I do's. Then Chuck takes Amy in his arms and dips her like he's a navy sailor in Times Square. Nick and I cheer for the happy couple and JP Elvis starts up "Love Me Tender." The newlywed Mr. & Mrs. Vegas begin dancing, swaying to the music.

Nick approaches me from across the aisle. "So how does it feel to finally be a bridesmaid?"

"Better than when I lost my virginity. What about you? How does it feel letting your ring go?"

"Better than when I got married." We turn our attention back to the dancing couple. Nick leans closer like he wants to tell me a secret. "*Love meat tender . . .*" he sings along, and I laugh, thinking of how ridiculous yet adorable Nick looked in that Elvis jumpsuit in Memphis.

The song fades out and the happy couple share in one more

kiss. Flashes spark around them as the photographer wildly clicks the camera.

"How about one more song?" Nick says, handing JP Elvis a twenty, and makes his request. Soon, our maestro picks the guitar strings in the lovely little melody—"Can't Help Falling in Love." Nick shyly offers his hand and I take it, trying to play it cool. Meanwhile, I feel like I'm back at the eighth-grade prom and my crush just asked me to dance. Only Nick is much more than a crush.

Taking the lead, he wraps his arm tightly around my waist and we sway to the soft music. This time much closer than we were at Graceland. It's hard not to grin from ear to ear. What a perfect ending to a great night with a great man.

Nick spins me around and brings me back into his arms. "Not to sound corny, but I think this is our song."

Our song. He thinks we have a song?

Don't freak out, Olivia. Just say something cute.

"Really? And here I thought it was 'Girls, Girls, Girls.'"

He lets out that rich laugh and it warms my heart to know I inspired it. "You're not like any stand-up I've ever known."

"Yeah, neither are you."

His soft, sweet smile falls. "Olivia, I need to tell you something," he starts, and I know he's about to say something important—something he hasn't had the courage to say yet.

"What is it?"

"I . . . um," he stammers, and stops.

"What? You can say it."

His eyes search mine like he's unsure. I watch him take a breath, then let it go. "I really want to kiss you again."

"Then what are you waiting for?"

Forty-One

Nick takes his time, leaning in slowly. Our lips meet in the kind of kiss even Elvis would write songs about. He tastes like champagne and mint—refreshingly intoxicating. Not a trace of smoke in the slightest. His hands press into my back, pulling me closer, and I fall deeper and deeper and—

"Hey, whose love story is this anyway?" Chuck yells, yanking us out of our magical moment. Nick and I share a *we've been caught* glance and I run my finger across my lip, feeling the buzz of his skin on mine.

Afterward, Nick takes my hand like I'm his girl and I hold on tight. The four of us cross the threshold, where a leather-clad Elvis waits, leaning against the roof of a white limo. "Nelson party?" he asks.

"That's us," Chuck says, and looks at his bride. "After you, Mrs. Nelson." She giggles then glides inside. We're ready to wave them off when Chuck offers us a ride back to the hotel. "Anything for the best man and maid of honor," he adds.

Nick and I share a look.

"When in Vegas?" I say, shrugging.

"Yeah, why not?" We climb in the back next to the newly-weds, where the Elvis tunes carry on and the minibar awaits.

Nick and I sit suitably shoulder to shoulder across from the bride and groom. Still, it doesn't stop me from imagining what I'd do to Nick if we had the limo to ourselves. By the look in Nick's eyes, he has a similar fantasy. Thank God the hotel's not far. These next ten minutes are about Mr. and Mrs. Chuck Nelson. The next ten hours . . . well, we'll see.

"So where's the honeymoon?" I ask.

"We're going to Hollywood. Amy's never been."

"That'll be fun," I say, thinking I'm also a Hollywood virgin. "Actually, Nick and I are playing a show in West Hollywood tomorrow night."

"Well, we have to come see you guys. You're our new best friends now," Amy says, reaching over to take my hand like we're practically sisters. I wonder if she'll remember me tomorrow, or if I'll just be the bitch who ruined her wedding photos with my aesthetically displeasing glasses.

"I'll get you tickets. Show's at eight at The Comedy Shoppe," Nick offers. "Consider it a wedding gift."

"Thanks, man," Chuck says, and cuddles closer to his new wife.

Soon, the limo pulls up to the hotel and we file out. "You guys wanna hit the tables with us?" Chuck asks.

I fake a yawn, stretching my arms wide. "I'd love to but I've got a big day tomorrow."

"Oh, right. Your show!" Amy says, sounding excited about the extra treat.

"No, she's got an audition tomorrow afternoon for *The Late Night Show*," Nick brags, and I tug on my ponytail. I can't believe it's almost here.

Amy gasps. "With Anderson Vanderson? My maid of honor's gonna be on *The Late Night Show*!" She flings her arms open and barrels into me. "That's so exciting! Congratulations!" God love her. Isn't she the cutest?

"Thanks," I say, praying I don't disappoint both of us. "We'll see you two tomorrow night."

Nick and I send the bride and groom off with a wave and wait for them to walk deep into the casino floor. The moment they're out of sight, we look at each other, communicating the obvious, and hurry toward the elevator. Meaning we attempt to restrain our excitement by hiking at a normal pace but somehow make it in record time.

Inside the elevator, we're alone. Finally. I rest against the mirrored wall, a hard rail against my back. The best man leans his body onto mine, kissing me again. This time it's hotter and hungrier than before. On our floor, we stumble over each other, crashing against the walls in the hallway like Ping-Pong balls. Soon we're locked in a room—his or mine, I can't keep track. My body responds to his every touch, even more than before. A shiver runs through my body and I roll my head back, giving a little moan.

I know we promised no funny business. But there's nothing funny about this moment. Not funny *ha-ha* anyway. I tangle my fingers in his hair and he slides my white top off, kissing my neck. The awkwardness of Atlanta and the restraint of New Orleans and every moment after that all fall away. Here in a room at the Isle of Riches Hotel and Casino, Nick and I are completely in sync. Our bodies harmonize perfectly the way our voices do when we sing classic rock. Only this is a lot more fun.

The pleasure he provokes builds and builds inside of me, heightening the way a good joke does before the punchline drops. I almost can't believe it. I can't stop it either. It's coming. The release I've been waiting for. The bliss I've been missing for so long. I belt a pleasure-filled cry. And there's nothing fake about it.

In the morning, I wake up to Nick's warm skin against mine, his heart beating steadily. I smile, biting my lip at the memory of last night and all the other little moments of the last ten days. He stirs and blinks his eyes open.

"Hi," he says, like he's just as pleased to wake up next to me.

"Hi." I take in his morning-after look, wanting to capture every second of it.

"I didn't hear you snore last night."

"You're probably getting used to it by now."

Nick grabs his phone from the nightstand. "What time is it?"

"A little after eight," I say, reading the hands on my watch.

Nick rolls on his back and lets out a soft, easy yawn that makes me want to hit the snooze button and stay in bed with him the rest of the day. "We should probably get up and get going."

"Just a few more minutes." I slink my arm around him, caressing the valley of his collarbone.

"Your audition's this afternoon. I thought you'd be jumping out of bed."

I glance up at him, resting my chin on his chest, and slip my hand between us. "Right now, I'd rather jump something else."

His head rolls back into his pillow, a naughty smirk on his mouth. "Mmm, how much time do we have?"

Giggling (yes, *that* kind of giggle), I rise up, hovering over him. Soon our bodies are intertwined once more. The rush and ecstasy return and I find myself close again.

Ding-a-ling-a-ling!

Ding-a-ling-a-ling!

Who could be calling me right now? Whatever it is, it's not more important than this. I let it go to voicemail.

It rings again.

"Dammit," I whisper, and find the phone on the floor next to my pants. "It's Bernie. I swear that woman has some kind of radar."

"Answer it. Could be important," Nick urges, wiping his lip.

"Hello?" I answer.

"Olivia, you're not still sleeping, are you?" she asks, the city street noise competing with her voice.

I sit up, covering my chest with the duvet. "No, I'm just getting ready."

"Good. Now, how are you feeling about your audition?" she asks.

"Great! I have an improved set. The bookers will love it," I say, attempting to trust my comedy.

"That's what I like to hear. Now try to leave as early as possible."

"My audition's not until two thirty. We've got plenty of time."

"In theory, but don't underestimate Los Angeles traffic. You didn't go all the way out there just to spend a few extra minutes at the buffet." Bernie may be referring to eggs and sausage but I've got a craving for breakfast in bed. Though, she's probably right—better not to risk it.

"I'll get there on time. Don't worry."

"Good," she says. "Call me afterward so I can follow up. Got it?"

"Got it. And Bernie?"

"Yeah?"

"Thanks. For setting all this up for me. It's been life-changing," I say, looking over at Nick, who's been patiently waiting.

"No sweat, kid. Safe travels."

I end the call and give Nick a long face. "I think it's time to go."

"Okay, we'll finish this later. Whose room are we in?"

I survey the hotel room and don't spot my chunky marshmallow of a suitcase so I say, "Yours. I'll meet you in twenty minutes." I give him one last kiss, then jump out of bed and head across the hall to my room with my pants unbuttoned and my top inside out.

After a speedy shower, I throw all my things in my luggage, then slip on a fresh pair of jeans and Nick's tour shirt for the drive.

Buh-bye, Vegas!

Out in the hall, Nick meets me with two go-cups of coffee. "Nice shirt."

I pull at the fabric. "Oh, this old thing?"

Nick grabs me by the waist and I fall into his arms again. If we keep this up, we'll never make my audition. Right as his lips graze mine, he pulls away. "Shit. I forgot we left the Jeep at the chapel last night."

I check my watch. "It's fine. We'll grab a cab and be there in no time."

Within five minutes, Nick and I secure a taxi and head up the highway toward the Elvis Chapel. I begin humming "Chapel of Love," singing, *"Going to the chapel and I'm gonna be on late-night TV."* Nick snickers then joins in with, *"You're gonna be on late-night TV!"*

When we pull up to the chapel, the cab driver congratulates us on our upcoming nuptials. This is the part where we typically flinch and make it clear that we're not a couple. We're not married. We're not together. Instead, we share a smile and say, "Thank you."

We walk around the building to the main parking lot, me dragging my elephant-sized case across the asphalt. The lot is practically desolate with the exception of triplet limos—one black, one pink, and one white. Something's missing.

"Where's the Jeep?"

Forty-Two

t's not here." Nick throws his hands at an empty parking space on the side of the chapel. "I parked it right here, remember?"

There are only so many things that could've happened to his beloved Jeep. The most obvious being very, very bad. "You don't think it was . . ." My heart sinks the moment I look at him, his worst fear realized. Someone stole the Jeep. This is a disaster.

A total disaster.

"No, no, no. This can't happen. I locked the doors. There's an alarm." Nick shakes his head, stomping toward the space as if the Jeep will appear if he just gets inside the lines. I've never seen this look on his face or shade of red on his skin.

"Try not to freak out," I say, addressing both of us, though my stomach's tossing and churning as reality sets in.

"Don't freak out? Don't *freak* out!" Uh-oh, he's about to blow. I brace myself for the fallout. "My Jeep is gone. Our ride is gone! Do you know what that means?"

"Yes, it means we need to find another way to L.A. My audition's in five and a half hours."

I can't give in to any other conclusion. My career and life depend on us finding dependable transportation. Pronto!

Nick pulls a cigarette out of his jacket pocket and lights up. Where's he been hiding those? "You know, you keep thinking this audition is everything. It's not everything."

Why is he being like this?

"Not everything to you. You don't need to be on late-night television. You have fans and a Comedy Channel special. You have a career. I need this. And right now, there's nothing we can do about your Jeep besides report it and get moving." Nothing I say seems to penetrate his clenched jaw or angered heart. "Look, I know you're upset but it's just a Jeep!"

"Spoken from the girl who keeps an antique in a storage garage."

Uh-uh. He's not bringing my dad's Jeep into this mess. "That's not the same thing and you know it."

"Actually it is, Olivia! Everything that meant anything to me was in that Jeep. Everything I owned. And now what . . . all of it's on its way to Mexico to be disassembled and sold for parts?"

Now I'm as lost as our ride. "What do you mean everything you own was in the Jeep? There's nothing in there but T-shirts with your face on them."

Nick takes off his sunglasses and rubs his eyes. When he looks up, it's not fury staring back at me. It's something else. "I got rid of my apartment in Brooklyn. Sold everything I could replace and took what I couldn't. I'm not going back to New York. I'm moving to L.A."

"Wait, what?" I shake my head, processing what he just told me. "Back up. You're moving to L.A.? To do comedy?" As the words barrel out of my mouth, details of the past couple weeks begin to click. The clinking in the boxes, not wanting to drive me home, shoving off the roommate stuff. "Why didn't you tell me?"

"Because I'm not gonna do comedy anymore. I got a job. A real one."

Okay, now my head hurts and it's not just all the champagne we drank last night. "You're quitting stand-up?" He answers with a look, and I know it's real. Still, this doesn't make sense. Something doesn't add up. "How can you quit after all that stuff you said? Why would you tell me not to give up comedy when you are?"

"I meant that. I did. But for me . . . it's more complicated than you know."

I must be an idiot. Why did I let this guy in? Why did I fool myself into thinking he was the answer I was waiting for?

I scoff. "You're so full of shit. *Stand-up's so great* and *I'm so great* and you let me think that we could be . . ." It's not just comedy he's walking out on, it's like he's walking out on me too. Why am I surprised? Everyone leaves eventually. "Never mind, I get it. You really are born to run, aren't you?"

"I'm sorry. It's not personal. I guess I thought it would be easier this way."

"Easier for you." Not only does he remind me of my father but now he's behaving exactly like my mother, sneaking out without a word, avoiding the hard conversations. "You know what, Nick. You're a coward and a quitter. And I don't want any more help from you. I don't want anything from you!"

I grab my suitcase in a rage and stomp off, but the damn thing digs its heels in the ground. And my dramatic exit's reduced to a humiliating waddle.

"Olivia, wait! Where are you going?" The sound of his boots crunching against the pavement draws closer.

"Don't follow me!" Using every ounce of strength I have, I keep going.

What a disaster.

Forty-Three

With tears streaming down my face (that's right, I'm cryin' in public), I search for the closest bus station on my phone. I need to get out of this town ASAP and it looks like the next bus leaves in an hour. Perfect.

Wait, no. It won't arrive in time for my audition. Crap! I search for the closest car rental and summon an Uber to find me somewhere on Las Vegas Boulevard. On the ride over, I call the rental place. It rings endlessly and my heart's pounding in my ears. Why is this happening?

I try again. And again. Same thing. My stomach twists as we turn the corner. Ugh, I'm gonna be sick. Should I call Bernie back?

No, Olivia, just stay the course. I'll make it. I have to.

Wait, where are my set notes from last night? My face feels feverish as I open my backpack and tear everything out of it. They're not here. Shit, shit, double shit. I need those notes. I mentally retrace my steps—I showed Nick my notes before

I went onstage, stuffed them in my back pocket, and that's it. They must be in my suitcase.

"Excuse me, I think I forgot something. Can you pull over so I can check my luggage?"

"Here?" the driver asks.

"Yes, anywhere and fast. Please!"

He yanks the steering wheel to the right and stops at the curb. I scramble out of the car and yell for him to pop the trunk. As soon as I'm in, I dig through the mound of clothes. Next time, if there is a next time, I'm not packing half this crap. My pleather performance pants surface and I check the pockets. Empty. All empty. The notes must've fallen on the floor at the hotel.

I glance at my watch, the hand ticking away the minutes I have left before it's too late. No, no, no, no, no. There's no time to go back. Dammit!

Scrambling back in the Uber, I attempt to calm myself with a few deep breaths. It's going to be fine. I'll figure it out.

Crowds of people surround the entrance to the rental place like it's Six Flags on a Saturday morning. No wonder they didn't answer. Oh, Lord. What if there are no cars left? If I don't get on the road in one hour, I'm toast. It takes both the driver and me to lift my suitcase from the trunk. Dragging it along, I pray to anyone, anywhere for a car. And fast.

"Olivia!" A woman's voice calls and I turn back. Chuck and Amy walk my way, wheeling their compact luggage behind them.

"Hey," I say, not wanting to be rude though there's no time for chitchat.

"What are you doing here?" she asks.

"It's a long story. Nick's Jeep was stolen last night and I need to get to my audition."

"Oh my god, I'm so sorry." The happy couple now look horrified. If it wasn't for them, we'd have picked up the Jeep in the hotel garage and be cruising toward California. The truth about Nick still concealed in his cargo. Win some, lose some, I suppose. But I can't afford to lose *The Late Night Show*.

"Thanks. It was nice seeing you but I really have to run." I start for the packed entrance again.

"Olivia, wait!" Amy calls. "We're on our way to Los Angeles too, remember? Why don't we save you the trouble and give you a ride."

Yes, yes! Maybe Chuck and Amy are my true guardian angels.

"Are you serious? You'd do that?"

"You're my maid of honor, of course we will."

I fling my arms around her. "Thank you, thank you. Thank you!"

"Happy to help. Where's your buddy Nick?"

I want to tell her he's not my buddy anymore but I bite my tongue. "He's got his hands full here. You know, police reports, insurance. Stuff like that. He'll get there later."

"That's a real shame," Chuck says. "I'm so sorry."

I don't feel sorry for Nick. Not one bit. "Trust me, he's fine on his own. But I really need to get to that audition so . . ."

The three of us haul ass out of there and speed off in a little Hyundai Accent toward I-15.

"Where's your audition?" Chuck asks.

"NBS Studios."

"Holy moly, Olivia! You're gonna be on *The Late Night Show*!" Amy squeals while Chuck plugs the destination in his GPS.

"ETA is 1:34 P.M.," Chuck announces, and attaches his device to a vent holder. As long as that number doesn't go up, I may actually pull this off.

I pop my head in between the front seats. "You two may have just saved my comic career."

The Mr. and Mrs. seem pleased with themselves and share a sweet kiss just inches from my face. For a split second, I almost miss Nick's kiss. Almost.

My phone buzzes in my pocket. Speak of the devil. It's Nick, the bastard. I send it to voicemail and catch a glimpse of his face on my shirt. Geez, what a terrible idea it was to wear this.

"Honey, can I play some music?" Amy asks, and her hubby replies, "Whatever you want."

You see. That should've been my first clue—what kind of selfish jerk makes me negotiate for one measly song an hour? Then the melancholy sounds of "Heartbreak Hotel" move through the speakers. Of course she's playing Elvis. One of his little helpers just pronounced them husband and wife last night. I hate that it reminds me of Nick. The way he kissed me last night. I should forget about it. Especially since he's just days away from forgetting about me.

How did I not know any better? And why, after I let him in, told him everything, did he still keep this from me? And what kills me the most is he's giving up a comedy career stand-ups like me would kill for. The guy must be a lunatic.

Then, as if he can feel me thinking of him, he calls again. This time I almost pick up just to tell him off. But I wouldn't know what to say, and I'm not in the mood to hear anything he has to say. So I ignore him once more.

I fuel all my emotion into reconstructing my set on paper,

listening back to my show from last night, and keeping an eye on the ETA—1:37 now. Still ahead of schedule.

After stopping by a drive-thru Jack in the Box somewhere outside the Mojave Desert, we get back on the highway. The new ETA is 2:11 P.M. Totally fine.

Crossing into Los Angeles, the clock strikes T-minus twenty minutes. I glance down at my outfit. Nick's face stares back at me. It's almost showtime and I'll be damned if I bring him along in any way, shape, or form.

"Hey," I call to my escorts. "I hate to do this but I can't wear this to my audition so I'm gonna need to change back here."

"That's fine!" Chuck says, and Amy smacks his shoulder.

"Save the show for the stage, okay?" she says playfully, but I'm already slipping a new top over Nick's Buh-Bye shirt, so that Chuck doesn't catch a glimpse of my goods.

Finally, I look the part of a late-night TV comic, but we're slowing down. Way down. Four lanes of cars sit bumper to bumper. Windshields glare in the hot afternoon sun. Current ETA— 2:18 P.M. No, no, no. I pull up the directions on my phone. That dreaded red line runs along the highway until just before the exit to the studio.

Fucking L.A. traffic! Is rush hour every hour out here?

Bernie was right to rush me this morning. And now I'm about twelve minutes from getting screwed. I didn't want to do this but now I have no choice. I dial Bernie—maybe she can push back the audition time, tell them I'm a Texas–New York transplant that didn't account for "the 5."

There's no answer so I leave her a frantic message. I don't have a number to the studio but I dial whatever I can find online.

It's nothing but operators with Valley girl accents giving me the runaround. The closer we get, the more the ETA increases until finally I see the source of this mess. A broken-down bus taking up a whole lane.

I think back to when I left my apartment—Imani and I joking about not getting hit by buses. That joke is officially retired. I will be too because now my ETA is 2:39 P.M. Ten minutes late— any chance that's on time by Los Angeles standards?

Traffic begins to move once more. "Hey, Chuck," I say, "is there any way you can pick up the speed? I don't know if I'm gonna make it."

"I'm going as fast as I can. Any luck getting your agent on the phone?"

I look back at the screen for any missed notifications though I've been white-knuckling the phone for the past thirty minutes. "No."

My head swims with what-ifs and fresh tears sting my eyes. I have to get there. I just have to.

Forty-Four

t's 2:33 when Chuck's rental screeches to a halt in front of NBS Studios. "Go, go!" Amy says, hollering at me like I'm yards away from the finish line.

"Thanks for the ride!"

"Thank us after you nail your audition."

I shut the car door, unload my luggage from the back, and race inside as fast as my baggage will allow. I'm only a few minutes late, that's not so bad. I really hope it's not so bad. Pulse racing, palms sweaty, and knees seconds from buckling, I say a silent prayer to the stand-up gods as the elevator climbs.

Ding!

The doors open and I start for the office, but I can't move fast enough. This shit has got to go. Without a second thought, I abandon my baggage in the hall and dash toward the glass door, sweat beading on my brow. I fling it open and shoot a laser-like stare at the receptionist. "Hi, I'm Olivia Vincent," I say, panting. "I have an audition."

"Uh-huh." I catch her lip snarling at me before she clicks around on her mouse. "You had a 2:30 P.M., correct?"

"Yeah, I'm a little late. I just came from Las Vegas. My ride's Jeep was stolen overnight, I had to get to the car rental place, but it was crazy packed, and this couple I witnessed get married last night were there, so they gave me a ride but then we hit some traffic on the way—a broken-down bus of course—I tried to call but I couldn't get through to the office because I didn't have much information and—"

She cuts me off with a wave of her hand. "Let me save you the rest of your breath. Your audition was the last of the day. The bookers just left for a company event. I'm sorry but you missed your chance."

"They're—they're gone? I'm only seven minutes late."

"Just late enough. You'll have to reschedule. And might I suggest leaving earlier next time?"

It's like my heart actually splinters and shatters inside my chest. "I missed it?"

"Yeah, that's what I said."

This is it. After everything I've been through to get here—the bad shows, the Elvis impersonators, Jeremiah's funeral and scorned wife, Midland and my dad, the wild ride with Nick—I completely missed the *Late Night Show* audition? Seven minutes. That's all it came down to, seven stupid minutes.

Just like I learned in comedy class. Timing really is everything.

I drag my feet to the hallway. My lump of luggage waiting for me like it wants to go home now. I do too. Though, I'm not even sure what that's going to look like anymore. I make my way out of the studio building, standing on the shady sidewalk with nothing. My entire comedy career flashes before my eyes—all that was and all that could be.

Then I hear footsteps close in on me and look up. We left the desert miles ago but I swear it's a mirage. "Nick?"

"Hey." He stands there steadily, dressed in his black leather moto jacket in this July heat, gaze exposed without sunglasses, looking at me like he has so much on his mind. I don't know what to say or how to react. He lied to me. But he's here now, and I'd be lying if I said it's not good to see him.

"How did you get here?" I ask, feet glued to the sidewalk.

He drops his head for a moment, then looks into my eyes. "Turns out my Jeep wasn't stolen. It just got towed." That damn chapel parking lot. "It took a while but I got it back. Everything's in it. Including your garbage bag pillow."

So Nick didn't lose anything that mattered to him. But I did. "Oh."

"Olivia, I'm sorry about this morning," he says. "I'm sorry I didn't tell you about L.A. I wanted to but—"

"But what?"

He releases a heavy sigh. "The thing is, when I was with you, it felt good to pretend like everything was okay. Like I wasn't just divorced. Like I wasn't about to quit stand-up. And like maybe things could turn out the way I wanted them to. I think a part of me didn't want you to look at me the way you did this morning. Like I'm just a big disappointment.

"I also don't want you to think that this was just another tour and that you're just another girl because you're not. I really care about you, and I really do wish things were different."

I wish things were different too. I wish I could pretend everything was fine the way I used to. But I can't run from reality anymore.

He hands me my set sheet, the one I had to reconstruct in the car. "Anyway, I came to give you this. It was on the floor in my room this morning. I was speeding my ass off to get to you on time but I guess I just missed it."

"You're not the only one."

"What do you mean?"

And when I can finally look into his now-honest eyes, I burst into tears. "I didn't make it in time either. I missed my audition. I missed my one chance."

He moves closer and sweeps a loose strand of hair away from my face. "Hey, it's okay. There will be other auditions. Bernie will see to it."

I cross my arms. "I don't know. I have to go back to work now so I can support myself. Comedy's going to have to take a back seat. Again."

"I know it's hard but you can't let this little setback stop you. You have to be relentless."

"Relentless, huh? Is that why you're quitting?"

"I'm quitting because I don't know that I'm getting out of it what I wanted. But you? You're just getting started. And you're good. You might actually make it. Headline shows I can't even afford tickets for."

"Like Ellen?" I say.

"Yeah, but much hotter."

A little laugh tumbles from my lips but the levity doesn't last long. "I have so much to figure out when I get back to New York. It's a disaster back there."

"Worry about tomorrow, tomorrow. Tonight we have a show at The Comedy Shoppe. You and me, babe. And the bride and groom from last night."

"Chuck and Amy." The heroes who almost got me here on time.

"Right, those guys. Let's just go all out. Let's close this tour and our time together with one last killer show. Let's get enough laughs to last us a lifetime. What do you say?"

Forty-Five

I stand off the stage, at the famous Comedy Shoppe on Sunset Boulevard, otherwise known as the Sunset Strip. Performing here is a pretty big deal, and I want to enjoy every second of it. I'm still really bummed about missing my audition. But things don't always go to plan. And when they don't, I have to figure it out. Bounce back.

It's like Nick said, *Worry about tomorrow, tomorrow.* So I am. Tonight is about going out with a bang—that's a bang, not a bomb, I hope. I stretch out my hands and mouth, shaking my jitters away.

"Hey." Nick pats my shoulder, startling me. "You ready to rock this club?"

I nod, pushing my glasses up my nose. "Yeah, that's one way to put it."

While the emcee wraps up my introduction, I look to Nick, knowing that this is the last night I'll ever open for him. The last night we'll ever tour together. There's so much I want to say but right now, there's only one thing that really matters.

"Wish me laughs."

Nick gives me a warm smile and nods. No doubt he's wishing me all the laughs.

"Please welcome to the stage Olivia Vincent!"

With a grin, I walk to the stage and grab the mic. All the electricity in my body begins to settle enough for my hands to steady.

"Woo!" I hear a woman holler from the crowd. Sounds like I've got a fan. I glance over the dimly lit faces and spot Chuck and Amy cheering their asses off like it's Friday-night football in Texas and I'm the star quarterback.

"All right, Los Angeles!" I say, and the audience cheers. Why do we love hearing our city announced onstage? I don't know but it works. Every time. Maybe I'm feeling wistful but there's a gorgeous energy about the dark, blue-and-purple-tinged room. Maybe it's the crowd's glowing skin and blinding white teeth.

"Happy to be here. It's my first time in L.A., so I thought I'd tell you a little about myself. I'm from the country in West Texas," I say with an accent. "You probably can't tell because I left my Wranglers at home. Anyone here from Texas?" A loud *yee-haw* leaps from the audience. No joke. "Now that's what I'm talkin' 'bout. Did you lose your virginity in the back of a pickup truck too?" This little crack gets a decent laugh.

"I was raised by a single dad"—I wait an extra beat then continue—"which explains why I'm now a stand-up comedian." Another laugh rolls in, boosting my confidence.

"I'm also a millennial, so I've got that going for me in this economy . . . I know, I know. We're entitled and we complain a lot. But there's one thing we've got over older generations. Millennials never have to worry about retirement planning. Because . . ." This is where I really take my time, let the tension build. "You'll never be able to retire." The crowd offers one of those *sad but true* laughs. The kind of joke that sticks because it's truly relatable.

"Seriously, it's not gonna happen if you're thirty and renting your parents' basement . . . Yeah, right, you can't afford your parents' basement! What are you, a thousandaire?" The sight of wide smiles and sound of sincere laughs slowly mend my afternoon heartbreak.

"Let me put it to you this way, if you clench up every time you log into Netflix, praying your dad hasn't changed the password, you'll be working for life. Luckily, my dad doesn't know how to change his password. But if he wanted to find out, he'd probably ask Jeeves.

"Any dads in the audience tonight?" I ask, and get more cheers than I expect. "Okay, I see you, rockin' those New Balances." Now here's where I share a little more about me. "My dad was into jokes. He was great at dad jokes. You know the ones with the corny-but-obvious punchlines? Here's one I remember well. He asked me, 'Why can't you hear a pterodactyl going to the bathroom?' And I thought about it. Then it dawned on me. I don't know how to spell pterodactyl." Another healthy laugh from the audience. Okay, I've got traction. Momentum. Now let's hope for magic.

The audience goes quiet again and I let the silence linger. "Actually, my dad kicked the bucket recently." I drop my head as if giving him a moment of silence. *Aw* reactions spill out from the crowd. "Yeah, he really doesn't like buckets. He just—" I grunt and mime the action. My Converse striking air. Laughter bubbles up.

"No, I'm kidding. He's dead. He died." This gets a nice big laugh. Bigger than expected. "I never know how to say that. Because if I deliver it straight-faced like I just did, people are gonna think *I* did it. And if I deliver it sad, which I am, then what do people say? 'I'm so sorry.' 'Sorry for your loss.'

"What am I supposed to say to that? *Thank you* . . . Why? It's not a compliment." I swagger across the stage like I'm checkin' someone out. "Wow, you're looking good. Did you just lose a parent?" Another solid laugh. So maybe death can be funny. I bet my dad would find it funny.

"I didn't tell my last boyfriend about my dad's death because, again, I didn't know how to say it. He was a really nice guy and suggested I invite my dad to dinner. So we had spaghetti . . . and a séance. It was nice." I love that this is going over so well with the L.A. crowd. Now I'm really hitting my stride and it feels amazing.

"After I lost my dad, I moved to New York City, which is totally different from West Texas. For instance, where I'm from you might see an old man on his front porch whittling a piece of wood. Whereas in the city, you might see an old man on the subway . . . stroking his wood.

"Yeah, it's a little scary braving the streets alone, especially late at night after performing in comedy clubs. To feel safe, I used to carry pepper spray. But now I carry a can of desperation. Because nothing scares a man more than a woman ready to commit." This time the laughter hits the ceiling. If only it weren't true.

"Seriously, I've been single too long. The only guy I see on a regular basis is the pizza delivery guy. And all I want is a man who makes me coffee in the morning and offers to buy Plan B. Is that too much to ask?" Now it's like the crowd's having multiple laugh-gasms.

"My favorite part of a relationship is the beginning. You know what I mean, before you meet his mother." Oh, the ladies get this one—guys too. "I love that initial stage when attraction sparks. You know, when your brain's hijacked by some boy-crazy spell with Siri's voice saying, *Crush activation complete. Loading romantic pop playlist.*" Giggles spill out of the girls in the audience, and I think about the way Nick made me feel the night we first met. "After two weeks of those Taylor Swift lyrics swirling in your lady brain, you start thinking—maybe it's a good idea to ask him to move in.

"It's not," I say with a cautionary-tale sigh. Now I'm going to get really personal. "Anyway, I've been on a bit of a losing streak lately. I lost my dad. Then my job. And my rent-paying roommate. If all that wasn't bad enough, I also lost my orgasm. It's true. I don't know what happened. It's just gone. Like it fell out of my panties' pocket or something. You know that weird, useless pocket in women's underwear? Turns out, maybe not so useless.

"I searched everywhere—couch cushions, Jacuzzi jets . . . my ex-boyfriend. Couldn't find it. So one day, I had too many mimosas at brunch and asked my girlfriend for advice. 'How can I find my missing orgasm?' And she said, 'Maybe you . . . should fuck a detective.'

"I figured it was worth a try. So I meet this guy. And I swear to you his name was Detective Cummings! This has to be my guy, right?" The audience is bursting with laughs and I hold them like a man waiting for a woman to finish in bed.

"So we're in bed together. It's getting late. By now he can't find my bra hooks. So an orgasm is out of the question. At this point, after a failed search, I have two choices. Recite the periodic table song to myself until it's over. Or . . ." I gesture to the audience with the mic and they holler back, "Fake it!"

"That's right. The tried-and-true method of faking it. Anyone here fake it?" There are a slew of *woos*, one from a guy in front. "Sir, you faked it? How?" I ask, and he shrugs, chuckling along with the audience. "That's impressive.

"Here's the thing, men know women fake it sometimes. But they're so cocky they never think we fake it with them. But I'm here to tell you, fellas," I say, then get really serious, "every five minutes, an unsuspecting man is the victim . . . of a fraudulent. Female. Orgasm." It's a lot of fun to see the ladies laugh more than the guys at this one.

"It's heartbreaking, I know," I say, lowering my head. "But we can do something about it, ladies. So please, let's stop faking it. Let's face it. Tell him the truth—he's not as good at sex as he thinks he is. Let him feel what you feel. Total and utter disappointment." Laughter swells from the audience and crashes onstage, washing over me.

And they're not faking it.

"That's my time, everyone. I'm Olivia Vincent. You've been great!"

Forty-Six

Nick waits for me off the side of the stage, grinning with his arms open. "That was awesome! You should be proud."

I crash into him, inhaling his familiar Irish-Spring-and-leathery-cologne scent. "Thank you," I say, my body still surging with energy. Things may not have worked out as planned but this isn't half-bad. The emcee calls Nick out to the stage and I realize that this is the last time I'll ever see him live.

"Wish me laughs," he says, and I nod, smiling as he heads up for the mic. The crowd grows louder, wilder. More than laughs, I wish he wouldn't give this up. Not yet.

"Hey, Liv," someone calls behind me. I know that voice. It's one of my favorite sounds in the world. But it can't be. Can it?

I turn around, finding Imani with a toothy grin, her arms stretched out, inviting me to her. It *is* her. Without a word, we crash into each other, embracing each other in a much-needed

reunion hug. Tears prickle at my eyes, and if I weren't still riding
the wave of my show's success, I'd weep on her shoulder like a
baby. It's good to see her. Really good.

"Damn, I missed you," I say, pulling away to make sure this
is all real.

"I missed you too. Are you crying?"

"Yeah, apparently I do that now." I fling a tear off my cheek
like it's a mosquito. "What are you doing here?"

"I couldn't miss my girl's last tour stop. Plus, I'm leaving for
Europe tomorrow and I didn't want to wait another three weeks
to see you."

"You know Germany is in the other direction, right?"

"So I see you've become a geography major since driving
across the continental U.S."

I laugh, still in disbelief over it all. "I can't believe you came
all the way out here for me."

She looks into my eyes, almost like she can't believe this moment is real either. "I thought about our conversation the other
night, and I wanted you to know that I'm not just the reality
police. I believe in you, Olivia. I want you to know that I have
your back. You're my penguin."

Resting my hand over my heart, I feel her sincerity. "Thank
you." Okay, now I'm really blubbering. "You're my penguin too."

Imani pulls me in for another hug. "All right, you crybaby." I
laugh, wiping my tears away. The one thing I didn't pack (besides floss) is tissues. "So that's the famous Nick Leto, huh?"

I look back at the stage behind me. "Yeah, he's my Jerry."

"Your what?"

"Never mind." Because soon it's gonna be buh-bye.

"Well, whatever he is, he's kind of a fox. Any sparks fly between the two of you?" she asks, and I avert my eyes, blushing. "Girl, you been holdin' out on me?"

"It doesn't matter anyway. He's not going back to New York."

"That's a damn shame."

Imani and I watch the rest of Nick's set from the back of the room. It's the most vibrant I've ever seen him. Maybe even more than his comedy special. Why would he want to give this up? He's practically raising the roof with trunkloads of laughs—enough to last a lifetime. Imani bursts into a big belly one, slapping her thigh at his punchline.

See!

I think of my dad giving up comedy to take care of his family. I don't know what Nick's hoping to gain by giving this up. Whatever it is, I hope it's worthwhile and full of love.

After the show, the three of us head back to the greenroom to celebrate our last night on our cross-country comedy road tour. Nick cracks open a mini bottle of champagne and pours it into a few lowball glasses on the table. I peer through the glass, looking for spots and dirt. So far it's cleaner than a comedy condo.

"To us and our last night on the tour. And to Olivia, the last comic standing," he says with his bubbly raised.

"Hear! Hear!" I say, toasting with my friends. As we sip our celebratory drinks, the door creaks open and chatter from the club spills in, along with someone else. I gasp, practically dropping my drink when I see him.

Oh my Lord.

It's Anderson Vanderson, the host of *The Late Night Show*. He towers over us like a Conan O'Brien but with the boyish face of a John Mulaney.

"Hey, guys, hope I'm not interrupting anything," he says with a smile that's much too shy for his superstar status.

"No, not at all. Come on in," Nick says.

"How y'all doing? I'm Anderson Vanderson." The TV host offers his hand to each of us. Holy crap. Am I even breathing right now?

"Hi, Anderson Vanderson," I say, starstruck.

"Hi." He grins at me like I'm funny. Funny-looking, that is. "I caught your show out there, it was very entertaining." *He* was in the audience? Oh, thank God I didn't know he was there, I probably would've choked on my nerves. He's a comedy genius.

"Thank you, *Anderson Vanderson*," I say, grinning.

"Call me Anderson."

"Okay." I haven't blinked since I touched his hand. Amy and my Aunt Carla are going to flip when I tell them about this.

"Any chance I could interest you two in coming on *The Late Night Show*?"

Nick's brows shoot up. "You mean a stand-up spot?"

Meanwhile, I'm totally speechless, so much so that Imani has to nudge me in the ribs. "On *The Late Night Show*?" I spit out.

"Yes, that's what I'm proposing." He must think we're a little high the way we're responding all slow and Herb-like.

"Just like that?" Nick asks. "No audition?"

"No audition. I've seen what I need to. The crowd loves you two. And I think America will too."

"I, um, I don't know what to say," I stutter.

"How 'bout yes." Anderson claps his hands once but it's not enough to break the spell.

"Yes!" I shout, flashing him the happiest smile of my life. "We'd love to come on your show. Right, Nick?"

"Absolutely," Nick says, and shakes the man's hand.

"Fantastic. Here's my card. Call my office tomorrow and they'll get you in touch with the booker to get you scheduled, all right? I'm headed out now but I'll see you on the show soon."

"Okay. Thanks! Bye!" We send him off, waving like we're characters in the Macy's Thanksgiving Day Parade. This is definitely something to be thankful for.

The moment the door closes, the three of us look to one another and cheer like crazy. "Aaahhhhh!" Hands waving in the air. Champagne spilling out of glasses. Jumping and dancing around like we just won all the laughs in the world.

"I just got a spot on *The Late Night Show*!" I say.

"I know. I just got a spot on *The Late Night Show* too!"

"Holy shit, Anderson Vanderson just saw your show and loved it!" Imani chimes in, and grabs me by the shoulders, bringing me in for another squeeze. When she lets me go, Nick and I go for each other.

"See, Olivia *Vincent*. I knew you were a winner," he says.

Without a word, and without regard for Imani standing right next to us, Nick lays a victorious kiss on me and I let him.

We may not have New York but at least we'll have *The Late Night Show*.

Forty-Seven

t doesn't take much for Imani to convince me to stay with her in her very chic hotel as opposed to another night in a skanky comedy condo. (Sorry, Nick, you're on your own now, buddy.) Plus the hotel is within walking distance of the comedy club. I forgot how great it is to let my feet take me somewhere new. Us ladies can't help but stay up the rest of the night, talking with the lights off just like our slumber parties in high school. I can't imagine spending Imani's last night here any other way.

In the gray morning light, I walk Imani out to the cab waiting to take her to LAX, where she'll fly across the Atlantic to Germany. Not only is my first and only comedy road tour with Nick over, but this chapter with Imani in New York is coming to a close too. I'm nervous, understandably, but at the same time excited for this next season in my life to unfold in unexpected ways. Be prepared for anything, right?

My friend opens the door to her cab, passport in hand, ready for her next adventure. "So this is where I leave you."

"Hey, I took off for my dream first, so it's only fair you do the same," I say, and she chuckles. "It means a lot that you came out here to see me."

She fixes her hands into a heart shape over the left side of her chest. "Like I said, you're my penguin."

"Penguins for life." Tugging her arm, I pull her close for one last goodbye hug. "Thank you for everything. I don't know if I could've gotten this far without you."

"You could've. You would've figured it out. Take care of yourself, Liv."

"I will. You too," I say as she climbs in the cab and closes the door. The taxi window eases down, her face coming clearly into view.

"*Auf Wiedersehen,*" she says.

"*Auf Wiedersehen.*" I wave farewell, watching the taxi drive off along Sunset Boulevard. Now it's just me, and I'm okay with that. I have to be. This is the new Olivia Vincent Plan.

I've got Imani's room all to myself until eleven. I should use this time to go back inside, pack my things (and nothing more), and get ready to head to the airport in a few hours myself. But I can't bring myself to do it. I can't get on a plane without seeing Nick one more time.

Another taxi pulls up in front of the hotel entrance and I snag it. Who cares if I'm in leggings and Nick's Buh-Bye shirt. The comedy condo is only about a mile from here. As we head up the hill, we pass The Comedy Shoppe and I imagine coming back to perform again after the *Late Night Show* taping. It'll be nice to have a reason to visit Nick again.

The driver drops me off in front of the apartment building, my stomach in tight knots. I've seen Nick every day for the last two weeks, nearly every moment. Why am I nervous? I rush up to the second floor and bang my fist on the door. No idea if anyone else is staying here. After a minute, I knock again. No one answers.

Oh, no, I hope I'm not too late. Where would he even go? Probably his new place—sounds like he made arrangements for everything. I pull out my phone to call him and—

"Olivia?" The sound of Nick's voice calling my name is something I will miss. I turn around and find him standing there with his coffee and a cigarette.

"So I guess this means you're smoking again?" I ask, walking down the steps with my arms folded. I wish he'd say buh-bye to that nasty habit.

He pulls the stick out of his mouth and flicks it with his thumb. "No, this is one of those fake cigarettes that help you quit smoking."

"You mean you're *faking* it?" I joke.

"I'm pretty good at it, right?" Nick's brows wiggle and he stuffs the faux smoke in his pocket. "What are you doing here? Don't you have a flight to catch?" he asks.

"I do, but I wanted to come see you and thank you."

"Thank me for what?"

I shrug, thinking the list is too long to say. So I sum it up. "For bringing me on this mind-opening, life-changing, classic rock–filled comedy road tour."

"You forgot orgasmic."

My cheeks warm at the memory. "That too. I can't imagine having done this with anyone else but you."

"Olivia—"

"Wait, let me finish." I step closer. "You and I aren't that different. Except you're much, much older than me," I tease, and he rolls his eyes. "I get why you want to start over after what happened, but you can start fresh in New York too. And if you really want to stay here, in a climate that's much more conducive to a soft-top Jeep, then at least don't stop doing stand-up. The world needs your help seeing the humor in life. To make us laugh because you're so incredibly amazing at it. Please, don't give that up."

He drops his head in a chuckle. "It's hard to take you so seriously when you're wearing a shirt with my face on it."

I glance down at my tee. "Oh, *hahaha!*"

"Is that all?" he asks.

No, but I think I'll stop here. For now. Maybe I'll have the courage to say the rest when I come back for *The Late Night Show*. "Yeah, that's all."

"I'm not quitting comedy." By the look on his face, he's not joking.

"You're—you're not?"

"No. I just got a nationally televised spot. I can't quit now."

"Oh, thank God." I drop my shoulders in relief, thanking the heavens. "So what are you gonna do about L.A.?"

Nick closes the space between us like he wants to tell me a secret, or maybe something better. He places his hands on my shoulders and says softly, "I'm gonna say *buh-bye*."

I smile so wide that my eyes squint in the early sunlight. "Wait, does that mean . . .?"

"Yeah, I'm going home to New York, where I can be near you." Nick tilts his chin, lowering his eyes to my parted lips, and kisses me like it's the first time. Like it's forever.

"Life's funny, isn't it?" I ask.

"It really is." He holds my gaze for another moment and I let myself imagine what's next. Imagine what we can be. What I can be. "You know, I have a pretty long commute back to the city, and I could use some company."

"Are you asking me to ditch my flight to JFK?"

"Yeah, I mean I *am* ditching Hollywood."

I tap my chin. "Well, when you put it that way, okay. I'll ride back with you."

"Then hop in the Jeep. We'll grab some coffee and pick up your *hella* heavy luggage."

I climb into my designated seat and Nick fires up the engine and selects a song for the road—"Home Sweet Home." We buckle in, and this time he takes my hand.

"I gave up my apartment in Brooklyn and I don't have a place to live anymore," he tells me, pulling out of the apartment complex. "You know anyone looking for a roommate?"

I smirk. "Yeah, I think I know someone."

"Think she'll waive the deposit for me?"

"That depends. Will you let me drive the Jeep on the way home?" I ask, hopeful.

The car slows to a stop. "Sure, why not?"

I look around, waiting for the Jeep to move but Nick puts it in park and unbuckles. "Wait, right now?"

"Yeah, you can drive. But I get to pick the music, *capeesh*?"

"*Capeesh.*"

Epilogue

H ow do I look?" I ask Nick, standing in front of him dressed in a pair of *real* leather pants and full face makeup.

"You look hot, babe," he says.

Don't hate me for this but if Nick Leto says I'm *hot* one more time . . . I adjust my glasses and rephrase the question. "Thanks, but how do I look for TV?"

"Olivia, you look great. Seriously."

"I'm so nervous," I say, waving around my sweaty hands. "Eleven million people are going to be watching me tonight."

His smile fades. "Shit, now you're making me nervous."

Nick and I managed to get our *Late Night Show* slots booked back to back. Or rather, Bernie arranged it. Somehow, I got the first spot. Ladies first, I guess. So, tomorrow we'll be back at NBS Studios, only Nick will be in full face makeup.

He wasn't kidding about being roommates when we left Los Angeles. He moved in just last week right after Imani officially moved out. And like the way things were on our tour, Nick and I are slowly becoming more than just apartment buddies, more than a Jerry and Elaine. Maybe it's fast, but right now, it's working for us. We spend our evenings bouncing around at our respective gigs and our days fighting over the stereo and watching our favorite comedies.

I've picked up a lot more work since we got back, and Nick's been instrumental in helping me be seen more throughout the city and beyond. We're talking about going on the road again soon. There's still a real possibility I'll have to supplement my comedy income until things really pick up, but I'm not at all discouraged. After everything, I feel confident in pursuing comedy wherever it leads—not just realizing my dream but my dad's too—however long- or short-lived it was. I know wherever he is now, he's lounging with a bowl of popcorn on his lap, the remote control on his chest, and he'll be watching me live.

"Hey! Did you forget about me?" Imani yells from my pocket.

"Oops!" I retrieve my phone and hold the screen to my face. Imani, Uncle Artie, and Carla are streaming on a video call. "Sorry, guys!"

"Let me see the set," Artie asks, moving closer to the screen as if that will change the direction of the camera.

"I can't take you on set but I can show you the greenroom," I say, and flip the view around, giving them a little tour of the backstage lounge. Definitely an upgrade from some of the greenrooms on the road.

"Why do they call it a greenroom when it's not green?" he asks.

I look to Nick for the answer and he shrugs, just as clueless. "You'll have to ask the internet about that one."

"We're so proud of you," Artie says.

"Yeah, Liv. I've got my NBS app all loaded up on my TV. You know I had to hire an IT guy just to get this set up," Imani says, sounding inconvenienced.

"Please, don't pretend you did it for me. I know you won't miss an episode of *The Bachelor.*"

"I mean yeah, I'll use it for that too."

"Olivia Vincent." A guy wearing a headset and carrying a tablet pops in the room.

"Yeah?"

"You're on in five." He disappears just as quickly, and my stomach jumbles and jitters.

"Oh my god you're about to make your *Late Night Show* debut!" Imani squeals, and I can't help but blush incredulously.

Nick steps in and takes the phone. "Hang on just a second, guys." Then he lowers my device. "Don't overthink it. Treat this show like the one we did in L.A. That's what Anderson Vanderson loved. Just go out and have fun. Everyone's gonna love you like we do, okay?"

I nod and take the phone. "All right, I'm heading to set. I'll call you after, okay?" My chosen family sends me warm wishes and waves me farewell. I take in a deep breath and head out toward the dark set, Nick right by my side, his hand in mine.

Anderson Vanderson steps out beneath a row of bright stage lights and the audience cheers him on until he hits his mark. "Thank you. Thank you! Our next guest is a very funny young woman from Midland, Texas. You may have seen her on the New

York comedy scene or at The Comedy Shoppe here in Los Angeles. Please give a warm welcome to Olivia Vincent!"

I stretch out my hands, my mouth, and adjust my glasses before looking back at Nick and saying, "Wish me laughs."

He smiles, and I know he's wishing me enough laughs to last a lifetime. My whole body trembles as I head out toward the light, the audience drawing me in with their welcoming applause. Then, I step up to the stand and take the mic.

Acknowledgments

In the early stages of this story, I kept coming back to the same Nichiren Daishonin quote—"The journey from Kamakura to Kyoto takes twelve days. If you travel for eleven but stop with only one day remaining, how can you admire the moon over the capital?"

The road to writing this book tested every creative bone in my being, but I kept striving toward that moon at the end of the journey. Throughout writing this, there were moments that felt isolating. But the truth is, support surrounded me at every moment. And I'd like to express my gratitude to those who helped me bring this book to life.

First, a special thank-you to my dad, who introduced me to stand-up comedy on vinyl. I know you were with me, helping me orchestrate this book from the other side. And my husband, Joe: it's been nearly twenty years and there's still no one else I'd rather watch stand-up with. Thank you for your undying support and for betting on me while I'm still learning to bet on myself.

I wouldn't have made it this far without my incredible agent, Suzie Townsend, and the team at New Leaf Literary & Media. I'm so grateful to have you all in my corner. Thank you, Kristine E. Swartz. You are the coolest editor ever! This book, which I'm beyond proud of, happened because of you. A special thank-you to the team at Berkley, who have been enormously helpful throughout the publishing process—Natalie Sellars, Bridget O'Toole, Stephanie Felty, Lindsey Tulloch, Randie Lipkin, Christine Legon, Nicole Wayland, and Megan Elmore. And Jess Cruickshank and Colleen Reinhart, for a cover I'm crazy about.

Thank you to my mom, Lorraine, for your love, support, and dedicated readership. A heartfelt acknowledgment to my grandma Merene Davidson, who passed away as I was finishing the draft of this book. Thank you for always supporting my career, even naming my first novel. You are deeply missed.

This last year was especially tough, and I couldn't have done it without the love and encouragement of my family and friends—Chantell Morales, my loyal lobster. Heather Hildenbrand, from day one you've been an incredible friend and my author ally. Kristina Robinson, my heart. Thank you Chelsea Fine, Kristina Harrison, Jessica Goldner Bowman, Robert Robinson, Rachel Linde, Mai Lee Aksel, Showlee Mendoza, Gil Mendoza, Masayo Ikeda, Cool Aunt Robyn, Helen Winslett (and your Midland roots), Angelina and Victoria Winslett, Autumn Winslett, Imani Pretlor, Alexa Lugo, Pamela Hopkins, Eric and Christy Bernal, Rachel Armstrong, Judy Glenney, Nana Miller, Chika O'Berry, Ram Surendren, Moonjung Cho, Daisy Pardasani, Willonda Brown, Sakura Detorres, Alisha Thapa, Kristen Bollman, Naima Abdul Khaliq, Monica Ohtsuka, Gina Rizzi, Steph Nuss, Lilian Monroe, Meredith Schorr, Devri Walls, and Rebekah Moan.

An enormous thank-you to my hilarious friends who shared their stand-up wisdom with me—Emily Paige, Amoreena Wade, and Joel Palilla Hicks.

And last but not least, a sincere thank-you to my mentor, Daisaku Ikeda, and all my fellow members of the SGI-USA. Each of you has instilled in me the never-give-up spirit so that I too can admire the moon over the capital.

No Funny Business

AMANDA AKSEL

DISCUSSION QUESTIONS

1. Olivia has no issue disrupting her life in pursuit of her dream of performing stand-up. Do you think she's irresponsibly impulsive or admirably decisive, and why?

2. What was the most memorable scene, and why?

3. Have you visited any of the cities on Nick and Olivia's tour? If so, how were their experiences similar to or different from yours? If not, which city would you most like to visit, and why?

4. Olivia wishes she could have one last conversation with her dad and ask questions that have been weighing on her heart. Who in your life, past or present, do you wish you

could have an important conversation with, and what would you ask?

5. According to Olivia, Whataburger is the best burger restaurant. Who do you think makes the best hamburgers?

6. What surprised you the most about Olivia's story?

7. Nick was all about classic rock tunes on the tour. Which songs mentioned in the book would you add to your road trip playlist? Or which songs in general would you blast with the windows down?

8. The comedy road tour forced Olivia down memory lane. While reading the book, were you inspired to recall any sweet or bitter memories from your past? If so, which ones?

Photo courtesy of the author

Amanda Aksel is a West Coast transplant whose curiosity about people led her to earn a bachelor's in psychology. Instead of pursuing a career as a couples counselor, she wrote about one in her first novel. You'll often find her writing stories about fabulous, independent heroines; pretending to be Sara Bareilles at the piano; watching reruns of *Sex and the City*; or sprinkling a little too much feta on her salad. Amanda calls Virginia Beach home but loves to travel the world with her high-school-sweetheart husband any chance they get.

CONNECT ONLINE

AmandaAksel.com
AmandaAksel
AmandaAksel

Ready to find
your next great read?

Let us help.

Visit prh.com/nextread